Jim Carley was born in Ashf... currently lives in West Lond... *Immortal Plastic* is his first n...

IMMORTAL
PLASTIC

Immortal Plastic

by

Jim Carley

Hamilton & Co. Publishers Ltd
LONDON

Paperback ISBN 1 901668 77 0

Publisher

Hamilton & Co. Publishers Ltd
10 Stratton Street
Mayfair
London

To Anne

Part One

The Chance Encounter

The Toy

As days went, the 17 June 1979 was about as bad is it got for Helen Bridgenorth. It was one of those rare, exceptionally hot, summer days. The kind you expect when you are on holiday in Spain, but are something of a freak in the Medway towns of Kent. It was the sort of day that, no matter where you went, it was still too hot. Indoors or outdoors, it did not matter. Cool places did not exist, just humid hell holes. The air was too heavy, and there were too many people. Anybody who was vaguely claustrophobic would have stayed at home.

The town centre in Maidstone was heaving, everybody was doing their summer shopping. The mid-season sales had just begun. Old dears were out looking for a bargain and mums were trying to get a good deal on next year's school uniform for their little ones. The kids themselves were just hanging about on the street corners, smoking cigarettes or chewing gum. It would be like that until they went back to school in September. Congestion wasn't the main problem for Helen Bridgenorth, though. Her real problem was her five-year-old son, and the tantrum he was currently throwing.

"I want one, mummy," he screamed. "I want one." He was a small lad for his age, with bony arms and legs. He was short sighted, which meant that he had to wear chunky National Health Service glasses. They were the type of glasses which had pale blue transparent frames, which all children's glasses seemed to have in the seventies. In addition, he wore the standard children's uniform of the decade; a loud T-shirt, short trousers, knee length socks and buckle-up sandals. Some might have referred to him as a "little dear", but Helen knew exactly how much of a handful her son could be. If only his father were here, he knew how to take a firm stance on these things. He wouldn't have tolerated such a public tantrum. Then again, he wasn't there. Although his office wasn't that far away it wasn't much use to Helen now. Her son just stood there, outside the toy shop, balling his eyes out. His face was scarlet red, with tears running down each cheek. His glasses had misted over, and his lower jaw had gone wobbly from his outburst.

"I want one," he screamed again.

"You can't have one," Helen shouted. She was at the end of her tether.

"But I want one," the boy continued.

"They haven't got any, though," said Helen. "Now come on, I need to get to the supermarket."

"But, mum, the others will have one," he persisted.

"No they won't, darling," his mother assured, "The man in the shop said they hadn't got any. He said that nobody had got them. There are only a few of them, he said, and they never had any in Maidstone. None."

"But, mum," the boy went on. There was nothing his mother could say to convince him otherwise. Her frustration mounted, as passers-by began to stare at the young lad and the scene he had created.

"Everybody is looking at you," Helen pointed out,

but it did no good. She was beginning to wish she had never taken him to see that damn film. She should have known he would be taken in by it. She had had no choice though, every little boy wanted to see that film. It wasn't just a children's film, though, it was the biggest film of the decade and it was costing Helen dearly. Not only did the tickets cost a bomb, it was everything that went with them. There were toys, and T-shirts, and pencil cases, and lunch boxes. Every little boy had something, something with that film plastered all over it. It wouldn't have been so bad if the merchandise was cheap and easily available, but it wasn't. Everything had a hefty price tag. It was absurd, the price they were asking for little bits of plastic. It was amazing how these big merchandising companies were allowed to get away with it. Their behaviour was normally scandalous, but that didn't excuse the fact that this one toy in particular had been marketed in the worse possible way. One little toy of which they had hardly made enough for one toy store, yet they had spent thousands telling all the kids in the world that it existed. It was every parent's nightmare. In the winter of 1979 thousands of kids had asked Santa Claus for the toy, only to wake up heart-broken on Christmas Day when it wasn't there. What sort of a way was that for a company to behave? It was nothing short of disgraceful. That didn't help Helen Bridgenorth now though. She was stuck on a street corner with a bawling five year old, who wouldn't move for anything less than the toy of his dreams.

"If you don't come now," she ordered, "I'm going to leave you there." The words seemed to stop the tears for a second. Sure, he wanted the toy, but the prospect of being abandoned in the middle of Maidstone was perhaps a price that was a little too high. He watched his mother turn and begin to walk away up the street.

"Mummy, wait," he screamed, as his skinny legs ran after her. He buried his head in her dress, and blurted out more tears. For now though, Helen had won. Her little boy had abandoned the toyshop for the day. As they walked away from the toyshop the little boy took a second to look back. He could still see the dark cardboard figure looming in the window. That was what he wanted. That was what he wanted more than anything in the world.

Helen Bridgenorth never bought the toy for her son. She never even realised how much the toy had dominated his life. She thought he was growing up like an ordinary boy. He had his quirks, like anyone else, but essentially he seemed sound. The boy was obsessed though, unnaturally so. Every day he carried the obsession with him, through childhood, adolescence, and the early years of manhood. He wished that one day he might at least see the toy, or maybe touch it. In his wildest fantasy he even owned it, but he never thought the day would come when that fantasy might come true. Twenty years after that sweltering day in Maidstone town centre, however, the dream began to turn into reality. The circumstances that brought it about were so complex that even the fertile imagination of a young boy could not have made them up. The little boy had become a man, but his biggest adventure was yet to take place.

The Best Looking Woman on TV

"So," said Ralph Lee, "who would you say was the best looking woman on TV?"

"Interesting," Brad Clusky replied, "I'm sure we have had this conversation a thousand times before." The two of them sat in the front seats of a blue Bedford van with false plates, parked up in a North London side street. It was mid-evening, a fairly dark night for the time of year. Ralph sat in the driver's seat, wearing his standard uniform of a rugby shirt and jeans. Brad, on the other hand, was dressed completely in black, and deliberately so.

"I've always had a thing for Dana O'Brien," Ralph went on.

"The girl from *Capital Night Out*, right?"

"Right."

"So what is so special about her?" Brad asked.

"Red heads, man," Ralph explained. "I've got a major hang up about red heads. I've been with blonde girls and brunettes, black girls and white girls, old girls and young girls, but I have never had it with a red head, and what a girl to make it with, huh?" He fired up a cigarette, and rolled down the window to let the fumes escape.

"Well, she's not my type," said Brad.

"Do you reckon she's ever shagged Marcus Clint?" Ralph asked.

"Who the hell is Marcus Clint?"

"Her co-presenter. You know, the guy with the really white hair and the suntan. He speaks with that fucking goofy tone, like he's just done it with your girlfriend and feels the need to explain to you how much better at sex he is compared to you."

"He sounds like he might have shagged her," Brad replied.

"What chance do you reckon I have then?"

"Well," said Brad, "if you ever meet her, which is highly fucking unlikely, I reckon she would blow you clean away."

"Thanks for the vote of confidence," Ralph sighed. "How about you though?"

"How about me what?"

"I asked you a question, remember. Who is the best looking woman on TV?"

"Oh," said Brad, "that is actually quite a hard question."

"What's hard about it?" questioned Ralph. "I don't think that is a hard question at all."

"It's hard," explained Brad, "because there are so many contenders with strong credentials who have to be considered on their individual strengths."

"Such as?"

"Well, for a straight mind-blowing shag it would have to be Jennifer Aniston, obviously."

"Obviously," Ralph repeated.

"For a sophisticated seduction, however, it would have to be Kirsty Young."

"Kirsty Young? She's a fucking news reader! How the hell could you want to shag Kirsty Young?"

"You asked me the question, so I'm answering it. You chose Dana O'Brien, and I didn't complain. I'm choosing Kirsty Young."

"But you already chose Jennifer Aniston," Ralph pointed out.

"For a different reason."

"So you get two choices?"

"No," corrected Brad. "I get three."

"Three?" Ralph questioned. "Why do you get three choices?"

"Because I haven't covered the novelty value shag yet. That would have to be Ingrid Bourgromenko."

"Ingrid Bourgromenko? She's a weather girl. Are you some kind of pervert or something, trying to assemble your own news programme to shag your way through. Besides, she's weird and Bosnian."

"Albanian," Brad corrected again.

"Whatever," Ralph replied. He flicked his cigarette butt out of the window. "I'm getting tired of this shit," he went on. "What time is it?"

"Eight fifteen," Brad answered, checking his watch. "It's time to party," he added. He took an earpiece out of his pocket, and slid it into his ear. Then he took the black balaclava off the dashboard, and rolled it on to the top of his head like a hat, stopping short of covering his face.

"All set?" asked Ralph.

"Yeah, I'm ready. I'll see you later." Brad opened his door and slipped out. In seconds he had vanished into the encroaching darkness outside.

The Gresham Corporation

Less than an hour later, Brad Clusky was in position. The closing darkness had all but erased his outline from the side alley in which he now crouched. He'd been there for almost half an hour, tucked away behind the bins and plastic sacks of trash. He was almost immune to the smell of rotting rubbish by then. Other people may have vomited at the stench, but not Brad. Years of training had meant he could tolerate a lot worse than bad smells. To him, and the rats that he was sharing the alley with, it was just part of a day's work. At least two unmarked security patrol cars with plain clothes teams had passed him in the time he had been there. Neither had detected him. Indeed, as Brad had suspected, the patrols were not very interested in the alley at all. Maybe they had checked it a thousand times before, and the best they had found was some homeless down and out, off his head on methylated spirits. Given the choice, they would probably rather not deal with that kind of company tonight.

Nine o'clock marked the end of the guard shift. It was time to go. Brad pulled the balaclava down over his face, and moved with slow precision out across the street. The weather was perfect. The cloud was thick, filtering a slow steady rain, and the wind gave a bite to the skin. It was the sort of weather that people didn't go out in unless they couldn't avoid it. The streets were thus empty, with not a potential witness in sight. Brad, covered from head to toe in black, wove between parked cars and the trash in the street. Always he had one eye on the windows of the terraced houses than bordered the road. A lucky onlooker might remember him, his tall frame and thick build. He could not afford to leave a single clue as to his identity. Nobody was allowed to get a glimpse of him, at any cost. This job was too important to get something that simple wrong.

Brad's target was the anonymous tower block which now stood before him in sleepy silence. Brad knew however, that the innocent façade of the building was just a cover. The locals thought it housed an insurance company, or an accountancy firm, or something equally as bland. In reality the dark tower housed something far more impressive and secretive. It was the sort of thing that nobody would expect to find, or want to find, at the end of their road. The people who ran the Gresham Corporation knew this, which is why they insisted on their policy of secrecy. In the wrong hands the things that were inside that tower could seriously undermine the British Space Industry.

The ten foot wall that acted as the first line of defence of the Gresham Tower had blended perfectly into its urban surroundings. Some architect had been told to design it that way. Just another innocent office block, but with more hidden security than Fort Knox. The heavy iron gates boasted a razor-sharp set of teeth on their summit. No fewer than sixteen closed circuit television (CCTV) cameras cased the perimeter. Not one of them had picked up Brad as he eased his way over the wall and into the compound.

He checked the tiny earpiece he was wearing, and the button microphone on his collar.

"Are you with me buddy?" he whispered.

Five streets away, in the back of the plain blue Bedford van, ex-military technical guru Ralph Lee checked his consoles. He was surrounded by thousands of pounds worth of computer equipment of various descriptions. All of it was switched on and whirring away frantically. At the keyboard where he sat, he had already ploughed through the first seven access passwords at the Gresham Tower. The seventh code had given him access to the main security computer. From there almost anything was possible.

"I've got you loud and clear my man!" Ralph responded into his headset. "What's your position?"

"I'm inside the complex, about twenty yards west of Camera Four." In a second Ralph had punched up the digital image from Camera Four onto one of his monitors whilst firing up another cigarette at the same time.

"I'm scanning baby, but I can't see you. You are one hundred percent in-fucking-visible."

"That's what I get paid for," Brad replied smugly. "Okay, I'm headed for the door. Are you in the main area?"

"I've got seven codes. Two more and this pussy is going to purr every time I hit the keys."

"How long?"

"With you in five."

Brad and Ralph had been working with each other for more than ten years. First in the marines, then the SAS. These days, however, they were freelance. Brad was always the front man. At thirty five he was still pretty fit, and could out run men ten years his junior. He worked out every day, a punishing routine. He had a thick set face, with a square edged jaw. His thick black hair was normally gelled back, but tonight it was messed up by the balaclava. He was well built, with just the right athletic frame for his line of business. He was both agile and strong, a perfect combination. His commitment to fitness, however, allowed him a few indiscretions. He smoked, but no more than five a day, and then only low tar cigarettes. He drank as well, but that too was in moderation. Other than that he never ate fast food, or drank anything with bubbles in it.

By comparison Ralph had lost it. He liked his drink, his cigarettes and his women. He liked them all so much he was constantly occupied by at least one, if not all three. His hair was almost gone, his stomach expanding, and these days he always wore his horn rim glasses in order to see what he was doing. His contribution to the operation, despite his appearance, was essential. Not only did he know computer systems better than Bill Gates, but he could also outrun a police patrol car in almost anything with four wheels. On one occasion he even managed this in a supermarket shopping trolley, just to prove a point. Ralph had five computers set up in the back of the van, linked to nine different monitors, two modems, and the smallest satellite dish hidden on the roof. The whole lot was being powered by a cable running out of the floor of the van and wired into the mains of a nearby house. Those people were certainly going to get a shock the next time they saw their electricity bill. From this control centre, Ralph had the whole situation covered. He knew the location of the nearest police patrols and he knew how many guards were in the tower. He knew their names, the type of gun they carried, and could even access their national insurance numbers if he wanted to.

Immortal Plastic

Back at the tower, Brad had slid up to a service door at the back. It could only be opened with a special swipe card, read with a laser. Brad had stolen such a card a day earlier. The guard concerned was still bound with tape in the cupboard under his stairs. Ralph had played about with the card by plugging it into one of his computers and upgrading the security clearance it had. With one swipe Brad was inside. Normally the central computer would register that the service door had been opened at 9.07 p.m. Tonight no such record would appear.

The Honey Bee

"Okay," reported Brad, "I'm in. How are those codes coming?"

"All nine hands to the dealer," Ralph came back smugly. "Thunderbirds are go!"

"Don't get cocky, mate!" Brad came back sternly. "It isn't your arse that will get peppered with lead if this goes wrong! Knock out the elevator monitor so we can get this done."

In the main guard office the conversation centred around the Arsenal match the night before. It took a systems expert six hours the following day to work out why the main computer screen in the office was still reading systems normal at that time. Two minutes later Brad was on the tenth floor which housed the AVREX stand alone facility. It was completely hack-proof to the outside world, even for Ralph. If you could reach its main interface, however, it was supposed to be like pinching sweets from the pick and mix counter. AVREX was so hot that only six scientists normally had access to it. It was entirely owned by the Gresham Corporation, Europe's leading company in space exploration. That was why Brad was there.

The ultimate goal in space exploration is to send a human further than the scope of the known galaxy. To coin a cliché, to boldly go where no man has gone before. The problem is that it would take longer than a human lifetime to make it that far. Scientists had long ago recognised two approaches to this problem. You could develop a space ship on which the crew could reproduce and create a dynasty that would last long enough to encounter the next intelligent life form, an idea known as the Noah's Ark theory. The alternative, and more favoured, approach, was to suspend human life for the duration of the journey, as happened to Sigourney Weaver in *Alien*. The Gresham scientists had just made a major breakthrough in cybernetics, long term animal hibernation. The experiment had involved a honey bee, an insect with a normal life span of no more than two or three weeks. The Gresham scientists had come up with a new technique for freezing the bees. After six months, when the bees were defrosted, they were found to be still alive. There were one or two side effects - the bees had become infertile and could no longer fly - but they survived the freezing process. This was even more remarkable when you consider the delicate biological structure that a bee has. The Gresham scientists were so taken by their success that experiments on primates were planned within three months.

Brad had never worked for the American Government before, but the USA wanted the details of how to freeze bees more than anybody else. It felt a bit odd, but to be honest he really didn't care as to who shook hands with aliens first, if they even existed. After all, we were all supposed to be part of one big sharing, caring planet these days, weren't we? The great big family of human civilisation, with petty differences left to history. As long as human kind could meet with aliens then nationality was a side issue, as long as he was an American. Brad didn't care about it really. If it ever happened he would be a long time dead. What he did care about was the money, and Uncle Sam had deep pockets. A million dollars to steal Europe's biggest science secret, and hand it over to NASA. It was the biggest job that Brad and Ralph had ever been offered. So much for the supposed Anglo-American special relationship! For a million dollars Brad was more than happy to stab the UK in the back. Any self respecting Briton would do the same thing.

AVREX was housed behind two air-locked doors. The inner chamber had every security gadget you could buy. CCTV, thermal imagers, humidity sensors, laser alarms. Almost as much hardware as AVREX itself. It took Ralph almost seven minutes of frantic work at his console to shut every system down, whilst at the same time making the guards believe it was business as usual. The ashtray on his work station was already filled with butt ends, and the van was thick with smoke. Finally Brad was in the main chamber. It was a tall room with brilliant white walls, no windows, and only one way in and out. AVREX itself was just a large grey metal box, the size of a car, that hummed and whirred to itself. Only one terminal was linked to it at a small black table with a standard office chair. Brad pulled up his balaclava and reached in his jacket for the special glasses Ralph had given him. Inside the lenses were minute cameras and a transmitter. From then on everything that Brad saw would be relayed to a monitor in the van half a mile away. Brad sat down at the table and pulled out two CD's from his jacket, one red and one blue.

"You still with me techno-boy?" he whispered to his collar.

"Absolutely, this is your outside broadcasting unit

ready to receive the live news bulletin."

"You ever tried talking English rather than crap?"

"Hey, I'm the doctor here," came Ralph's jovial response. "You are just my hands. Are we ready to operate?"

With that Brad booted up the terminal and loaded the red CD into the drive. At that point he didn't know that things were about to go horribly wrong.

Leibfield Space Port

The Centurion Angel, the fastest space frigate in the galaxy, blasted its way out of Leibfield Space Port. Jed Largo, a small time mercenary and ace star pilot, crammed himself in to the control seat. He was a confident, masterful individual, with wavy blonde hair and a gleam in his smile. Beside him in the cockpit his co-pilot Mahnja furiously worked the controls. Mahnja was a Smownork, a reptilian humanoid species, half man and half lizard. As they reached orbit the radar screen began to bleep frantically.

"Damn it!" exclaimed Jed (with a curiously American sounding accent for an alien.) "We've got a destroyer class battle cruiser coming right at us. Our cargo must be really hot this time. Quick, Mahnja, activate the main drive. We need to get to warp speed if we are going to out run that thing."

Mahnja croaked in his usual ominous fashion. Behind him Lady Carina of the Spendolini System appeared. She was a delicate, tiny woman, with long auburn hair in a weaved pony tail that reached down to the base of her back. Her innocent ivory complexion, however, was a mask for the fact that she had the temperament of a swamp beast. Her eyes quickly scanned over the sensors.

"What's happening?" she cried.

"We've got company!" exclaimed Jed.

Immortal Plastic

"That's a Glokorian ship behind us," she quickly deduced, "and no ordinary ship at that. That's the Cybercopter, Drax Mantis' own battle cruiser."

"Listen, baby, I don't need a lesson in Glokorian politics to recognise how bad this situation is," retorted Jed.

"Can you outrun it?" she pleaded. The first laser blast to strike the hull answered for her. The odds were slim.

"Mahnja, lock in the shields," cried Jed, "and get that main drive activated." The Smownork grunted in compliance. "Look, sugar," Jed turned to Carina, "I didn't invite this company. It's you they're after. What was on those disks you stole anyway?"

"They contain tactical data on the Glokorian satellite communication system. Enough to analyse a weakness and destroy the entire system. With this information the rebellion against the Glokorians could win a great victory."

Another blast hit the hull and sparks flew in the cockpit.

"Yeah, well don't count your blessings," said Jed. "It looks like we won't be around long enough to do anything with it."

Drax Mantis, First Admiral of the Glokorian Territories, stood on the bridge of the Cybercopter as it closed on the Centurion Angel. His ship was fifty times bigger than the Angel, and a hundred times more powerful. Victory would be easy. Drax himself was a vast being, head and shoulders above any other Glokorian, and twice as broad. His body was covered in black metallic armour, and was cloaked in black robes. He wore a fearsome black helmet and mask over

19

the pale limp flesh of his face. All that could be seen of his real body were his eyes, fearsome and fiery red. To look into those eyes was to look into evil itself. Around Drax, his hoards of officers locked the ship's weapons onto the Angel. A few more direct hits and it would all be over.

"Commander," Drax cried in his deep husky voice, "I want that ship destroyed and I want it destroyed now. What is its course?"

The Commander turned from his control panel to answer his leader.

"Sir, the ship will be destroyed in a matter of moments. We have knocked out its main warp engine. It can't out run us, and there are no planets on its current trajectory."

"They may try to land again," Drax pointed out. "Move in closer, Commander. We can not afford to let them escape!"

"Damn it!" exclaimed Jed back on the Angel. "They've knocked out the main warp engine. There's no way we can escape now. We're going to have to head back to Leibfield."

"They won't let us do that!" shouted Carina. "They'll destroy us before we get anywhere near the main docking bays!"

"Then I guess we won't be using the main docking bays," Jed replied.

"What is that supposed to mean?"

"This is a small ship," Jed went on. "There are only two ways they can effectively trace us. They can use the visual radar scan, as they are probably doing at the moment, or they can use thermal image sensors."

"*Thermal image sensors?*" Carina questioned.

"*They lock on to the thermal signature of our engine. If they do that then we can't hide anywhere. We will have had it for sure. Hold on!*"

The Centurion Angel careered back towards the skyscrapers and freeways of Leibfield, with the Cybercopter close behind.

"*They're heading back to Leibfield!*" hollered Drax. "*Increase power to all weapons. They must be destroyed before they can attempt a landing.*"

A blaze of laser bolts rained down on the Centurion Angel. The tattered hull was in flames. The ship, however, was getting closer to safety. It was small enough to mix in with the other family class cruisers floating over Leibfield, forming the morning rush hour. The Angel sent at least half a dozen other ships spinning as it rapidly descended towards the mist at street level.

"*They are disappearing into the mist,*" reported one of Drax's Commanders. "*Prepare a thermal image scan to pick up their engine signature.*"

"*Eroogh, scallee narook,*" Mahnja shouted.

"*I see it,*" Jed replied, translating the Smownork language in his head.

"*See what?*" asked Carina, who was not bilingual.

"*They are preparing a thermal image scan,*" said Jed, "*just as I suspected. Mahnja, do you remember that old chemical factory on the north side of Leibfield? I'm sure they used to have a big chilling plant there.*"

"*Yahgoa defrot,*" Mahnja replied positively.

"*This sounds like a plan,*" *said Carina.*

"*If we can make it to the chilling plant,*" *Jed explained,* "*we can probably mask our signature. The thermal image scan won't be able to penetrate the lower temperatures. The chances are they won't be able to see us!*"

"*It's a worth a try,*" *said Carina.* "*Let's do it.*"

With that the Centurion Angel veered around, and began to head towards the north side of Leibfield Space Port.

At that exact moment during the film, Walter Bridgenorth inadvertently knocked over the popcorn bucket of the guy sitting next to him in the cinema. It was to prove to be a big mistake.

Popcorn

"What the fuck are you doing?" shouted the guy sitting next to Walter Bridgenorth, in response to the loss of his popcorn. He was a big guy with a muscle T shirt, and too much gold jewellery.

"I'm so sorry," said Walter apologetically, hoping that would be the end of the matter. His attention returned to Drax Mantis's frustration on the screen, who was calmly breaking his Commander's neck for letting the Centurion Angel escape.

"What do you mean, you are sorry?" the big guy said. "I don't care if you are fucking sorry, dick weed! I want to know what you are gonna do about my fucking popcorn!"

Walter reached in his duffel coat pocket, sandwiched between his seat and his buttocks, and pulled out a pound coin. "Here," he said. "Will that do?" Already some people in the row behind were becoming agitated by this disturbance.

"Do I look like I eat money, dick weed? Does my home girl here look like she eats money?" he indicated a slinky looking babe in the next seat, with a dress that barely covered her underwear. Walter had already noticed the young lady a good time earlier and in honesty had found her legs a constant distraction to what was, of course, the greatest movie ever made. "I want you to go to the kiosk and get me another bucket, you putrid jerk," the muscle T shirt concluded.

"Look," replied Walter, "I have offered you adequate compensation and sincerely apologised. Since I am trying to follow the film I don't see that there is any more I can do."

"Oh yeah?" cried the big guy rising to his feet. "Maybe I should just give you a good kicking, you stupid fuck."

Immediately Walter realised that he should have gone to buy the man another bucket of popcorn, but that is easy to say with the benefit of hindsight. Unfortunately it was already too late to avoid a degree of personal injury. Walter was a skinny, sad little character who wore chunky glasses and whose hair would never comb right. He wore a black baggy woollen jumper under his duffel coat, with drainpipe jeans and Converse basketball boots. His face was thin and lifeless in a way that invited any passer-by to punch it, even if he hadn't just knocked their popcorn over.

Walter gulped as the blow struck, knocking the king size cup of Coke out of the hand of the girl sitting on the other side of him. The fizzy drink flew through the air and showered down on the occupants of the next five rows. Walter slumped over in his seat, a black eye already swelling. One of the arms of his glasses had snapped. All around people were on their feet trying to evade the scene. Two Coke-soaked lads from the row in front, who fancied themselves as hard cases, jumped on the big guy before he could get a second punch in on Walter. What followed resembled a miniature riot, with all sorts of people punching each other for all sorts of different reasons. Walter, however, managed to escape with just the one injury.

Immortal Plastic

In less than five minutes the whole thing was over. Cinema staff were closing in from all angles, brandishing their torches in menacing fashion. Since they had all probably seen the film at least three times already that evening, they were glad of some audience participation to liven things up. Their normal customer orientated dispositions went out of the window and were replaced with a savage desire to use their torches like truncheons. They approached the punch-up from all angles, and had soon overpowered the rabble. The end result was that Walter, the big guy, and his chronically underdressed lover, were all ejected from the theatre.

In a dejected state, Walter headed home to his flat above the shop where he worked. His argument with the cinema manager for a refund came to nothing. He had started the evening planning to enjoy the most celebrated science fiction event ever. *Galactic Encounter: The Special Release* - finally back on the screen after twenty years. Instead it had been an evening of complete disaster. His glasses were completely ruined, which would cost him a packet to replace. Worse still it was raining, and his duffel coat was getting soaked. Walter was a born loser, a typical geek. Physically he resembled a beanpole. At mid way through his twenties he showed no sign of filling out. He had few friends, and none of them female. Like most people who didn't have much in the way of looks, however, Walter made up for things in the form of his personality. The only problem was that his personality was as equally objectionable as his looks, but for very different reasons. He was one of those science fiction nerds, very likeable but not the sort of guy to get stuck in a pub with.

At the centre of Walter's universe was his shop, and even that wasn't actually his. He only worked there, but was the only employee. The shop was actually owned by Mr Chang, an entrepreneur from Hong Kong who had several varied business interests in London. Celluloid Space Cowboy was, however, one of the best science fiction nostalgia and merchandising stores you are ever likely to find. Thousands of Walters from all over Britain had travelled to London just to see it, and most had even bought stuff. As Walter wondered down the High Street that night, towards the shop, he couldn't help but feel gutted. This was the opening night of the special release. It was *the* night to see *the* film. The chances of the film being released again to mark thirty years, or forty, were slim. It would never happen again. It was a bit like losing your virginity, a real one off. Imagine being kicked out during your first sexual experience! For Walter though, that had actually been the case. It was a bad comparison to draw. He reached the door of Celluloid Space Cowboy. The closed sign looked him hard in the eye from the other side of the glass. Walter turned away, only to be met by a more piercing stare from a cardboard cut out of a green alien in the shop window. He slowly turned the key in the lock. As he did so the first police car zoomed past, splashing the contents of a large rain puddle all over him. The car didn't stop, but motored on with lights flashing and the siren on full volume.

"You swine," Walter shouted after the car. "You stupid sodding swine!" It was the last straw for Walter. He was drenched from the curls on his brow to the white socks in his trainers. Then the second police car zoomed by, and did exactly the same thing. It was closely followed by a third and a fourth. By the time all four had passed the puddle was empty, Walter was almost drowning, and the windows of Celluloid Space Cowboy had never looked so clean. Walter paused momentarily. Although he was soaked, and furious with it, he recognised the fact that it was unusual to see so many police cars charging around at that time of night. Stranger still, they were accompanied by a helicopter that was closing in overhead.

"Bloody hell," he said to himself, "something big must be going down." He opened the door to the shop, and trudged inside with his soaking clothes.

The Tenth Code

At about the same time Walter Bridgenorth entered his shop, Brad Clusky was preparing to hack into the Gresham Corporation's AVREX system.

"Okay," said Brad. "The disk is in. This had better work."

"Trust me," came the crackling voice of Ralph in Brad's ear.

The screen in front of Brad lit up with a message.

AVREX SYSTEM

PROPERTY OF THE GRESHAM CORPORATION LTD

UNAUTHORISED ACCESS STRICTLY DENIED

PLEASE ENTER YOUR USER PASSWORD

Brad hit the keys on the console. It had taken them three weeks to lift one of the top secret passwords. There were strict guidelines on those sort of things these days. Gone were the days when a password could be a wife's maiden name, or a nephew's birthday, or the name of the family dog. These were invariably the first things the modern hacker would think of. At the same time a password had to be memorable, short and snappy. The last thing you want to do is forget the damn thing. Gresham scientists were advised by security specialists on the choice of their passwords. They were told they should choose things of relevance, but with no immediately obvious link with them if considered by a third party. Suggestions included favourite snooker players, or least favourite towns, or a particularly memorable present, and so on and so forth.

Finding out things like that took a lot of work. In the end Brad and Ralph had paid a prostitute to seduce one of the top scientists. Of course, she was only given a few choice details of what she was actually getting involved with, only being told the right questions to ask. The hotel room was bugged, to ensure they were covered in case the hooker forgot to tell them anything important, and the boys tuned into the proceedings from their van outside. It was a bit like listening to a football match on Radio Five Live in terms of build up, anticipation, and finally the full on action. There was no need for commentary, Brad and Ralph provided that themselves with a little help from a box of Marlboros and several cans of draught-slow beer. When the password was finally disclosed it turned out to be "Drax Mantis" of all things, so obvious it was predictable. These scientist types were all the same. Eat science, drink science and sleep science fiction.

WELCOME TO AVREX
WHICH AREA DO YOU WISH TO ACCESS?

The red CD was already doing the work for Brad. It contained a specially designed virus which cut out irrelevant files in order to get to the good stuff. A whole series of menu screens came up and disappeared. In moments they were in the access area for the secret project files.

PLEASE ENTER THE FINAL ACCESS CODE
YOU HAVE TWENTY SECONDS TO COMPLY

"It's asking me for another code," reported Brad.

"Another code?" Ralph was surprised.

"Come on buddy, don't piss me about. I've only got twenty seconds to enter it."

"I know, I can see."

"So what the fuck is it?"

YOU NOW HAVE TEN SECONDS TO COMPLY

Ralph's eyes scanned all the screens in the van rapidly. What had he missed? There shouldn't be another code. Then he noticed that the screen linked to the police computer was going crazy. Two, four, ten, fifteen patrols were already deployed, and a helicopter!

"Oh fuck!" the cigarette he was dragging on fell from his mouth.

YOU HAVE FAILED TO ENTER AN
ACCEPTABLE
PASSWORD

SECURITY SYSTEMS NOW ACTIVATED

Brad hadn't stuck around to read the message. He dived out of the door as the air-lock sprung to a close. The red CD was still in the drive. The blue one had already fallen to the floor and shattered, as had his glasses which provided the video link to Ralph's van.

The evidence of leaving these things might prove incriminating, but that was no longer the number one concern of Brad Clusky. His only concern was to get out of the building, and fast, before he was caught. Alarms were already ringing throughout the tower. An automatic locking system was sealing off every escape route. Brad was thinking fast. There was no contingency plan for this. They had already reached the point of no return. As soon as Brad was inside the tower they were committed. Any fuck-ups from then on had to be dealt with on an "as and when" basis. As fuck-ups went this one was a howler. Twenty seconds away from stealing the goods, and the whole show goes pear-shaped. You had to love the irony of that.

Just then the elevator bell in the corridor went off, indicating the doors were about to open. Brad was about to come face to face with whoever was inside, a prospect he was not keen on. He instantly glanced across to the stairwell door; it was his only hope. The elevator doors sprung open, revealing two guards with their guns already drawn.

"Hold it there mate, or I'm gonna make bloody big holes in you!" called one of the trigger happy guards.

The notion was not appealing. Brad dived through the stairwell door as a round of bullets impacted in the wall around him.

The Escape

Outside Ralph had already abandoned his computers, and was now in the driving seat of the van. There was nothing he could do at the console that was going to help Brad now. Instead he decided to try and rescue him. He had turned the key but the engine jammed. Of all things, the battery was flat.

"It won't start," he screamed into his headset.

"What do you mean, it won't start?" a more desperate scream replied down the wire.

"I don't know. The battery must be dead, or something."

"Are you fucking kidding me? In case you hadn't noticed all that static in the background is gunfire! Don't make this any harder than it already is."

"The van has had it, Brad! I'm gonna have to leave it. Just get the fuck out of there!"

Brad didn't need any instructions. He was already at the fifth floor, pacing down the stairs. The stairwell design was on his side. It was almost impossible for the two pursuing guards to get a clear shot at him. Things, however, were about to get worse. Brad could now here the echo of guards moving up the stairs from beneath him. He had no choice but to abandon the stairs and crashed out onto the fourth floor through an access door. He needed another second to think. It was a second more than he could afford. He now found himself in a rather typical, but deserted, open plan office. Both the elevators and stairs were now out of the equation. Choosing either would guarantee a speedy encounter with a gung-ho security guard. The air shafts in the ceiling didn't look big enough for a man of his size. There was nowhere obvious to hide. The sound of the guards approaching the access door behind him was getting louder and louder. Things seemed pretty bad. In desperation Brad headed for the closest window. It was difficult to see anything outside from the reflection of the office lights behind him. The only clear things he could make out were the flashing lights on the security patrol cars outside, but he could also just about make out the roof of some sort of annex about two floors down. He wasn't sure whether or not it was far to jump, but he had no choice.

He grabbed an office chair and crashed it through the window. As he did so the guards emerged from the access door behind him.

"Kill that terrorist bastard!" one of them shouted, a description that Brad found curiously inaccurate. Before they could take aim, however, Brad was plunging out of the window. He landed hard on the roof below, and cut his hand on some of the glass from the broken window. If he had landed a metre to the left he would have impaled himself on the busted chair he had already thrown out, and would probably be dead. Luck still appeared to be on his side, but there was no time to be cocky and dwell on it. Already there was a guard at the window from where he had jumped, and he was carefully taking aim at Brad. The annex roof was fairly small, probably housing a kitchen, or something equally suited to be slapped on the side of an office block. Brad saw that he could reach the edge of the roof simply by rolling across it through the broken glass. As gunfire rung out again, Brad rolled sideways and fell from the annex, crashing to the ground below.

Pain swelled through his cut hand. The two falls had taken their toll. He was bruised and battered, but for the moment it seemed the guards had lost sight of him. In addition, it didn't appear that any of the guards above were keen to follow his direct route to the ground floor. Then Brad heard the first barks of the guard dogs and he almost felt like surrendering. The dogs sounded big, unpleasant, likely to cause him some serious damage, and far too close for comfort. He wondered how much more pursuit he could withstand. Surely he was only prolonging capture, and risking his life in the process. Then he noticed that the perimeter wall was less than ten metres away. On the other side he would have a good chance of escape. He mustered his strength and headed for the wall. The dogs were close by, barking madly, and there were more guards close behind them. Torch beams danced along the wall, searching for Brad's shadow. The occasional gunshot was let off at the slightest movement. Brad was tired, panting heavily, and nursing his wounds. It took all he had to pull himself up the wall. He took a moment at the top to get his breath back. It was to prove a mistake as a torch beam caught him head on. An orchestra of automatic fire tried to knock him off the wall like an empty beer can in a fairground attraction. There were no prizes for the punters tonight though. Brad toppled off the wall, and out of the compound.

"Ralph!" he called into his button mike. "Ralph, where the fuck are you?" The receiver crackled, but there was no response. Brad pulled his earpiece out and discarded it. He could now clearly hear police sirens coming at him, coming at him fast. He ran across the street and towards the alley where he had started out. Headlights caught him, but were no match as he clambered over the nearest fence and through the yard it encompassed. For the first time Brad began to feel confident. Every step, every jump, every clamber, every drop of sweat, every twinge of pain, everything was taking him further from the tower and the AVREX facility. The dogs had lost his scent, the patrol cars were aimlessly chasing through side streets which he had already passed. Then he heard the roar of the helicopter, and he knew it was not over yet.

Joy riding kids thought that helicopters were their very last worry. All you had to do, if they got too close, was hide up in a back lot or behind a wall. Brad knew better. He knew that police pursuit helicopters carried thermal image cameras. On that he would appear like a lighthouse on a dark night. His body heat was giving off a signal that was impossible to miss. The only escape was to find a source of heat to drown out his own thermal signature. Brad's desperation increased. As soon as the helicopter picked him out it would be over. With new found force he was throwing himself over wire fences and brick walls looking for an open doorway to carry him inside, to carry him to somewhere warm. As he crashed through a side gate on to the High Street he knew the helicopter was close, but his answer was already at hand. Not only were the lights on at the curious looking comic store across the street, but the door was ajar. With one final burst of energy he ran towards the shop as fast as he could.

Jed Largo

Jed Largo was wary as he entered the cave. His brain was telling him that this was a bad situation and that he should turn back, but his instinct was moving deeper into the cavern. The light was beginning to fade, and an envelope of murky shadow now surrounded him. He was protected from the frosty temperature by his all-in-one, combat issue, insulated space suit. On his feet was a matching pair of astro boots, ideal for the alien terrain. The cave itself was empty, with rough walls of stone for comfort. He could tell though that somebody, or something, called this place home. It was then that Jed heard the sound of footsteps behind him. He turned to face the direction the steps came from.

"Who are you?" enquired Jed of the dark cloaked figure who was emerging before him. The silhouetted creature pulled back the hood that covered its face.

"My name is Cardinal Fergus McTulip," the figure announced. Under the hood was an old man, with a grey beard and steel blue eyes. His voice was mellow, and had a warmth in his manner that a boy might expect to find in his grandfather.

"McTulip," repeated Jed, his hand nervously fidgeting near the holster of his laser blaster. He still wasn't sure whether or not McTulip was friend or foe. "I know that name," he went on. "Didn't you know my

father? His name was..."

"I know who your father was, Jed," said the old man, "and I know who you are too."

Jed was startled by this familiarity.

"What do want from me?" Jed enquired. McTulip did not answer at first. Instead he circled the cave and took a seat on a large boulder. It was clear that this was where the Cardinal lived, if you could call these conditions habitable. Then again, he was dressed like a hermit, and no doubt lived like one as well.

"Your laser," said McTulip, indicating Jed's belt with a bony index finger. He could read Jed's uncertainty at his arrival, and his eagerness to pull his gun. "If you are planning to shoot me, you'd best get on with it. I'm not one for melancholy."

Jed realised his error, and quickly dropped his hand to his side.

"Your time has come, young Jed," McTulip went on, feeling confident that the initial social barriers to conversation had been broken. "You have come of age, and your learning must now begin."

"My learning?" Jed laughed. "I don't know what you are talking about!"

"The training you now face is intensive. It will require all of your mental and physical capabilities. You will need to open your mind to new thoughts, and sharpen your senses in order to control your emotions."

"Old man, you've got the wrong boy. I quit school years ago. There ain't no future in it! Besides, I do just fine doing what I do. There's an honest living to be made in smuggling."

"Your ignorance will be remedied," McTulip added undeterred. "You do not realise that your

potential is far beyond bar fights and petty smuggling. You are from a stronger bloodline than you give credit to."

Jed grew annoyed. "Stop mixing your words McTulip. If you only have fancy things to say then you have come to the wrong man. Where I come from we use straight talk, we say what we mean."

"Maybe I have come to the wrong man," the old man drew back. "I thought I was talking with Jed Largo the Skellern Warrior. It is unlike me to confuse a thuggish brawler like yourself with such a great leader. It seems we all make mistakes. You must be on your way, I'll waste no more of your time." He rose to his feet and pulled his hood back up around his face, trying to make himself look busy.

"Wait, wait!" said Jed in dazed surprise. "Did you say Skellern Warrior?" He thought he had missed an important part of the conversation.

The old man turned to face him, and spoke slowly. "It is your fate. I have forseen it."

Walter Bridgenorth sat behind the counter reading the comic. It was the first ever issue of the *Galactic Encounter* comic, first printed in 1980 in New York and priced in the shop at forty pounds. It was based on the original movie script, and included the pivotal moment when Cardinal Fergus McTulip tells Jed Largo of his destiny as a Skellern Warrior. Not as good as the movie, but a good substitute. It was the best he could have hoped for, considering the blow out at the cinema. His duffel coat was hung up on a hat stand near the door, desperately trying to dry out. The rest of his clothes he had exchanged for his tartan pyjamas and a fluffy C & A dressing gown, which his mother had bought him for Christmas two years ago, along with his trusty pair of slippers. He had fixed his glasses with a strip of masking tape as a temporary measure. He couldn't wear them, though, due to the fact that he was nursing his black eye with a bag of frozen peas. As a desperate attempt to compensate for these things, he had made himself a mug of hot chocolate, and had picked out the comic from the appropriate rack in the shop.

As it was only just gone ten it was a bit too early for bed, and there was nothing on television. Instead he sat back in the chair behind the counter, which was his personal favourite, and rested his feet on the cash register. Life wasn't such a bad place, sitting there with hot chocolate and a classic comic, even though he must have read this comic a hundred times before. As tranquillity seemed to return, however, the shop door flew open with a tremendous bang, and a complete stranger, dressed from head to toe in black, burst through the door.

Celluloid Space Cowboy

Brad Clusky crashed through the shop door, and slammed it shut behind him. Walter threw his comic and bag of peas in the air in surprised horror, and jumped to his feet.

"Please don't kill me!" he begged, assuming Brad to be an opportunist burglar. "Take what you want, but let me live."

Brad ignored him, but checked outside to see how close the helicopter was, peeking out from behind the green cardboard alien in the window. He still didn't know if he had escaped. A crack firearms unit could smash the door down in seconds and splash his guts all over the shop. The thought was not comforting.

"I beg you," Walter went on, fighting back tears of terror, "Please don't hurt me. I can open the till. I think there is about thirty pounds in it."

Thirty pounds. It was the notion of an amount of money that small that first seriously drew Walter to Brad's attention. Thirty pounds, it was enough to make Brad want to laugh. Moments ago he was executing a million dollar hoist, but now this idiot thought he was robbing his comic store for a mere thirty quid. Did he really look that unprofessional?

"Look mate," Brad finally spoke, allowing his attention to be drawn from the window. "I don't want your comics and I don't want your money. What I want is for you to shut the fuck up, kill these lights, and turn the heating up."

"Turn the heating up?" Walter found the request most unusual.

"Yes," shouted Brad. "Turn the heating up, and no more questions." Walter quickly complied, and scuttled over to the thermostat. After increasing the heat to maximum he switched the lights off. Brad checked the sky out of the window, the helicopter's spot light beam passed along the High Street, past the comic shop and down towards Superdrug and Dorothy Perkins. It did not sweep back again immediately, although that was no comfort for Brad. He knew that beam was almost certainly going to pass up and down the street at least a dozen more times over the next hour before the search was abandoned. Two more police patrol cars zoomed by outside, too fast to make out Brad's outline at the window. Brad knew though that his pursuers were close now, too close. Any mistake would give him away.

Walter was still trying to gauge the situation. He thought that it was in his interests to put his hands in the air. He didn't think Brad had a gun, even though he was obviously dangerous, but he felt more comfortable in a submissive position. He tried to work out what Brad was all about. Turning off the lights was one thing, but turning up the thermostat seemed more than just a little strange. Anyway, what sort of man would be being pursued by this many police cars? A serial rapist? A mass murderer? A drug baron? Oh yes, this man must be dangerous, and a lot more dangerous than the thug at the cinema. Despite Walter's fears, he remained confident with the situation. There was obviously a large police presence in close proximity. It would only be a matter of minutes before two portly coppers would stroll into the shop. After a few moments of 'ello, 'ello, 'ello patter, the man in black would be suitably handcuffed and carted off to be detained at Her Majesty's pleasure. It was thoughts like that which made Walter sleep soundly at night. Unfortunately for Walter, his two portly policemen were not forthcoming. Indeed, his face became more intense with fear as the sound of the helicopter grew more distant and the patrol car sirens seemed to move away.

Conversely, Brad's anxiety was starting to diminish. As his safety became more of a certainty his body gradually sunk to the floor of the darkened shop. He was exhausted, filthy, and his face was sticky with drying blood where he had wiped the cut on his hand against it. He lay there on the floor taking deep breaths, and trying to work out his next move. He wanted to be somewhere else, somewhere safe. He knew, however, that he would have to stay in this shop until daylight. The police would stay in the area at least until the morning, if not longer. Any men caught out walking by themselves would be stopped and questioned. The way Brad looked at that exact moment it wouldn't take Sherlock Holmes to work out that he was the boy they were looking for. Instead he would have to wait until the streets filled up with people. Only when the street outside was full of shoppers would it be safe to disappear again.

"Can I put the light back on?" asked Walter.

"No lights," Brad replied, reaching inside his jacket for a cigarette.

"Ah, there's a no smoking policy in the shop," Walter explained apologetically. Brad fired up regardless. He felt he had earned it. Besides, he had only smoked two earlier in the day, leaving the remaining three of the day's quota to be enjoyed after the job had been pulled off. Walter felt he had to justify himself. "You see, some of these comics are over thirty years old. They have already faded. The smoke damages the paper." He picked up his broken glasses from the counter and tried to straighten them on his nose in order to get a better look at Brad. Once he had got them more or less right, he put his hands up again.

"Why are your hands up?" asked Brad, deliberately ignoring the comments about his cigarette. Walter sheepishly dropped his arms to his sides. For the first time that night everything was silent to Brad. No screaming guards, no menacing dogs, no static from Ralph in his ear, and no helicopter. He took the opportunity to survey the shop for the first time. Celluloid Space Cowboy. He had noted the name as he crossed the street. He knew nothing about marketing, but the name did nothing for him. Then again what would you call an odd ball science fiction shop? The clientele were probably all sad sods who would think that a name like Celluloid Space Cowboy was really cool. In truth, the shop had a certain atmosphere in the darkness of night. It was a dingy little cabin, stuffed so full of memorabilia you could hardly move. The walls were lined with original movie posters from a range of space films ranging from the 1950's to the present day. The racks were filled with comics, some sealed in plastic. Other racks held postcards of science fiction heroes, or key rings with plastic figures on the end, or other such tacky crap. Plastic space ships, with a coat of dust, hung on wires from the ceiling. There was something almost sinister about such a curious collection of artefacts.

Brad found himself staring at a poster on the far wall. It was a portrait shot of Drax Mantis. The pose was fairly standard, with Drax just standing there looking menacing. The name Drax Mantis bounced around Brad's head. He could see himself typing the words on the AVREX keyboard only a short time earlier. In that moment he found that he could identify with the film *Galactic Encounter*. He was just another poor sod who had been defeated by the evil Drax. Another character who had bitten the dust in the opening scene. A get-it-man. Hell, it was almost poetic.

The Flat

Brad dragged hard on his cigarette, then he turned to Walter. He was just the sort of guy you would expect to find in a shop like Celluloid Space Cowboy. Chronically underweight, no dress sense, gimp glasses. He guessed that his personality would score a big zero on the party scene. Then a much darker thought came to him. This pathetic man had seen him, seen his face. He reached around for the balaclava but it was gone. Where the fuck had he lost that? There was nothing to protect his identity from this man.

"Why did I have to turn the thermostat up?" asked Walter, sheepishly trying to kickstart the conversation from the safety of the far side of the counter.

"Heat," said Brad, "the helicopter looks for body heat. The only way to stop it is to drown out your signal, either by hiding somewhere cool or hot. Room temperature is probably safe enough, but a few extra degrees never go amiss."

Brad kept the explanation brief. Anything he said was a clue to his identity. After all, how many guys are likely to know about the sort of gear they carry on police helicopters? Of course, Walter did not know Brad's name, but that was irrelevant. Both MI5 and MI6 were certain to have files on ex-SAS men. The investigating officers would know that the attempted theft of the AVREX system would have required that level of expertise. Assuming the perpetuators were British, they would not have to show Walter too many mug shots of ex-servicemen for a positive identification. Brad knew that would be just the beginning. When they had his name they would find him, and then it would be over. He could hide in the remotest corner of the world, but he would not be safe. He would be dead before he was even aware that the slightest thing was out of place, and no one would ever find his body.

"What happened to your eye?" enquired Brad.

"I, er, I got punched," Walter replied.

"Not your day, I guess," said Brad. "What's your name?"

"Walter, Walter Bridgenorth. I work here. I live in the flat upstairs."

"Well, Walter," Brad said rising to his feet. "I need you to hide me. I'm going to be hanging out with you until tomorrow. There's too much heat outside for me to go anywhere tonight."

"Are, I mean er, are you a killer?" Walter asked tentatively. Brad laughed at the question. Sure he had killed. He estimated that the total was twenty seven, but that was a very different Brad Clusky. During the Gulf War he had participated in special operations to neutralise Iraqi strategic targets behind the lines, taking out scud missile launchers. Things were going well until they were sent in to take out a small operational control centre. One of the guards was a girl of no more than fifteen, practically dwarfed by her machine gun. She came out of a doorway and fired about ten rounds at Brad. He had no time to think about what he was doing, and accidentally hit her with so much firepower she was practically torn in half. She never had a chance. That was why Brad left the SAS, and that was why these days he had a no guns policy on his jobs.

"Sure," he finally answered, "I've killed people." He omitted the fact that he had not done so since 1991, but he wanted to keep an upper hand with Walter by maintaining the dark psycho image.

"You can stay in my flat upstairs if you like," Walter offered, now with his worst fears confirmed. "The way up is though that door on the side."

"Let's go up together," smiled Brad. "I wouldn't want you trying any crap on me. If you even think of calling the police or running off then I am going to have to be extremely unpleasant with you."

Walter nodded that he understood. He wasn't too sure how unpleasant Brad could be, but he imagined that it was probably pretty bad. The two of them climbed the narrow stairs up above the shop, and through the door into Walter's flat. For a moment Brad thought he was just in another section of the store. The flat was filled with more science fiction memorabilia than the shop itself. It felt like it was some kind of sick museum. The door lead into the lounge and kitchen, which were joined. More Airfix space ships dangled from the ceiling. More posters covered every square inch of the walls. Even the carpet had UFO shapes on it. Most of the stuff in the flat was *Galactic Encounter* merchandise. There was a Mahnja the Smownork coffee mug in Walter's kitchen, along with a Fergus McTulip lunch box. A *Galactic Encounter: Special Release* calendar hung from the back of the door. The picture for this month was of Lady Carina in a scantily clad pose with a laser pistol. On the table a big hardback book was open showing how the film was made. The most amazing thing however, was the cabinet in the lounge. Could it have been specially made for this purpose? Wooden panels comprising countless shelves, with a glass sliding door on the frontm, almost as tall as the wall Every shelf was covered with little plastic figures, no more than four or five inches high. There must have been hundreds of them, and each one was a different character from the *Galactic Encounter* Trilogy.

"You must be quite a fan!" Brad stated, feeling uncomfortable at being enclosed with such an obsessed fanatic.

"Do you like them?" asked Walter, for the first time losing his defensiveness and feeling much more confident in his own space. "I have three hundred and twenty one," he went on, "They are all originals, manufactured by the Bravado Toy and Game Company of Chicago between 1979 and 1986. I've got almost every one of the original set, one hundred and thirty three to be exact. Each one with it's original plastic gun. These ones down the bottom, they still have their original packaging. That makes them worth more, about thirty quid each. I've got a lot of duplicates, of course. There are fifty two Glokorian Soldiers, thirty seven Rebel Star Pilots, twenty two Glokorian Star Pilots, nineteen Glowba Bears, sixteen Rebel Aqua Troopers, fourteen Skellern Warriors and eight Jed Largo's, plus a few odd ones. The whole collection I reckon must be worth £2,000."

Brad was speechless. Only a guy like Walter could spend up to £2,000 on a pile of plastic. He couldn't think of anything meaningful to say so he didn't bother.

"Do you have a sink?" was his alternative line of question. "I need to wash this blood off, and clean myself up."

"Uh, yeah," Walter replied. "The bathroom is through there."

Brad moved off towards the bathroom, but before he did so he crossed over to the phone. It was simple enough for a man of his strength to snap the cord.

"Hey," shouted Walter. "You can't do that! I said I wouldn't call the police. You can trust me. You don't have to go round braking things!"

"The door key," Brad replied, ignoring the concerns.

"What?"

"The key to the flat, give it to me."

Walter reluctantly walked over to the coffee table where the door keys were resting in a plate the shape of the Centurion Angel. He passed them to Brad who went straight over to the door and locked it from the inside.

"Is there a spare set?" Brad asked.

"No."

"Good," Brad went on. "I'd best look after these then." With that he walked into the bathroom and closed the door behind him. Walter collapsed into an armchair. There was no escape from the flat. He knew if he tried the man in black would only stop him. He made a mental note to himself that he should never leave the shop door unlocked after hours. You just never know what sort of lunatics might walk in.

The Camera

Two hours had passed since Brad first entered the shop. He had washed his face and generally cleaned himself up, and had gone on to blow his cigarette quota for the day. He was already on eight, but was justifying this by the fact it was now gone midnight, and he was into the quota of the next day. Every now and then he would tell Walter to make him a cup of coffee, which he did, in order to rotate the tastes of caffeine and nicotine. The combination was enough to keep Brad from feeling too drowsy. Walter was less scared of Brad now, although he was beginning to find him quite objectionable. It was bad enough that he was smoking in his flat, something which was normally a forbidden activity, but the fact that he was just making himself at home was completely irritable. Who the hell was this guy, to order him about and make him brew cups of coffee? How dare he sit there with his feet on the coffee table reading yesterday's paper! How dare he break the telephone and confiscate the door key! Walter certainly didn't need coffee and cigarettes to stay awake, even though he was exhausted by the day's events. His increasing rage with Brad was taking care of that.

"Chill out," said Brad, "It's going to be a long time until morning. You may as well get some sleep if you like. I'm sure I can find my way round your kitchen if I need anything."

"I'm fine," Walter replied, with heavy eyelids, from the armchair opposite Brad.

"Want to keep an eye on me, huh?" smiled Brad. "There's no need for you to worry. I'm not here to rob you. I appreciate that all this stuff might be worth a few quid, but I don't know the right people to fence it through. It's not my scene, if you take my meaning."

"Why haven't you killed me?" asked Walter, using his arm as a jack between the arm of the chair and his chin.

"I haven't ruled it out," Brad came back. He was starting to become annoyed with Walter's odd character, and wishing that he had picked a different shop to hide in. Walter wasn't satisfied with the answer. He wasn't satisfied at all. First of all this man bursts into his shop with no explanation, whilst police cars and helicopters hunt him outside. In that situation it was fair to assume the man was probably dangerous, and likely to get violent if provoked. Since then, however, he had failed to give the impression that he was really a violent criminal at all. He didn't seem to have a gun, or any weapon for that matter. He wasn't especially threatening, even though he was rude, and failed to express the sophistication that a criminal being pursued by half the Metropolitan Police would deserve. Walter's thoughts became more systematic. He started to compare the man in black with Drax Mantis, the only criminal with whom Walter had any real empathy with, even though he was fictitious. Drax had many of Brad's characteristics. He was brash, thoughtless and essentially a bully. Drax, however, had a much larger bark than his bite. He rarely actually did bad things, as opposed to ordering other people to do them for him. In addition, from a cinematic point of view, he was a criminal who could easily be sympathised with. He was in many ways an anti-hero, his badness making him cool and therefore likeable. Walter sized Brad up along these lines. There was no reason to assume that the man in black had anything in common with Drax Mantis, but Walter considered it nevertheless.

"I tell you what I think," began Walter, "I think that if you were really a killer you would have snapped my neck or something the second you came in the shop. I mean, the police seem to want you pretty badly. That must mean you are pretty ruthless, huh?"

"It's none of your business," replied Brad, picking up the paper again and turning to the sports pages.

"Do you want to hear a theory?" Walter asked, chancing his arm.

"No."

"Good, here it is. You are a Norman Bates type serial killer on the run. The police are on your trail so you hide in my shop, but you have forgotten your ice hockey mask that you always wear when you hack people's insides out. So, not wanting to ruin your cool, you decide not to dice me but to take me hostage instead while you work out your next move. How am I doing?"

"You read too many comics and watch too many films," Brad replied, not looking up from the paper.

"So what is it you have done?" asked Walter, trying to give Brad a chance to provide his own explanation. "Are you a terrorist perhaps, or maybe an escaped convict?"

"You ask too many questions, Walter."

"Well, this is my flat, and I didn't actually invite you in. I don't like you drinking my coffee or reading my paper. I especially resent the fact that you are smoking in my flat. I think I deserve to know a little about what all this is about, considering the circumstances."

"Look," said Brad lowering his tone but leaning forward, "You are right, I'm bad news. I've had a very long night being shot at and chased by dogs. I am also very tired. All I need is one night of your hospitality, then you will never ever have to see me again."

"How do I know I will never see you again?"

"If it makes you feel better I'll add your name to my Christmas card list."

"That is not what I mean," Walter continued, standing up and walking slowly towards a small cupboard across from the chairs, "I mean what if you send somebody to hurt me after you have gone? You may have powerful friends. Maybe I know too much? I have seen your face, I could describe you to the police." The cupboard door eased open.

Walter wasn't exactly sure what he was about to do, but he was confident that it was going to work. In the panic and confusion that had occurred when Brad had entered the shop it had seemed like Walter was very much in danger. Walter was now starting to realise that the situation might be the other way round. He was working on the assumption that the man in black needed him alive if he was going to make it through the night avoiding a police cell, or worse.

"Look," said Brad, "I'm not going to send anybody to hurt you." As he said it the flash of the camera blinded him.

Brad cursed. How could he have been so stupid!

Walter was smugly standing there with the Polaroid camera he had taken from the cupboard in one hand, and wafting dry a photograph in his other.

"What the fuck are you doing?" Brad blurted, jumping out of his seat. He knew the answer already. He had been set up. "Give me that photo," he demanded.

"Hey," replied Walter. "This is my insurance."

"Give it to me," insisted Brad. "Give it to me, before I kick the crap out of you!"

"Is that a threat?"

"Just give me the sodding photo!"

"So it's not a threat?" Walter's questioning continued.

"What?" said Brad in confusion. "What are you going on about?"

"I am trying to establish whether or not you are a kicking the crap sort of person. It seems to be you are not. All mouth and trousers, I think, is more accurate."

"I'm warning you!" screeched Brad, reaching for another cigarette. "Do you want another black eye to have a matching pair?"

"I told you once that we have a no smoking policy," Walter stated forcefully. "Am I going to have to tell you again?"

Brad paused, and slid the cigarettes back inside his jacket. He knew, as much as he wanted to, he wouldn't be able to bring himself to hurt Walter. It would be easy enough to punch him, and richly satisfying. Such an act, however, might provoke an unpredictable response. Up until now Walter had been on side. He had played along with the whole hostage thing, and seemed unlikely to phone the police even after Brad had left. Physical violence now might jeopardise all of that. Brad was resigned to the fact that he would have to use reason, and that would mean letting Walter have his way. Sure, he would play along for now, but he would also have to see where things went. He decided to let Walter keep the photo if it made him feel better. The chances were it was blurred or over exposed. There probably wasn't anything to worry about.

"Look," said Brad, calmly taking a seat again, "I need your help. I'm not saying that you won't end up in jail for doing it, because you might. You could always say that I forced you or something, or I held you hostage. I just need to keep my head down for a few hours, then I'm out of your life."

"What's your name?" asked Walter, who sat down opposite. Brad thought about making a joke by saying he was Richard Kimble from *The Fugitive*, or something similar, but he thought better of it. He certainly felt like a fugitive. Instead, and for reasons beyond his own comprehension, he told the truth.

"It's Brad." With that every army protocol he had ever learned seemed to disappear out of the window. He had given up both his face, and now his name. It wouldn't have surprised him if he had started giving a lecture on the layout of the Gresham Corporation tower next.

"Well, Brad, or may I call you Bradley?" asked Walter, not waiting for a reply. "It seems as though you and I are going to make a little deal about who gets to keep this little photograph here." Brad couldn't believe it. This sad arsed little fuck was about to come up with some stupid blackmail scam. It really had been a disaster of a night. He had no choice but to play along. If he had known then what he was about to get himself into, he might have chosen to come out of retirement and kill Walter there and then. This, however, was just the beginning.

Part Two

The Plan Is Hatched

Robin Hood

Six years before the night that he met Brad Clusky, Walter Bridgenorth had been a student at Warwick University studying philosophy. There was no particular reason why he had chosen philosophy; it just seemed to be a bit different. It turned out that he would have been better off picking a different subject, and probably a different university. He was, to be blunt, crap at philosophy, only managing to scrape a third, and he was hopelessly unpopular. Things could have been worse, though. If you are going to be an unpopular student it pays to be a philosophy student because, in the main, they are all unpopular. Walter thus became a member of an unpopular circle of male philosophy students who, despite spending all their time together, all hated each other. Walter felt his reasons for hating his group of peers were more than legitimate than most. He actually had dozens of reasons, but his top five were as follows:

1. Their disturbing addiction to *Monty Python*, especially the films.

2. Their ability to quote large sections of *Mein Kampf* by Adolf Hitler.

3. Their ability to always end up shagging the girls he wanted to shag, even the ugly ones.

4. Their addictions to girly drinks such as Taboo and Mirage instead of good honest beer.

5. Their complete hatred of science fiction.

On one particular damp February morning, Walter found himself sitting drinking coffee and eating Kit Kats in the student canteen with his group of philosophy associates; Randy, Jez, Mike, and Tony. The fact that it was damp and that it was February was more or less irrelevant. The five of them tended to resort to coffee and Kit Kats on most days. The only thing that ever seemed to change was the context of the conversation. Today's conversation was a creative debate on the social motivations of Robin Hood. The first hour had centred around his name. Robin Hood, as is well known, descended from a wealthy aristocratic blood line and his true title was Robin of Loxley. Naturally, as Mike had pointed out, Robin was sensible enough to recognise that such a name would not be popular with the poor, whose loyalty and support he was seeking. Jez challenged this by suggesting that a formal title would have held more weight with the aristocratic classes, whose support may have been more useful in bringing down the Sheriff of Nottingham. Having not considered this option, Jez added, it was reasonable to assume that Robin was not the intelligent man which legend wishes us to believe in. Mike retorted, by arguing that many successful public figures had only become so by allowing the public to choose their titles. Eddy "the Eagle" Edwards and *The Gladiators* were cited as good examples.

"Errol Flynn or Kevin Costner?" asked Walter, snapping a finger of Kit Kat.

"What?" questioned Randy.

"The best Robin Hood," Walter explained. "Who do you think? Errol Flynn or Kevin Costner? Please don't say Jason Connery. I refuse to accept that Robin Hood was a blonde."

Nobody answered the question. It was instead treated with instant contempt, and the conversation moved on.

"Was Robin Hood a good guy or a bad guy?" asked Tony.

"Please," sighed Jez, implying that the question was almost as daft as Walter's, "he was obviously a good guy."

"Indeed," added Mike, "anybody with socially driven motives to improve society can only be classed as a hero. Robin Hood arguably has a greater claim to the foundation of communism than Karl Marx."

"Wait a second," Walter interrupted, diverting his attention from the model space ship he was making out of the tin foil wrapper of his Kit Kat, "Robin Hood wasn't a good guy, he was just portrayed that way. Sure, he was a socialist, I can handle that, but he was also an anarchist. He murdered soldiers and robbed people. Just think about that for a second! He well and truly gave the authority of Britain a two fingered salute."

"But Robin Hood was a populist," said Mike. "He had huge support for what he did. Besides, he was protecting the throne for the true king in his absence."

"So, by comparison," Walter went on, "what you are saying is that if I considered that a modern day Chancellor of the Exchequer was planning a cabinet coup to overthrow the Prime Minister, who is incidentally a very patriotic man, I would be well within my rights to kill the Chancellor and any member of the Treasury who supported him in the name of Great Britain. Is that right?"

"Don't be a fucking prat," said Jez.

"You always have to be an arsehole, don't you,"

added Randy. "Of course murdering the Chancellor of the Exchequer is completely different to murdering the Sheriff of Nottingham, as was. The sooner you recognise things like that the sooner you might start getting somewhere on this course."

"You are completely incapable of social interpretation aren't you Walter?" added Mike. It was the sort of girly remark that Walter expected from these misfits. The slightest challenge to their pointless concepts was always brutally dismissed.

"I've got a lecture," Tony said, almost embarrassed at having been seen with Walter. "I've got to go." He stood up to leave. Mike and Jez went with him, only pausing to give a pitiful stare at Walter. Walter wasn't at all convinced that they actually had a lecture, they didn't normally start that early.

"Why don't you think about it," Randy said to Walter, as he also stood to leave. "It might do you some good."

Walter was left alone at the table with his empty polystyrene coffee cup and his tin foil space ship. Somehow, most of his conversations with Randy, Mike, Jez and Tony seemed to end in this way. They would treat him like an idiot, and then just leave him. Cretins! Walter pondered the Robin Hood question further. He was certain he was right, Robin Hood was a bad guy. He was a rogue and a law breaker. As Walter sat there he approached the issue from a number of angles before the idea came to him. If Robin Hood was a bad guy portrayed as a good guy then the opposite must also be possible. It must be possible to have a good guy portrayed as a bad guy, and it was. The answer was Drax Mantis. Walter cursed himself for not thinking of this earlier. Drax Mantis, the embodiment of evil, who actually turns out to be quite good. If only Walter had thought of that example when the other guys had still been there. The whole concept opened up numerous trains of thought as to how you could actually define a good guy and a bad guy. Indeed, the question had to be asked whether or not there really was a difference between good guys and bad guys. Ironically, six years later, during the small hours of the morning when Walter was trying hard not to fall asleep in case Brad Clusky should try something on, these thoughts came flooding back. How do you define good guys and bad guys? Was Drax Mantis really good, and Robin Hood really bad, and what about Brad Clusky? Where would he fit in the spectrum of good and bad? What about Walter himself? So many questions to be answered and issues to be debated. It was that kind of daydreaming that had cost Walter any chance of a career in philosophy. On the other hand, it was that kind of questioning that was going to make the encounter with Brad Clusky a lot more than a coffee time debating point.

Warren Kingburger

The immaculate stretched limousine cruised through the West End of London. It was jet black, the colour limousines are supposed to be. The bodywork had recently been washed, waxed and polished, so that any passer-by could clearly make out their reflection in it. The engine purred smoothly, turning over with a precise hum. The windows were blacked out, to avoid unnecessary attention. This was the definition of style, the plaything of millionaires. The car pulled up into a side street just off Leicester Square. The driver scuttled out of his door, like a well dressed beetle, and opened the near-side door at the back. Warren Kingburger stepped out of his limousine and slipped his Ray Bans over his nose. It wasn't sunny, that was just his style. He took a deep breath of air, and exhaled as if he were in the countryside. The pollutants in the air seemed to intoxicate him into thinking the stuff was actually good for him. A few passers by seemed obviously disappointed that someone of recognisable fame had not stepped from such an impressive automobile. Warren Kingburger was a big American, with a plump stomach and a round tanned face, who not only looked like but also dressed like Boss Hogg from the *Dukes of Hazard*. No one ever had the guts to ask him whether or not that resemblance to the TV character was intentional, or whether he really was stupid enough not to notice the similarity. He fired up a cigar as his personal assistant, Dilly Foxtrot, eased her incredibly long and shapely legs out of the car behind him. The driver obediently shut the door, and scuttled back to the driving seat. Warren Kingburger and Dilly Foxtrot stood there on the pavement side by side. They were as much alike as chalk and cheese. He looked like he was just out of the freak farm, with his whiter-than-white three piece suit with matching shirt, silk tie and Stetson. Dilly, on the other hand, looked sensational in a tight blue business suit that showed all of her curves. She looked sensational even when she hadn't eaten, slept, or had a manicure for three days. Some girls have it and some girls don't, and Dilly definitely had it. Of course, she didn't have the slightest drop of business acumen, but that was not what Warren Kingburger was looking for when he hired her. He just needed somebody who looked good beside him. If he was trying to seal a big deal over dinner, he could guarantee that the brush of Dilly's hand along the thigh of his intended target would be enough to crack their concentration and allow Kingburger to clean up. She more than paid her way in those sort of situations. Dilly, meanwhile, was blissfully unaware of all this. She genuinely thought she was making a constructive contribution to Kingburger's business.

"Well, Mr. Kingburger, this is the place," said Dilly in her sumptuous American Deep South tones.

"It sure is, honey. It sure is."

In front of them was a large vacant restaurant unit. Although there were no customers yet, the place was still a hive of activity. Carpenters were putting up partitions. Electricians were wiring in neon signs and sound systems. Couriers were delivering special equipment, ordered to strict specification. Painters were scurrying round to get work finished. A frantic foreman, who had not yet realised who had just arrived, was screaming obscenities at almost everybody.

"So what do you think baby?" Kingburger asked Dilly, who was busy adjusting her chest for maximum impact factor on passing males.

"It's fantastic. I've never seen anything like it," she pouted.

"I don't know whether it's as good as the one on Broadway," he went on, "but it knocks fucking spots off Tokyo, Berlin, and the shitty mistake we made in San Diego. Yes sir, this town ain't gonna know what has hit it! Try and picture it Dilly, my girl. Kids eating Drax Mantis Burgers with fries, or Skellern Fillet Sandwiches, and mom and dad feasting on delicious Jed Largo Chicken Buckets. Waiters and waitresses dressed up as your favourite Orbit movie characters. A huge video screen showing selected shots from the films, and trailers of all our forthcoming pictures. Plus more memorabilia than Planet Hollywood and the Hard Rock Cafe put together. This is going to be London's essential dining experience."

"I love it when you're being creative, Mr Kingburger," complemented Dilly, flicking her streaming blonde hair down her back, and placing a tender hand on Warren's shoulder. He almost purred in response, hinting that something far more depraved might follow later, after dinner, back at her hotel.

"So where are we at, Miss Foxtrot?"

"Well, sir," she maintained the formality. "I'm told that the main construction phase should be finished sometime next week. We've got the boys from

Vision and Wizardry arriving on the twenty third to add those special touches you asked for, and we have already started recruiting waiting staff. I have a couple of interviews for security staff to carry out today. Other than that, everything is on schedule."

"Is the bar done yet?"

"No, sir, but it's well on track."

"Pity, I could murder a Jack Daniels. How about the props?"

"Well, Quentin back in LA has managed to come up with some really great stuff. We've got the original Cybercopter model from the first film, plus Fergus McTulip's original costume. He's even managed to find one of Jed's original laser guns. I've got a full inventory if you need to check. There must be near on a hundred items."

"Good, I like that! How about a Drax?"

"A Drax, sir?" Dilly was confused.

"Yeah, a Drax action doll," Warren continued, puffing on his cigar. "Did you ask Quentin to get that yet?"

"We have all of the original toys on order, sir." The response didn't quite meet Kingburger's expectation. He wasn't used to second class service.

"Did I ask that? No, I didn't," he was getting angry. "Let me use more simple terms. Do we, or do we not, have a Drax Mantis action doll?"

"I believe..."

"You believe? Now honey, you know I don't like it when you only give me half answers. We need a Drax Mantis action doll. Original box." He drew his face closer to hers to emphasise his words, but his voice grew softer and sterner. "When you get it , and you will get it, make sure he has a rocket pack. You remember the scene, don't you? In Galactic Encounter? Drax Mantis has a rocket pack which he uses to defeat and kill Cardinal McTulip in their final battle. He goes on to wear it in the second and third films when he is trying to destroy Jed Largo. Only two hundred were ever made."

Kingburger's face was getting closer and closer to Dilly's. As it did so his bottom lip seemed to curl over, as if he were reprimanding a dog for chewing on his slipper. Dilly didn't like it when Kingburger was like this. She scrunched up her face and shut her eyes in rejection.

"This action figure," Kingburger went on, breathing cigar fumes all over her, "is very, very special." He drew a smile, and Dilly tried to draw away. "More special than you are sometimes sweetheart!" he went on menacingly, "Am I making myself clear?"

"Yes, Mr Kingburger. Absolutely!" Dilly muttered, her lips wobbling.

"Good. Well, shall we take a look inside?" he said, becoming upbeat and removing his face from the space directly in front of Dilly's own. "The boys could probably do with some motivation. I want to make it clear that I want England's first ever Orbit Studios Experience to open on time, and no excuses!"

His fat little frame waddled over to the door of the shop, and Dilly reluctantly followed on behind.

Orbit Studios

Warren Kingburger was a Texan, son of Bobby Kingburger the famous oil speculator. Bobby had struck liquid gold near Madisonville in 1951, one of the biggest fields in Texas. The Kingburger Corporation was established soon after. It produced so much oil that it effectively had a licence to print dollar bills. The business boomed, and moved to one of the biggest office blocks in Dallas. Warren was born a few years later, the only son of his millionaire father. His daddy tried to install the virtues of oil upon him. It was Bobby's only wish for Warren to take over the business when his time came. Warren, however, had other ideas. Money to him was the key to everything, and he didn't much care for which type of rigging gear delivered it to his back pocket. He used his father's wealth for his many dubious pastimes. He casually picked up a cocaine habit, which helped him get all the girls he wanted. Trashy girls, black or white, with false accents, acting like sophisticated college girls, whilst underneath hiding some unhealthy history nurtured in the slums. Girls who liked to party, and party hard. The girls and drugs were partnered by fast cars, designer labels, and endless travel between the likes of Monte Carlo and Vegas. Bobby was powerless to stop his boy. He had put enough money in his trust fund to bank roll his demeaning behaviour. Of course, he could have cut him out of his will, but his wife died too soon from cancer and Warren was all he had. So it came to be in 1978 that Bobby died. It wasn't a dramatic affair, the type of death that millionaires were supposed to have. There was no bedside scene with crying relatives giving their last emotional regards. There were no immortal last words to be handed down through the generations. The event was due to Bobby's fading eyesight. He was gunning his car down a side street in Houston that afternoon. Witnesses said he couldn't have seen the stray mongrel, chasing newspaper in the wind, until the last second. He swerved hard into a tree. It should have been over a cliff, or under an oil tanker, but it was only a tree. There was no explosion, the car was hardly marked, yet Bobby's neck was cleanly broken. No blood, no gore, but a straightforward fracture. The dog was unscathed.

Warren inherited the corporation, the ranch, the yacht, and the football team. At the time he was renting an apartment in California. His habits had cost him a lot of friends, and the bank balance wasn't as good as it used to be. On hearing of his dad's premature departure, and that he was still the only benefactor, he got blindly drunk and slept with five different whores on the same night. He knew even then, however, that things would have to change. The Kingburger Corporation was worth billions of dollars, but he knew that in his hands he could reduce it to nothing. So, for the first time in his life, he set about making some tough business decisions in an effort to turn over a new leaf. He sold the oil business within a week. Wall Street pundits estimated that it went for less than a third of its market value. A Japanese company snapped it up, much to the horror of Middle America. A week later he made his first and only company acquisition, the Orbit Studio Group. Orbit was a small movie company based in San Francisco. In 1978 its founder and only director, Todd Orchard, was working on a dodgy science fiction picture called *Galactic Encounter*. Five top studios had already turned down the production. The story was just so far out that it was perceived as a guaranteed flop. Spacemen, evil empires, talking lizard men. It was all too much. Todd Orchard needed five million dollars to finish the picture or drop the project, leaving Orbit to liquidation. Warren and Todd had met at a party at the time, which neither had been invited to. Somehow they had drifted together. Warren, who was more than stoned that night, lapped up the plot as Todd wept his funding gap into his cocktail. Within twenty four hours the deal was signed. Warren became the sole proprietor of Orbit, a move Todd would later regret, and funded the completion of the film with a small part of the revenue from the corporation sale. Twelve months later *Galactic Encounter* opened in LA. Within weeks it had become the biggest film in movie history, and made Orbit one of the biggest film studios in Hollywood. Jed Largo and Drax Mantis were household names, and Orchard was the hottest director ever. The film won no fewer than seven academy awards, including Best Supporting Actor for veteran star Callum Caffreys (who played Fergus McTulip). The *Galactic Encounter* phenomenon had been born, and America loved it. It was a Class A drug that nobody could resist. It had obvious appeal to kids, but it also drew in college nerds, hormonal girls who fantasised about Jed, and every other American with a dream to fulfil. Within months it went on to top box office charts in Japan,

Germany, France, Canada, Britain, Australia, Spain, Brazil and many more. In 1982 *The Glokorian Revenge*, the first sequel, was released. It almost matched *Encounter* in terms of revenue. The trilogy was finally completed in 1984 with the release of *Rise of the Skellern Warrior*. A movie legend had been created which went on to shape America for twenty years. The Orbit Group became hot property, with its share prices leaving the Kingburger Corporation in the dust. Warren, whom economists and analysts had originally perceived as one of the greatest threats to American commerce, had become one of its greatest pioneers. Numerous big hits followed, mainly science fiction, and mainly directed by Orchard with Kingburger as the producer. The Orbit stable rolled out such classics as *Cybercop*, *Dino Island*, *The Galactic Noonies Trans-Universal Vacation*, and *Gloopy: The Friendly Alien*. Twenty years since it all began, at the end of the century, it was time for something special. America was hungry for a classic. The value of such masterpieces as *Galactic Encounter* had been lost. They had given way to an era of crash and bang special effects, bad language, and increasingly gratuitous sex. The special release idea was Todd's, but Warren loved it and adopted it as his own. The three biggest films of the century, back again on the big screen, for a generation who had previously only seen them on TV or video, and for the rest of the world to see again as they were intended. Orbit's own in-house special effects team, Commercial Vision and Wizardry, had been given a $20 million budget to come up with the most awesome overhaul imaginable. New characters, crisper images, improved surround sound stereo, and the most adventurous effects that Hollywood could only have dreamed of in its most desperate nightmare. A whole six minutes of new film were added to *Encounter* alone, including a new scene with Klaxto Miraz, the notorious and fearsome alien gangster who had previously only appeared in the last film. Warren, however, wanted more. He wanted his fantasy world of another universe to become a reality. He wanted merchandise, he wanted corporate deals, he wanted toys, he wanted limited edition board games. He wanted it all, and the only way he could do it was to start to turn the real world into part of his giant fantasy. Bit by bit, in every major city of the world, he was buying restaurants. These were to be the tools of his success. These were to be the places where the world of science fiction became science fact. So far these places had opened in a dozen cities around the world, but now it was London's turn. Warren Kingburger just couldn't wait until the opening night.

All Day Breakfast

A week passed before Brad Clusky and Ralph Lee were due to make contact. That was the plan if things went wrong. No phone calls, no bumping into each other, no unscheduled meetings. If the police had one of them under surveillance then it was critical that he didn't lead them to the other. The meeting venue was an all-day breakfast cafe in Camden, a seedy place. The tables were made of thick chipboard, covered with a marble patterned plastic. The walls were painted white, and had faded over the years. The kitchen was separated from the tables by a traditional glass-fronted counter. A black board hung behind the counter with chalked-up prices of an assortment of fry-ups, which more or less consisted of all the same items. Ralph arrived at the canteen first. He ordered a full English with coffee, and sat down to read a tabloid paper. A waitress in her fifties, puffing a cigarette, delivered the plate to his table. Bacon, eggs, sausage, beans and mushrooms. He drowned them with sauce and tucked in. Brad arrived a short while later. The black clothes which he had worn to break into the Gresham Corporation had long since been incinerated. He was now in his more natural attire, a leather jacket, lumberjack shirt and jeans. The only clue that he had been involved in the AVREX job was the bandage he was wearing on his right hand, protecting the cut he had sustained jumping from the window. He walked across the cafe, and sat down at the table with Ralph.

"What happened to your hand?" asked Ralph, briefly looking up from the paper.

"It's just a cut," Brad replied. "Did they follow you?"

"No," said Ralph, chewing on some bacon. "I showed them a clean pair of heels on the night. Looks like you made it too. I thought you were fucked back there."

"Thanks for the vote of confidence," said Brad.

"How bad was it?"

"The usual. Getting shot at, running from menacing dogs, jumping out of windows, being chased by helicopters. A normal day's work, really. What happened with you anyway?"

"The van was shagged," replied Ralph, devouring a sausage. "Flat battery, of all things. I managed to jump start it a couple of days later. It's back at the lock up now."

"I didn't mean the van," said Brad. "I meant the tenth code. Why didn't you know about the tenth code?"

"I had no indication," Ralph said defensively. "It wasn't my fault. It was a ghost code, no signature anywhere else on the system. Even if I knew about it the chances of breaking it would be slim. Still, we need to start thinking about that."

"Ghost code, huh?" Brad was not satisfied with the answer. "I thought that was why the Americans were paying us all that money? We're supposed to be professionals. We're not supposed to get caught out by ghost codes. That's why they chose us!"

"Look, I told you," said Ralph raising his voice.

"I'm sorry that you got shot at, and I'm glad that you got out, but that code was invisible. I doubt that any of the top five hackers I know would have cracked it. It was a fucking mess, but next time we will get it right."

"Next time?" Brad sighed.

"We still have to get into AVREX. Don't forget who is providing the greens here. At the present time we belong to Uncle Sam, and he badly wants to know how to freeze insects and send them off to the outer reaches of fuck knows where!"

"Come on, Ralph. Wake up and smell the coffee! We aren't going to just waltz back in to that tower. There isn't going to be a sodding door man waiting there to hand over AVREX, and sincerely apologise that his colleagues were not more forthcoming the first time round. Gresham probably have a fair idea that the States were behind the break in, and that is going to worry them a whole fucking lot. Right now they are probably mounting more cameras, hiring more trigger-happy guards, and adding more fucking ghost codes! We can't touch it, not now. There's too much heat!"

Ralph finished his breakfast by wiping a slice of bread round his plate to soak up the mixture of egg, sauce, and fat. The waitress came over to the table.

"Anything else for you boys?"

"Can you get us two coffees, thanks?" Ralph replied. He fired up a cigarette and pulled over the large glass ashtray as the waitress disappeared back to the counter.

"Look," he went on, "we have to get back in. We have already been paid a lot of money, and we know too much. The Americans are not going to ignore it. If we don't deliver then they'll take us out. No debate. We can't hide from people like that."

"It's not that simple," winced Brad, staring hard at the sauce bottle to avoid eye contact. The waitress brought over the two coffees, with sashes of sugar resting on the saucers.

"I know it's not simple," replied Ralph. "We have no choice!"

"That's not what I meant," Brad replied sheepishly. "We can't do AVREX now, even if we wanted to. We've got another job."

Brad raised his cup in an effort to trivialise the comment, but Ralph wasn't that stupid.

"Another job? What other job?" Ralph asked suspiciously. "Does it pay us millions, I wonder? Does it reward us with a new life style in South America? Do they chuck in cosmetic surgery, and false passports? Is there a lifetime guarantee that we won't be shot one day by some American mercenary on a CIA salary? Please tell! This had better be good!"

"Look," Brad dropped his voice, but kept his stare. "I got seen."

"You got seen?" Ralph laughed. "What the fuck is that supposed to mean? Who saw you?"

"This guy. I was on the run. I thought I was clear, but the helicopter was close. I didn't want to chance the thermal camera, so I looked to get inside. There was this shop, a comic store place. I went in and he was there, and he saw me."

"Christ, I thought it was something serious," smirked Ralph. "A nerd in a, what did you say, a comic store! Why didn't you just kill him? No, sorry, I remember. You don't do that anymore. I could get someone to kill him. I could do it myself. This is not a problem!"

"I don't want you to kill him."

"Don't get sentimental on me, Brad," Ralph said stiffly. "If it's him or us it is going to be him. I'm not ready to die for some jerk who works in a comic store. Oh no, this is not debatable, that guy is dead."

"I said I don't want him killed. Besides, he knows my name."

Ralph took a gulp of coffee, and raised his eyebrows at his colleague. "I have to say that was pretty fucking stupid," he said. "However, when the little shit is dead it will be very hard for him to tell anyone."

"And he has a photo of me," Brad added with a tone of embarrassment.

"He has what?" Ralph exploded. "I can't believe that. You are so fucking stupid. How on earth? No, don't tell me. He has your photo! I can't take much more of this. You are determined to get us killed. Is he a sodding relative or something? How did he get a photo?"

"He took it. I wasn't expecting it."

"Why didn't you bust the camera?"

"It was a Polaroid."

"Easier still, tear up the picture!"

"I couldn't. He wouldn't let me."

"He wouldn't let you! You are fucking ex-SAS, for God's sake." Ralph sank back in his chair. He just couldn't comprehend his partner's stupidity. When you are up against it you just don't take chances. Any witnesses are killed without question. Sure, it's not very pleasant, but it was just the way it was. Them or us. In order to survive you have to prioritise. You don't go round telling people your name, and you certainly don't let them take pictures to keep as souvenirs.

"So what does this prick want us to do?" Ralph

concluded in defeat.

"I don't know yet. He wants me to meet him tonight, at a cinema."

"Maybe he's not so stupid, meeting in a public place. If it's money he is after don't take any chances. I can transfer funds out of any account in Switzerland to any other account at the touch of a button. Just say the word."

"Sure," replied Brad. He suspected, however, that it wasn't going to be anything as simple as robbing a bank. Walter was a lot of things, but greedy wasn't a word that instantly sprung to mind. He was sad, fanatical, devious, and gimpish, but not greedy. Brad suspected that what Walter wanted was something much more complicated than money.

"So what happens next?" asked Ralph. Brad pulled a scrap of paper out of his pocket and eased it across the table to his colleague.

"It's the number of the hotel where I'm staying," Brad explained. "It's the Strand Palace. I've reserved you the room next to mine. I want you to check in as soon as possible. I'll call for you there in the morning."

With that Brad stood and turned to walk out of the cafe.

"Hey," Ralph called after him. "Don't fuck up!"

Brad just smiled back. He walked out of the cafe and turned up the street. Ralph gestured to the waitress, and settled the bill.

Comics

It was 9.30 am. Walter always opened the shop at 9.30 exactly. He flipped the card over on the door, so that the word "open" was now pressed against the glass and the word "closed" faced back into the empty shop. He turned the bolt on the door and unlocked it. Celluloid Space Cowboy was open for business. Opening at 9.30 am in itself was a little pointless. It was too late in the morning to attract any school kids, and too early in the day to attract anybody else. This in itself didn't especially bother Walter as it gave him a chance to straighten the shop out. He changed the receipt roll on the till, straightened up the comics in the racks, filled out purchase orders, and played about with the window display. There was something very therapeutic about doing those sorts of things. When all the little jobs were completed it was time to make a mug of coffee, take a seat behind the counter, and pull out a good comic to read. Walter was a great fan of comics. It wasn't that he was incapable of reading anything more substantial, he purely saw them as works of art that needed to be appreciated. The story lines were normally more intricate than most of the novels he had ever read, the characters were razor sharp, and the artwork had its own niche in social history. How many icons of the twentieth century had evolved from this route? *Superman, Tin Tin, Desperate*

Dan, Batman, Judge Dred, and many, many more. They all started out as simple illustrations. That morning Walter had chosen a mid-seventies edition of *Planet of the Ant People*, but was having a problem concentrating on the story line. His mind kept drifting back to the events of a few days earlier. The man in black, or Brad as he chose to call himself, had been constant in Walter's mind. He felt that he had a moral obligation to do something about this man. On several occasions he had come uncomfortably close to calling the police and telling them everything, but for some reason he had thought better of it. He still wasn't completely convinced that he had figured Brad out. Walter had initially been proud of the fact that he had taken the Polaroid picture. He felt that he had shown Brad that he was no dimwit to be pushed about, that he was more than capable of standing up for himself. The photo had certainly been a turning point in the evening's proceedings. From the second the flash had gone off, Brad was on the defensive. It seemed like he was taking more care about what he was saying and doing, carefully not trying to let anything slip. To an extent he had been successful. Walter still really didn't know who Brad was, or how he had ended up in the shop. The whole thing left so many questions unanswered. Was Brad really that concerned about the photo, or was the defensive thing just an act? Did Brad have powerful friends who might torch the shop in the middle of the night, leaving Walter to die from smoke inhalation and incinerate any trace of the photo? Alternatively, was he being honest? Walter knew that what he should have done was put the photo in an envelope and given it to a solicitor, only to be referred to in the event of his death. Better still, he should have taken it straight to the police. The photo now lived in the till. Walter opened the cash drawer by hitting the "no sale" key to check it was still there. It hadn't, of course, gone anywhere. Mr Chang, who owned the shop, rarely came in to check up on things. Walter did all the paper work, and paid the money into the bank. He had done more or less everything for the four years he had worked there since leaving university. He glanced briefly at the photo, and slid the cash drawer shut again. On that night he hadn't let the photo out of his sight. He had strained to stay awake until morning, but had somehow managed it. He didn't even risk falling asleep when Brad dozed off at about three in the morning. He couldn't risk him waking up and destroying the photo, possibly choosing to slit his throat in the process. When daylight had finally arrived he was relieved. Brad didn't seem to have any intention of hanging around, and hardly even seemed interested in the photo anymore. This made Walter slightly mad, after going without a night's sleep to protect the bloody thing. It was then that he came up with the idea. He hadn't planned on it, it just came out. He regretted it immediately as it might have provoked Brad into violent retaliation.

"If you want this picture," Walter had said, "you are going to have to do something for me. If not, I give it to the police!" It had taken barely two seconds to say it, but the potential ramifications were enormous. Brad, however, had reluctantly stopped to listen to the proposal. This had caught Walter out as he hadn't actually thought of what he was going to blackmail Brad for. Instead he suggested the most stupid thing he had come up with all night. He asked the man in black to meet with him again. As for a time and venue he said the first thing that came into his head. He was already planning to go and see *The Glokorian Revenge: The Special Release* anyway. He had checked out the times and prices, and the rest of the details seemed to spill out. Remarkably, Brad had agreed. The only problem now, having taken this enormous risk, was to work out what Brad would give him in return for the photo, in addition to a guarantee of security. Whatever he was going to come up with, he had to do it fast. He was due to meet with Brad again that same evening. He scratched his head and thought. He sipped his coffee as Ngan Klux, leader of the ant people, was about to order his troops to execute his human prisoners, unaware that Captain Kane was fast approaching on a rocket cycle to save them. The shop door opened, and Oswald Moriarty hustled his way inside. He always came into the shop just after ten, but today he seemed to have more of a sense of purpose in his step.

"Walter, guess what?" he shouted, even though they were the only two people in the shop.

"What?" Walter replied, not looking up from his comic.

"The coolest thing is about to happen," Oswald continued to blurt. Little did he know how right he was, or how much of a catalyst the following conversation was going to prove in Walter's aspirations for blackmailing Brad, the man in black.

Oswald Moriarty

Oswald Moriarty was the most regular customer at Celluloid Space Cowboy. He had two things in common with Walter Bridgenorth. He had the same huge admiration for the *Galactic Encounter* films, and he was twenty-six. The similarities ended there. Oswald was a tall, lanky, buck-toothed lad. He had frizzy blonde hair and freckles. He wore jeans with a sports sweatshirt which was clearly too big for him. He had two sweatshirts, to Walter's knowledge, which were almost identical and were alternated while one was in the laundry. Today he was wearing the red one. Oswald was unemployed, and lived with his mum in a terraced house nearby. His mum kept the household afloat, working as a checkout girl in the local supermarket. Oswald paid her a mere ten pounds housekeeping a week, and spent the rest of his dole money at Celluloid Space Cowboy. With anyone else, such a slack attitude to life would have appalled Walter, but not with Oswald. Oswald was Walter's golden goose. Since Oswald's money was guaranteed to be spent in the shop, the trick was to get him to buy the crap that nobody else wanted. The hot lines sold themselves. Anything that had been made into a film or a television cartoon would move fairly quickly out of the door. Posters, key rings and mugs sold themselves to people who liked to give their friends naff presents.

Jim Carley

The trick was to move the obscure stuff, like the Japanese imports, or the battered copies that had been thumbed by too many time wasters. These things were reserved especially for Oswald. Walter had no less than four great techniques for selling these things to Oswald:

1. Explain to him the item was particularly rare, and therefore valuable, and that he was doing him a favour by letting him have it so cheap. In a few years time it could be worth a fortune.

2. Tell him that somebody exceptionally famous (e.g. an extra on *Star Trek: The Next Generation*) had been into the shop earlier and had picked up that very copy. If you look hard you can still see the fingerprints!

3. Tell him that it's the last one in stock, and that he has already had a number of enquiries over the phone. If he didn't buy it now, it was unlikely to be there in the morning.

4. Tell him he could buy two for the price of one, and give the extra one away as a present. This only applied to really slow lines. To Walter's knowledge, Oswald's mum normally received a comic for both her birthday and for Christmas as a result of this practice.

Sure enough, one of these techniques always resulted in a sale. Normally Walter would jump up to greet Oswald, and deliver his latest sales patter. Today, however, it was Oswald who was full of beans.

"What happened to your face?" Oswald asked curiously, although he was more surprised at Walter's lack of enthusiasm than his black eye and broken glasses.

"Nothing," Walter replied, "I just walked into a

door. What can I do for you today?" He didn't normally ask a question like that. He would recommend, direct, advise, or instruct, but never normally ask such an open-ended question.

"It's more like what I can do for you!" Oswald hollered back triumphantly, slapping a magazine down on the counter in front of Walter.

"What's that?" asked Walter.

"The latest copy of *Space World*. Have you seen it?"

"No."

"Oh, man, you should get it! It's got the latest news on the Orbit Studio Experience in it. It's cool man, it's really cool!"

Walter was, of course, familiar with the impending arrival of the Orbit Studio Experience. A designer concept restaurant, based on his favourite films of all time. It would have been impossible for him not to have been aware of it. He knew it would contain a number of props from the film which he would have to inspect as soon as possible, and was therefore preparing to dine there at some point during the opening week. He had thought of inviting somebody to go with him, but nobody sprung to mind.

"Everybody knows about the Orbit Studio Experience," he said. "It's been featured in every science fiction magazine I've read this year."

"I know," said Oswald, "but this one has got the scoop, man. This one has got the hot story."

"Which is?"

"They've got a Mantis, a Mantis action figure!"

"A Drax Mantis action figure? Give me a break! Everybody has got a Drax Mantis action figure. I've got four myself."

"You got one with a rocket pack?" Oswald asked smugly.

Walter lifted his face from his comic for the first time, as Oswald's words began to bounce around inside his head.

"A rocket pack?" he asked slowly, making sure he hadn't misheard anything.

"That is what I said," replied Oswald. "A Drax Mantis action figure with a rocket pack. Bet you haven't seen one of those before?"

Walter was stunned. His memory flooded back to 1979, when he was a mere child. He remembered that day, that really hot day, standing outside of the toy shop in Maidstone. He remembered his mother's anger, and his tears of frustration. He remembered it all. He remembered how much he wanted a Drax Mantis action figure with a rocket pack.

"I tell you, man," Oswald went on. "I have just got to see that thing. That is the only one in the set I haven't got. Just to see it! Wow, that would be something!"

Walter was too startled to reply. He was too startled to do anything. He had never wanted much in life. He was never into cars, or sport, or girls, but he had always wanted that action figure. It was the only status symbol he coveted, and one of the rarest. What was more, he already knew how he was going to get it. In a split second, his whole life seemed to fall in place. It was an amazing feeling.

"Walter," said Oswald with concern, leaning over the counter. "Are you all right?" The prompt was enough to make Walter snap out of his daze.

"I'm, uh, fine. Yeah, I'm fine."

"Do you want to borrow *Space World*?"

"No, that's all right. Our order should be in later this morning."

"Sure."

There was a moment's pause between the two of them, before Oswald asked if Walter still had anymore of those Japanese comics. This was a new experience for Walter, which took his mind off Drax Mantis. Oswald had never asked for anything under his own steam before, without any pressure. Perhaps this wasn't going to be such a bad day after all.

Drax Mantis

The flooded world of Aquaticacia, in the furthest quadrant from the bright centre of the galaxy, is one of the most inhospitable planets imaginable. Ocean storms, hurricanes, sub zero temperatures. Not a first choice vacation destination. Yet, on this mass expanse of water, the rebellion against the Glokorians had established a secret base. In a vast, submerged space port the Centurion Angel was parked up. Mahnja the Smownork was wandering about on the roof, trying to rewire the main navigation systems.

"How's it going up there?" called Jed Largo from the ground below. Mahnja let out a confused roar which suggested all was not well. "Okay, okay!" cried Jed. "I'll be back to help you in a minute. I've just got a few things to do. Fix what you can, and get one of those maintenance droids to help you out." The answer didn't satisfy Mahnja, but he was used to his buddy disappearing when there was anything vaguely complicated needing doing. Jed strolled off down an access tunnel towards the main control room. The dark and dowdy control room contained a jumble sale collection of old computer gear. It was hardly cutting edge, but under the circumstances it was working and managing to power a deflector shield around the base in the event of a Glokorian attack. The menagerie of rebel commanders were scattered about, discussing what to do next. Lady Carina sat at a console, monitoring the outer perimeter.

"How's it going?" asked Jed.

"Fine," she replied, fixing her eyes on the screen. "All the time the Glokorians are on the other side of the galaxy I think we will be okay."

"Listen," he said coyly. "Now that things are a bit more stable, I'm going to take off. I still need to find that alien scum who killed my mother. You understand, don't you?"

Carina turned slowly to look at him. "If that's the way it is Jed," she replied smoothly. "It's a shame, you're a good pilot."

"I'm a good pilot?" he responded, expecting her response to be somewhat different. "What the hell has that got to do with it? Look, I sympathise with your rebellion and everything, but I've got my own battles to take care of as well." He pulled away, and stomped off down the corridor.

"Jed! Wait," she called after him, reluctantly abandoning her position. "There's no need to be like that."

"Like what?" he snapped.

"We are going to miss you, I never said that we wouldn't."

"We are going to miss me?" He turned to face her. "What about you? Are you going to miss me?"

"I don't know what you mean."

"Sure, you do. Or are you going to deny the way you feel about me?"

"You're deluded!" she shouted.

"Yeah," he replied turning again to continue down the tunnel. "I guess maybe I am."

"Okay, Mr Hot Shot!" she called. "Go ahead and

89

leave. Go and find that alien and take your revenge, for what good it will do you. It won't bring your mother back, that's for sure. I expect you'll just end up being blasted."

"I can look after myself," he shouted back.

"That just about sums you up!"

As Carina shouted the tunnel rumbled, and a sheet of metal fell from the ceiling. At first she was taken aback. Could her voice have started some weird sort of avalanche? Jed turned and stared, but said nothing. No one was arguing any more. When the tunnel shook again it was clear that it wasn't Carina's voice that had disturbed the structure. These were tremors like an earthquake, yet Jed and Carina both knew that Aquaticacia was a stable planet. No, something was outside. Something big, with enough power to destroy the base.

"Drax!" muttered Jed, waiting for the next impact. It came with such force that it knocked Jed and Carina flying. "Come on," he cried, grabbing her arm. "Let's get out of here!"

"Am I going to have to watch the whole film before you tell me what is going on?" asked Brad Clusky.

"Sshh!" replied Walter. "This is a good bit." A week after Walter's last unfortunate outing to the cinema he was back again. Some people preferred *The Glokorian Revenge* to *Galactic Encounter*, but not Walter. Although *Revenge* was a much darker and sinister film than its predecessor, it lacked that final touch that was the difference between a really great film and an all time classic. It didn't matter much to Orbit Studios anyway. They had all three of the original films being re-released over a three week period. The box office takings were just mounting up.

"Look," Brad came again. "When you said you wanted to meet me at the cinema, I didn't think I would have to sit through an entire film first!"

"I don't understand you," said Walter, not moving his attention from the screen. "This is a great film. Considering I paid for the tickets, and this is the opening night, you should feel privileged. If not privileged, then grateful."

They were sitting in good seats. Upper circle, central to the screen, and about three rows back. The tickets came in at a pound dearer than the stalls. Walter had deliberately avoided the stalls, because that was where the incident of a week earlier had taken place. He hadn't noticed his assailant on the way in, but he couldn't be sure he wasn't downstairs amongst the sea of darkened bobbing heads. Anyway, this time he wasn't so scared. Even if Brad was a closet pacifist he still looked hard, and he was with Walter.

"If you are going to watch all of this," Brad tried for a third time, "I'm going to wait outside."

"You are staying put," Walter said firmly. "If you want to talk business, we'll talk business. It's a waste though. I'm beginning to think I'll never get to see one of these all the way through without interruption."

"So, what's the crack?" Brad asked with relief.

"Well, you see that big guy there, in the black?"

"Where?" questioned Brad, scanning the audience.

"Not in the audience, you morose fool, I meant on the screen!"

"Drax Mantis?"

"Well bless my cotton socks!" exclaimed Walter. "After all that it seems you are capable of some form of concentration."

"Everyone knows who Drax Mantis is," retorted Brad. "He's like Kermit the Frog, or King Kong, or Elvis, or..."

"I can assure you," interrupted Walter, "he's nothing like Kermit the Frog!"

"You know what I mean."

"Ssshh!" exclaimed a fat woman sitting next to Brad. She had been annoying him all night by taking up half of his leg room as well as her own. Plus she had the arm rest. Brad just gave her a fuck off kind of stare and she got the message.

"I want him," Walter continued.

"You want Drax Mantis," Brad repeated, making sure he had all the facts.

"That is correct. I want Drax Mantis."

"This isn't some kind of perversion thing is it," joked Brad. "I really don't think he would go for you. You're not his type."

"You really are immature aren't you?" condemned Walter. "Of course I don't want Drax Mantis himself. I should point out, after all, he is only a fictional character."

"So what do you want? Do want to meet the actor? Do you want to try on his costume? Do want to go behind the scenes? Do I look like the kind of guy who can procure those sort of things? Maybe you have me mixed up with Jimmy Saville, or perhaps even Cilla Black? Maybe you could come back on the show next week and tell me how you got on? I mean, please!"

"You remember my collection of action figures?" said Walter, ignoring Brad's immature little outburst.

"What, those expensive doll things?"

"They are not dolls," Walter reprimanded. "They are action figures."

"Whatever," Brad replied. His eye now caught the back of a girl sitting a few seats along in the next row. From the back she looked good, a slim neck and a bob hair cut. Maybe looking at her would ease the pain of two hours of Drax Mantis kicking ass and Walter Bridgenorth sprouting bullshit.

"There is one missing from my collection," Walter explained. "Drax Mantis."

"No, wait," said Brad, momentarily snapping out of his trance. "I'm sure I saw a Drax Mantis in that cabinet!"

"You did, I already have the original doll."

"Hah," shouted Brad. "You said doll!" He turned to the fat lady. "He said doll! Did you hear him?" With a look of indignation the woman stood up and grabbed her young son who was sitting in the next seat. As she dragged him from the theatre he burst out crying, and now it appeared that everyone in the circle was looking at Brad and Walter.

"At last," sighed Brad. "Some fucking leg room."

The Rocket Pack

"Why not shout a bit louder," Walter said sarcastically, "I don't think everyone in the theatre is looking at us yet." The comment seemed to temporarily kill the conversation. Attention turned again to the film for another five minutes. During that time Drax Mantis had completely obliterated the planet of Aquaticacia, but Jed, Mahnja and Carina had safely escaped on the Centurion Angel. The silence between Brad and Walter was uncomfortable. Both knew that the other wasn't really watching the film anymore, but instead trying to anticipate the other's next move. Walter was wondering if he was going to get away with his rapidly forming elaborate plan. Brad, on the other hand, was in a constant state of wonder at how bad the situation was becoming. He didn't enjoy the silence, or the film, and he was starting to care less and less about the attention he was attracting. For all he knew the fat lady may have already reported him to the cinema manager, and where would that lead? Would the police be involved? Would he match the description of a man witnessed only a week earlier seen breaking into the Gresham Tower?

"So," Brad finally said, "if you already have a Drax, why do you need another?"

"This is no ordinary Drax," Walter replied. "I want a Drax Mantis with a rocket pack. They were a limited edition, only two hundred were ever made."

"But it's only a toy!" exclaimed Brad. "Don't get me wrong, the sooner I get you out of my life the better; but, if I'm your genie in a magic lamp, I don't get why you only want a doll. Why not money, or something worth while?"

"These things have an auction value of ten thousand dollars!"

"Is that all? Hell, my associate could wire an amount like that out of any international bank and they wouldn't even know it was gone. You could just go ahead and buy one with that."

"You don't understand," Walter frowned. "Although that is their auction value, these things never come on the market. No, people don't sell that sort of thing. You could get money if you wanted, but what I have in mind will need more than that."

Brad scratched his head. How had he ended up in this situation? The AVREX job was a complete fuck up, but that in itself wasn't so bad. Sure, it was a disappointment, but you should just be able to walk away from that sort of thing. You get it together, and just try again. You don't blow your identity when you are undercover. You don't get photographed, and, most of all, you don't get blackmailed into stealing toys. Walter's photo should have been an insurance to save his own life, to spare him from Brad getting Ralph to get a hit man to take him out. Yet, although Walter was a geek of the first order, he was also very shrewd. He knew he had Brad in a corner. He was like a beetle kept in a matchbox by a school kid. The photo had already accumulated in value. Not only was it going to keep Walter alive, it was also going to get him more, much more. Things like this didn't happen everyday,

95

and certainly not to Walter. He was already considering Brad as a real life Jed Largo. In fact, the more Walter thought about it, the more he saw similarities between Brad and Jed. They were both experts, and knew how to handle themselves when they were up against it. They were both crude and rugged. They also had the same knack of attracting bad luck. Things just go wrong for guys like that, but they normally come out on top in the end. Since Walter had talked to Oswald Moriarty, the plan had matured in his head. Drax Mantis was just the start of it. In addition to that, Walter wanted to be part of Brad's scene. A real life adventure, something he had only ever dreamed about. Brad was his ticket, and the photograph was his receipt.

"So where are we going to find one of these things then?" Brad asked submissively.

"Most of them are owned by Orbit Studios," explained Walter, "the people who made these films. At present there are twenty seven in Europe, all in private collections. Soon there will be a twenty eighth. At the end of this month Orbit are opening a new theme restaurant. It's a bit like Planet Hollywood, or the Hard Rock Cafe. There will be a museum display, including a Drax Mantis action figure with a rocket pack."

"Where is this place?" asked Brad.

"Just off Leicester Square. Do you think you can do the job?"

"Well, it will take a few days to put a plan together," Brad sighed, "but it should be straight forward enough I would imagine."

"Good," said Walter. "But I have two more conditions."

"What conditions?" Brad asked suspiciously.

"Number one, we do the hit on the opening night."

"Are you crazy! Do you have any idea how much harder that will make it? There's bound to be extra security, especially if there are going to be celebrities. No, I can't do that."

"Would you rather I posted my photograph to Scotland Yard?" Walter asked menacingly.

"You're pushing it son," Brad replied in reluctant consent. "That photo is only going to buy you so much time. Pretty soon you are going to run out of luck. Anyway, what is the other condition?"

"I want in on the mission."

"Now you're just taking the piss. How many times have you been on this kind of job? I'll tell you, none. You have no idea what is involved. It's just not going to happen."

In response Walter gave a stare. He said nothing, he didn't have to. Already both men knew that this was the way it would be.

"I can't believe this," said Brad in defeat. "I just don't believe any of this. "

On the screen in front of them Drax Mantis was patrolling the bridge on the Cybercopter. His fists were clenched and his expression was stern. Once again he was preparing to do battle, and on his back he wore a special rocket pack.

Jim Carley

The Hot Tub

Although Dilly Foxtrot was staying in the Grosvenor House Hotel, Warren Kingburger had made other plans for himself. He was staying at his luxury mansion in Kensington. He actually owned no fewer than five homes. In addition to Kensington, he had a millionaire's condo in Los Angeles, a country retreat in Colorado, a designer apartment in New York, and a play den in Monte Carlo. He spent his time more or less evenly between all five. There were two very good reasons why he wouldn't let Dilly stay in the mansion with him. Firstly, there was the problem of the media. Kingburger had long been a favourite target of a number of society magazines. Most of his girlfriends, at one time or other, had ended up being featured. This in itself was not so bad, but it had added significant weight to the civil divorce actions of each of his four ex-wives. In grand total the four divorces had cost him over thirty million dollars, and divorce number five was already well in hand. The other reason that Kingburger did not allow Dilly to stay was because he found her quite objectionable at times. Sure, in the throes of passion she was hard to beat. She did, however, have an unfortunate habit of wanting to tidy things up, and never ceased to have a go about Kingburger's bad habits. If Dilly was around it was impossible to leave the toilet seat up, or leave an empty

98

bourbon glass out for more than fifteen minutes, or discard a pair of underpants without placing them directly into the appropriate laundry basket. It was that sort of thing that really pissed off Kingburger. As a result of these things, Dilly was only allowed to visit the mansion at Kingburger's request, and today was one such day. She had arrived at the mansion in her blue business suit, carrying a briefcase. To any hidden photographer the scene only depicted a senior employee visiting her employer at home. There was no scandal in that. Mr Charlesworth, the housekeeper, opened the door. He was a crusty old squire in his autumn years of life.

"Ah, Miss Foxtrot," greeted Mr Charlesworth. "Mr Kingburger has been expecting you. He is waiting to receive you in the conservatory."

"Thank you Mr Charlesworth," she replied. "I know the way." She walked off through the house, and towards the conservatory at the rear.

The mansion itself was a large Victorian town house. There were a number of similar properties on the same road, and each owned by absurdly rich people. Kingburger's house had wooden floors and tall walls, lavishly decorated with antiques from around the world. The conservatory, although clearly visible on the outside by neighbouring properties, managed to maintain its own secret charm. It was full of a wide variety of tropical plants, giving it a jungle like atmosphere. The furniture and floor had been constructed with panels of mahogany, giving it a rich warm feeling. The centrepiece of the conservatory was the hexagonal hot tub. Kingburger sat there in the hot tub, bubbles frothing all around him, naked all but for his Stetson (which he rarely removed) and a thick gold chain around his neck with a large K-shaped pendant. A Jack Daniels rested close to his left hand, and a large cigar was wedged in his right. He licked his lips approvingly as Dilly walked in.

"You wanted to see me, Mr Kingburger," she announced.

"Come now, Dilly," Kingburger replied. "We're not at school now. Why don't you dispense with the formalities. It's play time!"

"Okay, sugar," she replied, kicking off her stilettos and throwing her briefcase onto a chair. She walked over to a small bar in the corner, and fixed herself a Martini.

"Quentin tells me you managed to get a Drax Mantis with a rocket pack," Kingburger went on, puffing his cigar.

"Sure did."

"Well that is good news. You know how much I like to hear good news. Why don't you come on down here into the hot tub, and let me reward you?"

"Why, Warren," Dilly replied teasingly, sipping her drink. "You know I haven't brought my bikini with me!"

"So what," he replied. "If I can go commando, I'm sure you can too. Now why don't you take those clothes off and come down here?"

Many women would find such an offer from Kingburger repulsive. He was a blubbery old man, with numerous chins, reeking of cigar smoke and with bourbon flavoured saliva. Dilly, however, could see past that. She knew that there was a gentle, caring, loving side to him. She didn't, however, give a toss about that either. The only two assets of Kingburger's she was interested in were his money and his influence.

Sex was just something she had to endure to get to them. With that thought in mind, she began to take her clothes off.

The Contact

Ralph Lee had checked into his ordinary room at the Strand Palace Hotel. It was fairly small, with a single bed, TV, coffee making facilities, and an ensuite bathroom. The view was of another wing of the hotel, as opposed to any glimpse of London's magnificent skyline. He had unplugged the phone and replaced it with a modem, linked to a lap top PC. Sitting on the bed, he adjusted his glasses and set about his work, although he was less than motivated.

"I can't believe what you have got us into," he snorted.

"Get off my back," said Brad, slumped in the only armchair in the room.

"I mean," said Ralph, "why the opening night? It's bad enough doing something like this, but why the opening night?"

"That's what he wanted," replied Brad, firing up his third cigarette of the day.

"Smoking, huh? I guess the little dick is getting to you as well," said Ralph. "You know, it's not too late to have him taken care of."

"No, this isn't his fault. I don't want him killed. It's our fault for fucking up the Gresham job. It's up to us to put it right."

"What if he doesn't stop there?" asked Ralph disconcertingly. "What if he wants us to do a raid on

Toys R Us to get him a complete Action Man set? Maybe he's also got a thing about Lego? They do some neat stuff these days."

"Hardly likely! Anyway, have you got any plans yet?" Brad sucked hard on his cigarette, and puffed out a lingering cloud of smoke.

"It's amazing what you find on the web," Ralph replied. "They have a full breakdown of the restaurant which I've down loaded and cross matched with the planning application from the local authority. It breaks down like this. It's a four storey set up. The museum will be on the ground floor, with the restaurant on one and two, and offices on three. Kitchens are in the basement, could be a good start point. They're putting in a service lift at the back with access to all floors. There is also one handy emergency exit on the back, leading into a side street. It's not near a sewer or the underground, so there is no access from below. There are two skylights, but they look too high profile to use.

"Various exhibits will be all over the place, although the Drax doll is listed as a museum piece. That means it's on the ground floor, which should make our job easier. I can't say exactly where it will be though, and if it's only four inches big you might need some time to find it. Then you've got to work out how to get it. Chances are it will be in a glass cabinet. I doubt it would be wired."

"What about other alarms?" asked Brad.

"Standard system. Emergency exits are wired to the fire alarm and the main alarm. CCTV is dead cert'. I reckon about twenty cameras throughout. I've managed to link into their invoicing system. They have Capital Entertainment Security on their books. If they are working the show then you can expect some of the guards to be packing automatics, although most of them will just be beef cakes in DJs."

"What about a contact?" Brad continued.

"Well, there are a few names linked with the gig. We could go for a guest. So far they have a good number confirmed. We've got Fuzzy J and Jimmy Lambourne. Then there's your favourite Russian sex pot Ingrid Bourgromenko."

"I told you before," Brad butted in, "she's Albanian."

"There are a few other celebrities as well," Ralph went on. "Then there's the man himself, Warren Kingburger. He owns the whole show. The head chef is called Dominic, although they haven't appointed any junior staff yet. Other than that there are a few maintenance guys. Any runners amongst that lot?"

"I don't think so. I can't stand Jimmy Lambourne. His radio show sucks! No, I need a better way in."

"What about Ingrid?" Ralph asked. "I mean, she is one of your favourite women on TV, as I remember you saying. Who knows, you may even get to score."

"No chance," Brad replied. "Much as I would like to, she is just too hot. The chances are some scum tabloid journalist will link us together, and take a few glossy pictures. The last thing I need is to see my face in a national newspaper."

"Well, there is no one else in....no, hold on a second!" Ralph hit the keys, and the images on the screen changed. "Hello baby!" he exclaimed.

"What have you got?" asked Brad, sitting up in his chair.

"May I introduce Miss Dilly Foxtrot."

"Dilly who?"

"Dilly Foxtrot. She is Kingburger's left hand lady.

Get the details. Age twenty four and single. Originally from Jackson, Mississippi. No education to speak of. Why would a man like Kingburger hire a girl like that? She must be red hot. She must do amazing things to his dick!"

"So what's her role?"

"Project Manager. Can you dig that? All American bimbo overseeing a project like this. Maybe this is going to be a lot easier than we thought! I think we have our opening. She's at the Grosvenor House Hotel in Mayfair. Booked in until the opening night. She's got a booking on a flight to Los Angeles the next day."

"Okay, I'll accidentally bump into her," said Brad.

"What about Walter?" enquired Ralph.

"What about him?"

"I thought you said he wanted in. I could put him in the van with me, so I can keep an eye on him."

"No that won't work. I can't risk him touching the computers and fucking everything up. Besides, I don't think he would want to be on the outside. He'll go in with me. That way if he gets busted he's on his own, and if that happens we torch the comic shop. We can't risk that photo falling into the wrong hands."

"Okay, I can handle that," Ralph replied.

"Good," said Brad. "Let's go to work!"

The Genuine Fan

Dilly Foxtrot began to peel off her clothes as part of a demeaning strip tease show. She unbuttoned her jacket and slid it off her shoulders. Normally she would have looked for a hanger, but that would have ruined the seduction. Instead she let it drop to the floor.

Warren Kingburger still sat in the hot tub, his stare fixed on Dilly's figure.

"I've been thinking," Dilly said, as if it were something she didn't often do. As she did so, she unclipped he skirt and let it fall away to reveal the full length of her stockings, and her fairly insubstantial briefs.

"Oh yeah?" Kingburger replied, only half listening. He was more concerned with the shape of her legs and thighs, and what was still to be revealed.

"You know the opening night," she went on. "I've had an idea about the guest list." She unclipped her earrings, and placed them on the rim of one of the large conservatory plant pots.

"What about it?" asked Kingburger.

"Well, all the people on it are famous, right?"

"Right."

"Do you reckon that will have the best impact?" She began to unbutton her blouse.

"I'm not with you," Kingburger replied.

"I was thinking," Dilly went on, now revealing a

column of flesh from her chin to the line of her briefs, only broken by the white silk of her bra. "Maybe you could invite some other people."

"Other people? What sort of people?"

"The fans," she replied, easing off her blouse. "The genuine fans. The sort of people that saw the movies twenty years ago, and still think they are the hottest thing going. People who are really going to dig all the memorabilia. People who are going to be blown away by the whole show. Can you imagine how cool that will look on TV?"

At this point all Dilly was wearing was her underwear. Most of her body was on show now. Her golden arms, leading to her slender neck, panning down to the perfect curve of her waistline.

"That's cool," replied Kingburger, in response to both Dilly's body and her idea.

Dilly wasn't really the idea-generating type, she never had the "vision" thing. Having said that, Kingburger liked the idea. Normally he was dismissive of most of Dilly's suggestions, like he was of most people's ideas. This idea, however, held water. Indeed, it was enough to momentarily distract him from the centrefold figure in front of him.

Kingburger didn't just see his films as business propositions. He was a genuine fan as well. He was addicted to the whole buzz of cinema, from the popcorn, to the trailers of forthcoming presentations, to the surround sound stereo. He pined for the days when there were short cartoons before the main picture, and there were girls with trays of ice creams in the aisles during the intervals. More than that, he loved the concept and philosophy of the cinema. He loved the merchandising, and the marketing, and the whole way of life that the cinema provoked. The only problem was that this wasn't endemic in everyone in the movie industry. Most of the young stars in the industry these days were preoccupied with sex, drugs, more sex and more drugs. There was no substance anymore. It was highly likely that most of the guests at the opening night of the Orbit Studio Experience would be from that mould. They would be more concerned with snorting lines of coke rather than admiring the fantastic memorabilia. Where was the news in that? No, Dilly was right. The genuine fans were what were needed. The sort of people who could go on *Mastermind*, and choose *Galactic Encounter* as their specialist subject. It was a peach of an idea. By the time Kingburger snapped out of his daydream, Dilly had removed all of her clothing, and now stood before him completely naked.

"Uhm," dribbled Kingburger, "that's more like it."

"So you like my idea?" said Dilly, a question which seemed to lose its impact in the face of her nudity.

"Absolutely," Kingburger replied. "I shall personally go out there and find some genuine fans to come to our party. In the meantime I'm planning a little party of my own. Now why don't you get that cute little butt down here into this hot tub."

"Yes sir," she replied. She stepped down into the hot tub, the bubbly water reaching up around her ankles and onwards up her slender frame until she was submerged up to her neck. Her hands moved gently over Kingburger's body under the water, bringing an instant grin to his face. All was well in the world of Warren Kingburger. He had his films, he had his restaurants, and he had a woman in his hot tub who was exceptionally perverted. Add to that a Jack Daniels and a cigar, and you end up with something that makes the Garden of Eden look about as attractive as Milton Keynes.

Indeed, everything was perfect, as perfect as it could be. What Kingburger didn't know, however, was that an elaborate plan was being hatched at the Strand Palace to steal the prize exhibit at his restaurant. That was pretty bad. Bearable, but bad. There was something else though that was worse than that, much worse. At about the same time Dilly Foxtrot had entered the hot tub, an American assassin had boarded a plane on the other side of the Atlantic. Neither knew, at that time, that they would soon be spending some quality time together. Just the two of them, a few friends, a couple of uninvited guests, and three dead bodies.

Part Three

The Uninvited American

Food

The end of Spring was approaching, and the nights were drawing out. It was still cold though, and generally overcast. The poor weather, however, did not prevent the droves of tourists from arriving in London. They were mainly American and Japanese, although there were a fair number of Europeans as well. London seemed to have endless variety to offer them. They visited the Tower, the National Gallery, and Madame Tussaud's. They visited Buckingham Palace, the Trocadero, and Camden Market. They visited everywhere. Anywhere that would take their money. Sightseeing in itself, however, was not enough to sustain the visiting hordes. In between their busy schedules they needed food, and plenty of it. They needed burgers, fries, pasta, pasties, ice cream and chocolate. The only thing that eclipsed the amount of food that was required was the variety of establishments from which it was supplied. These days there is no shortage of places to eat in London. For starters, there are the mandatory MacDonalds and Pizza Huts for those who like that kind of thing. No thrills, good honest grub. Wherever you come from in the world there are a few commercial emblems that are instantly recognisable. There is the red tag of Levis, the flamboyant curl of the Coca Cola signature, and the hopelessly infuriating Microsoft flag. The golden arches of the McDonald's "M" is right up there with the best of them. No matter what language, English, German, French or Japanese, the term Big Mac seems to easily translate. Then there is China Town, always good value for money if you can endure the famously rude oriental waiters. There are the minimalist noodle bars, or the upmarket brasseries in the five star hotels. There are the bistros of Mayfair, and the designer restaurants of Canary Wharf. In contrast, there are the notorious kebab houses and greasy spoons of the suburbs. To top it all there are the thousands of pubs which the city offers, serving ploughman's lunches, pork pies or jellied eels, depending on whereabouts in London you happen to be. Then, of course, there are the theme restaurants. The Hard Rock Cafe, the grandfather of all theme restaurants, originated in London. Since then there have been many imitations. Planet Hollywood, although a major contender, was never the only pretender to the throne. Following on there has been the Fashion Café, filled with designer dresses across the decades, and the Sports Café, laden with sporting nostalgia. Indeed, for every aspect of social life there seems to be a theme restaurant in London to follow. As if they weren't enough, they were about to be joined by a new competitor, the Orbit Studio Experience. Not just a restaurant, not a mere museum, but the ultimate dining and entertainment experience. Needless to say, Orbit had the other restaurant proprieters of London worried. Very worried.

Danny Dellapicho

Danny Dellapicho had an executive seat on the morning flight from Washington DC to London Heathrow. He was a short, stocky man, of Italian dissent. The muscles of his arms bulged inside his Armani suit. His face was stubborn and serious. His hair was cropped short and his dark bushy eyebrows met in the middle of his olive coloured face.

"Can I get you another drink, sir?" said the busty Caribbean airhostess.

"Bourbon, neat, and no ice" replied Danny. There was no please or thank you. The hostess fixed the drink with a warm smile, and moved onto the next passenger. Danny fingered the edges of the brown envelope he had been nursing since take off. He was waiting to open it, but wanted to make sure the other passengers had settled into the flight first. The last thing he wanted was some hyperactive kid looking over his shoulder. Instead he sipped the whisky. The sour taste hit the back of his throat and sent a wave of warmth around his body. He was at ease, perfectly relaxed. His index finger ripped the top of the envelope in a near straight line and he eased out the contents. He checked around him. The guy in the next seat was asleep, and no one was chatting much. Those who were not asleep had the in-flight headphones on, and were watching the movie on the screen up in front. It was a space film. The one with that bad guy all dressed in black, and the good guy has a lizard for a sidekick. Danny had seen the film before, but wasn't sure what it was called. Science fiction wasn't really his scene, and besides, wasn't that film at least twenty years old anyway? He sat looking at two black and white photographs of two different men. There was a name written on the margin of each. The fatter of the two was called Ralph Lee, and the hard looking one was called Brad Clusky. With the photographs was a briefing note. Dellapicho's task was laid out in simple terms. These two men had been hired by the US Government to obtain confidential information from a UK company with potential benefit to the United States. No more detail was given, and it was not necessary. Danny didn't need to know what these two men were supposed to have done, all he needed to know was that they didn't pull it off. The situation was clear. An American operative had located and hired the men. In order to do so he had had to divulge key information, not only his identity, but also the specifications of the project. This information had to be safeguarded. Of course, there was no reason to suspect that Brad Clusky or Ralph Lee would spill the beans. Then again, you can never be sure. Better to have all the loose ends taken care of. Danny Dellapicho was being sent to London with a simple remit: find these two men and execute them. There were no other rules to obey, but that wasn't a problem. Killing was Danny's speciality. The CIA considered him as one of the best. He had only scraped through the entrance tests at Langley to join the CIA, but he had proved his worth taking care of some business in Miami some years ago. It was that performance that had earned him his current job, taking care of people who needed to be taken care of.

Danny was a natural killing machine. He could handle a gun with ease on the practice range, and the rounds he let off always made a tight cluster in the head of his cardboard target. He could manage unarmed conflict as well, and regularly upstaged his instructors as a young recruit. He was fit and agile, with an instinct for survival. He was the immaculate product of American intelligence, a sophisticated device for extermination. He was ideal for a job like this. The two targets were somewhere in London. Danny had been there before, three times. The first time it was for an Irish terrorist who had seriously threatened Anglo-American relations. The second time took care of a senior civil servant who had some funny ideas about international trade. The last time he went for an ex-patriot who was using London as a base for a drug ring which included Las Vegas as one of its key distribution centres. Yes, Danny had first class knowledge of London. He knew the secret underworld community that resided there. Men like Brad and Ralph would be known in those circles. Any one of a number of informants might be able to confirm their whereabouts. Maybe they recently stayed in the same hotel, or purchased some hardware from a particular surveillance dealer. It would all be very easy. Maybe he would even have time to see a few of the sites if he had time to spare.

Danny reclined his seat, and slid the copy of the *International Herald Tribune* off the lap of the guy sleeping next to him. He wanted to read the report on last night's Giants game. For a moment he glanced up again at the screen at the front of the plane. *What* was the name of that film?

Cinderella

Walter Bridgenorth stood across the street from the Orbit Studio Experience, as he had done so for the last five evenings. There were two reasons for this. Firstly, and most obviously, he was genuinely fascinated. Prior to the construction of the Orbit Studio Experience, the extent of his world had rarely extended beyond the ensemble of science fiction bric-a-brac that resided with him in his shop. This creation, however, blew all of that into oblivion. This restaurant had it all. It had priceless exhibits from the movies, as well as that certain glittery, sexy, show business something. More than that, it had a Drax Mantis action figure with a rocket pack. Even if Walter had never met Brad Clusky, he would still want to be one of the first people to eat there. He would need to see the Mantis action figure with his own eyes. This tied in neatly with the second reason for Walter's presence. As the newest member of Brad's crack team he felt slightly obliged to case the joint, even though Brad hadn't actually given him anything to do as yet. Despite this, he wanted to feel as if he were making some sort of contribution. Checking out the location of the hit seemed to be the most obvious thing for him to do, even though he didn't really know what he was supposed to be looking for. The restaurant itself was shaping up nicely. The exterior had been painted bright blue, and a large electric sign lit up the famous Orbit logo. Some exhibits were already on display in the windows. Couriers constantly arrived with boxes, and Brad wondered with glee if Drax Mantis might actually be inside one of them. Well, he thought cynically, if he was in one of those boxes he wouldn't stay in the restaurant for long. Soon he would be in his new home, in Walter's flat, above the Celluloid Space Cowboy store. Removing himself from this fantasy for a moment, Walter tried to make a constructive appraisal of the building. There was only one obvious entrance, through the main door. Above it was a small remote controlled camera, monitoring all those who entered and left. Walter wondered how Brad would get them past that. Maybe they would go through a window instead, or possibly try and get in round the back.

"Hi there, buddy!" came a voice from behind Walter. It startled him, and snapped him out of the little world where his mind had run away to. He was even more shocked when he realised who it belonged to.

"Are you...," he began with some trepidation. "Are you who I think you are?"

"That's right son. I had a feeling you might recognise me. Warren Kingburger, at your service!" Kingburger, as ever, was clad in a white suit and puffing a cigar. His Stetson rested on his head like a crown. He looked kind of smug that he had caught Walter so much by surprise.

Walter, in contrast, was almost in trauma. This man was Mr Galactic Encounter, and he had just walked up to him to start a conversation. How weird was that? First of all some terrorist crashes into his shop and practically takes him hostage, and now he found himself in confrontation with one of the biggest studio bosses in the world. As Walter was speechless, his mouth hanging open embarrassingly, Kingburger continued to do the talking. "I've noticed you son, if you don't mind me saying. You've been stood out here almost every evening this week. Just stood out here, looking at my place. I wonder why that might be?"

Walter panicked. Shit! Had he blown the whole operation already? Was it all over before it had even begun? Were there armed police waiting around the corner to drag him off to jail? Was Brad behind this? Had he been set up? What the hell was going on?

"I didn't mean anything by it," said Walter apologetically.

"Hell, of course you didn't," laughed Kingburger. "I bet you just can't wait for this place to open. You're a big fan, am I right?"

"Uh, yeah," replied Walter, still not really sure what was happening. "Yes, I like the films."

"I knew it," shouted Warren. "You looked like a *Galactic Encounter* man the moment I first saw you. How many times have you seen it son?"

"Thirty seven," replied Walter. Was there any harm in being honest about something like that?

"Thirty seven! Hell, I ain't seen it that many times, and I paid for it. I bet you don't know why I came out to talk to you, do you?"

"Well, no," replied Walter. "I can't imagine."

"Well, you obviously know about me opening this place pretty soon. The problem is son, that it is going to be full of journalists, critics and bullshit movie stars on the opening night. I can't really stomach people like that. Of course, some of these guys are really famous stars, but they are only coming to pose for the cameras.

Can you see where I'm coming from?"

"No," repeated Walter. It wasn't really any clearer.

"Maybe I should explain some more," Kingburger went on. "You see, I'm a movies man. I like people who like movies too. That means I like people like you. I want some of the first people to celebrate the Orbit Studio Experience to be the sort of people who will really get off on it, if you pardon my terminology. You see, my friend, I need people who have seen *Galactic Encounter* thirty seven times to be there on the opening night. I want you to be there!"

"No way!" exclaimed Walter in astonishment. Wait until Brad hears about this! A man on the inside, what a result! There would be no need to worry about security if you have a bonafide invite. You can just stroll right on in there and steal the goods. This must be some sort of blessing. Maybe he should try to get Brad in as well. That might earn him some serious brownie points. This was just too cool.

"I take it that means you will come?" asked Kingburger.

"You bet! I mean, thank you. Thank you very much. I would love to. Can my friend come too? He is as big a fan as I am. Bigger! I mean, when I say big I mean huge. He is the fan, the fan's fan. He just loves it."

"Calm down, little fella. Of course there is room for two." Warren pulled out two tickets from inside his jacket. "The security boys don't know I'm doing this," he explained. "They are gonna be a bit pissed when they find out. Still, I pay them after all, so I don't care too much. They are gonna need to know who you are though. I'd best make a note of your name."

Walter suddenly panicked. There was no way he

could disclose his identity. That might blow the whole game. He had no choice but to make a new name up, but what? He needed inspiration. He looked up and down the street for a clue, a hint of a name. The first thing he saw, the first thing that jumped out, was a Marks & Spencer store, squeezed in between a branch of the National Westminster Bank and the Post Office.

"Mark Spencer," he blurted, without even realising he had done it. "My name is Mark Spencer." Kingburger pulled out a small note pad and a gold fountain pen. He scribbled the name down.

"How about your buddy?" he asked.

"Uh, Nat West. I mean, er, Nathan West," cringed Walter. Surely anyone with half a brain could see exactly what he had just done. What sort of names were they? Maybe though, just maybe, a foreigner might not recognise the obvious connection.

"So," replied Kingburger. "Let me check I've got that. Mark Spencer and Nathan West."

"That's right," Walter replied.

"Well that is just dandy," said Kingburger, handing Walter the tickets. "Those names sure seem familiar though. Are you sure I haven't met you guys before? Perhaps at one of our conventions?"

"I can assure you, I would have remembered," said Walter.

"Yeah, I guess so. Anyway, I got to be heading back to stoke up those builders. We've only got a couple of days to go, and they need all the encouragement they can get. Maybe I'll bump into you again on the big night?"

"Maybe," Walter responded. Warren Kingburger wandered back across the road to his new restaurant. Walter slumped back against the shop window behind

Immortal Plastic

him. Had that really just happened? Surely it was a dream! A sad, sick dream. In a minute he would wake up, in his flat above the shop, and it would all be normal again. He pinched himself, and it hurt. No, this was no dream. The two tickets were still in his hand. He had just become Mark Spencer and, just like Cinderella, he was going to the ball.

Dilly Foxtrot

Brad Clusky was beginning to regret the idea of trailing Dilly Foxtrot. His first reaction, when he saw her for the first time in the flesh at the Grosvenor House reception, was instant sexual magnetism. No wonder Warren Kingburger hired her. She was sex on a stick! Brad almost choked on his spit. Flowing blonde hair, ample full breasts (probably silicon), a tight waste, honey coloured skin, and legs that went all the way up. If there was ever a woman that made Brad want to bark like a dog, it was Dilly. She wore a slinky designer business suit, that sent off all the right kind of messages. Today must have been her day off. Brad followed her out from the hotel, keeping a safe distance behind. She took the first cab outside, and he took the second.

"Follow that car," he said to the driver. It was something he had always wanted to say. He had expected her to head for Leicester Square and the restaurant. The restaurant, however, was not on today's itinerary. Six hours of serious shopping was today's alternative. The two cabs came to a halt on Oxford Street, and dispatched their passengers. The plethora of shops was unbelievable. Brad followed Dilly to Wallace, Jane Norman, Karen Millen, Liberty and Selridges. There were shoe shops, clothes shops, underwear shops, jewellery shops and accessory shops.

Shops that Brad had no idea existed. He had always thought that his mother was pretty lethal when she was going round Littlewoods, but that was nothing compared to this girl. What made things worse was that Brad had no excuse as to why he was following this girl into the various shops, especially considering the obviously feminine nature of most of them. On a number of occasions Brad had come up with the excuse that he was browsing for a birthday present for his mother when approached by a sales assistant. The assistant in the lingerie department at John Lewis was, however, less than convinced. Finally, many hours later, Brad got the opening he was looking for. Dilly, now laden with designer shopping bags, had decided to have a break at a 'twee' coffee bar. Somehow Brad wished she had chosen a pub with a satellite football match on show, but he was grateful of any opportunity to sit down. Dilly had taken a corner table, and ordered a cappuccino. Exhausted, Brad pulled himself across the bar to where she sat.

"Do you mind if I join you?" he asked. She was genuinely surprised by the advance, which confirmed that she was unaware that she had been followed all morning.

"Sure," she replied, and he sat down.

"I always like to take coffee with other people," he said to justify his intrusion. "Coffee to me is such a social drink."

"You look very tired," she commented.

"It's been a very busy day," he shrugged, and called over a waiter to order a coffee. "Do you mind if I ask you your name?" he went on, returning his attention to Dilly.

"I'm Dilly, Dilly Foxtrot."

"That's a nice name. A bit unusual. You're an American right?"

"Mississippi originally. I live in California now though."

"I spend a lot of time in California myself. It's not really my scene though. I prefer Colorado."

"What would a guy like you be doing in California?" she asked as the waiter delivered the coffees.

"I do what everyone in California does. I'm in the movie game."

"No," said Dilly, seemingly falling directly into Brad's little trap. "I'm in the movies too." This girl really was a sucker.

"Well, that doesn't surprise me. I have to be honest. When I walked in here I thought that you must be in cinema. You just have that Hollywood glow about you."

"Do you think so?" replied Dilly. She was really starting to enjoy the conversation. She liked being the centre of attention, and this guy was pretty good looking as well.

"For sure," replied Brad. "So what is it exactly that you do?"

"Well, I work for Orbit Studios. I'm a Project Manager."

"No shit! You must know the big man Mr Kingburger in person?"

"Yeah," she smiled in embarrassment. "We have a close working relationship."

"He's a great guy isn't he? He helped me a lot when I was starting out." Brad didn't know which part of his brain was concocting this story, but he thought it was shaping up quite nicely.

"I don't believe it," gasped Dilly. By now she was hooked. "You know Warren too? What is it that you do?"

"Oh," paused Brad, thinking of something original. "I'm a, a producer. I've worked with most of the studios. I'm currently doing the new Schwarzenegger vehicle with Pacific Western." Was that going a bit too over the top? Maybe she would see through such an ambitious lie.

"Schwarzenegger!" exclaimed Dilly, still lapping it up. "My God, he is so cool! I would love to work with him."

"He's pretty ordinary really," added Brad, sipping his coffee. "Most of the big stars are. You must have worked with a few big names yourself?"

"Well," shrugged Dilly. "I'm still sort of new to it all. So far I've only worked on the *Galactic Encounter* special releases. They were all filmed twenty years ago though, so you don't tend to meet too many big stars."

"They are pretty big films," Brad reassured. "You can only go on to great things from a start like that. Hell, I know I could use a girl like you on a lot of the work that I do."

"You're just saying that," laughed Dilly.

"No way, I reckon you've got what it takes. I've got an eye for that sort of thing."

"You're very kind," she blushed.

"Say," continued Brad. It was time to go in for the kill. "You must be involved in that new Orbit restaurant they are opening in the West End?" To be honest Brad thought it would take a lot more small talk to come round to this point. Dilly, however, had made it simple. He wondered, briefly, whether or not it had been her leading him on, rather than the other way round.

"It's my main project at the moment," Dilly responded. "It's going to be a great opening night. So many big names are going to be there. I'm really excited!"

"That sounds like one hot party," Brad complemented. "I wouldn't mind having a slice of that myself. I should really be there. Perhaps you could get me an invite?" The deed was done. The delivery was perfect. Indeed, Brad thought his performance was worthy of an Oscar. This movie lark wasn't so bad after all.

Dilly's face, however, did not reflect his optimism. What had he done wrong? Had he asked too soon? Had he blown his cover as an opportunist? Did Dilly simply just not like him?

"Any chance of that?" Brad asked again, but with a more earnest tone.

"I would love to," Dilly replied, "but it's not up to me."

"Hey? But I thought you were a Project Manager? Surely that cuts some ice?"

"Well, yes," Dilly shamefully replied, "but Mr Kingburger has prepared the guest list personally. There is no way anyone gets in without his say so."

"Couldn't you put a good word in?"

"It's just not that simple, I'm sorry."

Shit! Shitty shitty shit shit! All Brad could think of were words which all related to excrement in some way or other. What the hell was he supposed to say now? He considered the options. "Of course you can get me a ticket, Warren and I go back a long way!" No, too smug. "If you don't get me a ticket I'll get my nutter associate to savagely murder you!" No, too brutal. "Okay, I wasn't so fussed about a ticket, but

what exactly are your views on casual sex?" Brad liked
that line. Who knows, it might even work? In the end,
however, he chose none of them. There was one of
those long painful silences. It was only broken by the
sound of a mobile phone ringing. Brad wanted to
thump the jerk who it belonged to, before he realised it
was his own. He reached inside his jacket for it, and
apologised to Dilly. She smiled, and drained her coffee
cup.

"Hello?" Brad asked the receiver. The crackling
voice on the end belonged to Walter Bridgenorth. The
beeps told him that he in a phone box somewhere.

"Brad, it's me. Walter." The name made Brad
shiver, and he fought hard to hide his visual distress.
His hand slid over the receiver momentarily.

"Excuse me," he said to Dilly. "This is an
important business call. It's, erm, Mr
Schwarzenegger's agent." With that he stood from the
table and shuffled over to a quiet corner of the coffee
bar. Dilly found it curious, but she was prepared to
wait for him to finish. The conversation might end in a
career move for her. Even if it didn't there was always
the possibility of a memorable one night stand.

Nathan West

"I told you only to use this number in an emergency, you stupid shit!" It was hard to demonstrate his anger on the phone whilst in a crowded coffee bar, but Brad was trying his best.

"That's charming," replied Walter, partly distracted by the broad and enchanting selection of advertisements for prostitutes which were sharing the public phone box with him.

"Is this an emergency?" Brad asked, passing a false smile back to Dilly who was still waiting patiently at the table.

"No," replied Walter.

"Well, why don't you bugger off then?"

"Because I have some very important news."

"Yeah, I'm sure whatever it is is ultra urgent, but I'm currently in the middle of a key part of the stupid plan which should soon result in you owning your poxy Drax Mantis doll!"

This news provided sudden excitement for Walter. "What is it you're doing?" he asked. "Are you undercover or something?"

"Look, this is hardly the time or place for me to be giving you a lecture on what I am doing. Just tell me what you want then piss off!"

"Well, you are just not going to believe this! You will never guess who I met today?"

"I don't know. H.G.Wells in his fucking time machine perhaps?"

"Nope. I met Warren Kingburger!"

"What?" cried Brad. "What the hell do you think you are doing? At no point have you been instructed to make contact with Orbit personnel, least of all Mr Big. Are you a total idiot? Are you trying to jeopardise this whole operation? Let's not mess about here. If this goes wrong then everybody goes to prison. That includes you, arse hole!"

"Take it easy," replied Walter. "He approached me, not vice versa."

"What do you mean?" Brad was really fuming. "Why on earth would a guy like Kingburger want to talk to you? He is a multi-millionaire movie studio icon. You are a low life anorak nerd with the charisma of a dung beetle. There is no reason in the known universe why he would want to associate himself with you!"

"Actually, he gave me two tickets to the opening night of the Orbit Studio Experience. I thought you might be interested."

"This is a joke, right? If this a joke then any deal we previously had is off. I may even have to kill you myself."

"No joke."

"But how?" asked a bemused Brad. "Why?"

"I don't really know myself," replied Walter. "It's all a bit of a blur."

"You didn't tell him our names, did you? Please tell me that you didn't blow our cover?"

"Who do you think I am? I can play James Bond as well, you know. I invented a couple of cover names for us."

"Why do I not like the sound of that?" replied

Brad. "What are they?"

"Well, I am to be known as Mark Spencer, and you are Nathan West."

"That sounds familiar. Are they real people?"

"No, not exactly. They came to me in a moment of inspiration."

"Okay," concluded Brad. "Well, hang on to those tickets until I can get to you. Where are you now?"

"I'm on Long Acre, the Leicester Square end, near Dillon's book shop."

"Wait there, I can be with you in about fifteen minutes, and don't talk to anyone, especially not anyone famous!" With that Brad hung up. He looked across to Dilly, still with a smile to die for. He wandered back to the table, and ushered the waiter to bring over the bill.

"I take it all is not well with Arnie?" asked Dilly.

"Who? Oh yeah, Schwarzenegger. Well, you know how it can be with these big stars. He wants me to fire one of the supporting actors."

"Tough, huh," she responded. "Look, about those tickets. I might be able to get you in some how." The waiter delivered a small plate with the bill neatly folded.

"Isn't that ironic," laughed Brad, tossing a ten pound note on to the plate. "You know Arnie's agent just told me that he had a ticket going spare. It looks like I will be going anyway!"

"That's great," she replied.

"Look," said Brad as he stood to leave. "I've got to shoot off. There's a city financier I need to catch. Maybe I can see you again at the party?"

"That would be nice," Dilly replied, "but having dinner tomorrow night would be nicer."

"Dinner?" questioned Brad. This was something

he had not anticipated. His brief was to get hold of the tickets, nothing more. He knew Ralph would blow a fuse if he accepted. The more time he spent with Dilly the more she was likely to find out about him. The risk was particularly heightened by her closeness to Warren Kingburger. Then again, to refuse would look just as suspicious. He had already showered her with compliments, and no one could argue that she wasn't stunning. To make things worse, a little voice in the back of his head was reminding him that he had to get to Walter as soon as possible to make sure those tickets were safe. He had to make a quick decision.

"Sure," he said finally. "I'd love to." He wasn't sure whether or not he was already regretting it.

"Great," she said. "Meet me at my hotel. I'll be in the lobby around eight."

"Sure," he smiled as he turned to leave. "Eight o'clock at the Grosvenor House."

"How do you know I'm staying at the Grosvenor House?"

"Uh," stuttered Brad, cursing his error, "you just struck me as a Grosvenor House kind of girl. Besides, I thought Orbit had one of those special deals with the Grosvenor?"

"You are very perceptive."

"Hey, it's dog eat dog out there." He made his way towards the door, anxious not to allow Dilly to dwell on his mistake.

"Wait," called Dilly. "I don't even know your name?"

"It's, erm, West. Nathan West."

"Gee," she replied. "Have we met before? That name sounds familiar!"

Brad just smiled back.

"Tell me about it," he muttered to himself as he left.

Surveillance

Danny Dellapicho had been in London for twenty four hours. In that time he had hardly slept or eaten, even though he had booked into a five star Kensington hotel. He had a hunger though, a hunger to kill. Killing people was almost the ultimate adrenaline rush. The only thing that actually provided more of a high than killing was the pursuit of somebody to kill. You could get off on tracking down your prey almost as much as putting a bullet in his head. So far, however, the leads had not been good. He had tried a few clubs where he still had good contacts, but they were not the kind of guys likely to hang about with Brad Clusky and Ralph Lee. He had tried everything from society bars to snooker clubs. No result. Zilch. It was obvious that Brad and Ralph were not the socialising kind. At least not in the circles Danny moved in. They probably kept to quiet nights out in suburban pubs. Hardly the sort of places where the landlord was likely to remember a face. A different approach was necessary. Rather than checking out pubs and drinking clubs, Danny decided to try potential suppliers. He had studied the profile of Ralph in particular. This guy was a hardcore techno-guru. The sort of purchases a guy like that might be making are only going to be from a small number of less than reputable retailers. The sort of men who could provide the latest military hardware across the counter in back street shops. Most people would be shocked to think that such things were possible, but you just had to know the right people. One such retailer was a guy called Buster Urman, who had a computer store off Tottenham Court Road. It was a tiny shop with a large glass frontage, and a crude ambience more appealing to the less scrupulous consumer. Buster mainly dealt in PCs, and there were plenty of buyers. He traded in PCs in the same way most of the local dealers did, buying in bulk cheaply, and hitting hard with sales. No warranties, and discounts for cash. Although it looked shady, the business was legal. As a front it had to be, to avoid unnecessary attention to the other business activities. Behind the counter was the real action. Buster was ex-army, and had used his time in the forces to build up enough contacts to see him through on civvy street. Espionage and surveillance equipment were his specialities. The goods came in from the back door of the Ministry of Defence, and there were plenty of buyers, involved in all sorts of shady activities. Anything could be procured for the right price.

When Danny entered the shop, Buster was serving a couple of nerdish students. He was a slightly obese, bald man, with a blond goatee beard. He wore a green T-shirt and 501s. His arms were heavily tattooed, and one ear was pierced. He looked like a typical hard man, the last person you would expect to find in a computer store. His strength, however, was not just in his size, but also in his ability to negotiate. In short, he had the gift of the gab. He clocked Danny, in his expensive suit, as far more likely to make a purchase than the lads he was currently dealing with. He watched Danny with one eye as he browsed over the latest offering from Apple. Perhaps he might even be a special customer. The thought of this made his manner towards the students more abrupt, in an attempt to usher them from the shop. It worked, and soon it was just Buster Urman and Danny Dellapicho alone in the store.

"Can I help you?" Buster asked hopefully. Danny pulled out the photo of Ralph from his jacket, and laid it down on the counter.

"You seen this guy?" he asked in monotone.

"What do you mean?" laughed Buster. "This is a computer shop, not a missing persons agency!"

"Just look at the picture," Danny firmly continued. Buster looked down, and in that instant Danny knew that it was a familiar face. He could read body language like an ABC book. The signs were good. Buster tried his hardest to conceal his recognition. He wasn't in the habit of disclosing details of any of his customers, especially an old friend like Ralph.

"Never seen him before," Buster lied. "Is he a relative of yours?" It was the wrong answer. Danny reached inside his jacket again, but this time it was to reach for his gun inside its holster. The silencer was already screwed on. He pointed the barrel directly at Buster's head, without a care that the shop's door was unlocked and more customers could enter at any second.

"What the hell is this?" cried Buster, taking a step back and raising his hands in a futile attempt to protect himself. "Who are you?"

"I asked you if you knew this guy, but I don't think your memory is working so good. I figure my little friend here might help you remember. You do know him, don't you?"

"Okay, I know him. No big deal! You don't need

to shoot me!"

"You sold him some kit in the last few days?"

"Yeah, a few things," Buster answered, his panic increasing. He glanced at the CCTV video behind the counter to make sure it was recording. It was. "Do you want to know what he bought?"

"No, I want to know where he is. Did he pick the stuff up, or did you have it delivered?"

"Uh, delivered. Yes, definitely. It was a plain package, brown paper. A couple of tracking sensors, no bigger than a tube of glue. He asked me to drop it off at a hotel. What was it? Yeah, the Strand Palace, that was the one."

"You see," Danny smiled, "that wasn't so hard". With that he let off three rounds. Each one hit Buster in the head, splattering his blood across the counter and the far wall. His dead body instantly slumped to the ground. Danny carefully walked round the counter, avoiding the pools of blood, and slid his gun back into its holster. He ejected the video cassette from the CCTV recorder. Evidence had to be destroyed. All the evidence. He thought for a moment about pursuing the two students who had previously been in the shop, and killing them too. Witnesses were always a liability that needed taking care of. He was certain though that he had successfully hidden his face from them, and at best they could only describe him as a guy in a suit. Instead he left the shop, walked down towards Oxford Street, and hailed a cab to the Strand Palace Hotel. He had drawn first blood for the day, and he was hungry for more.

Light Bulbs

Ralph Lee was feeling pleased with himself, very pleased indeed. He had calculated exactly how the Drax Mantis action figure would be stolen. It wasn't an overly complicated plan, but it was full of deviousness and cunning. Whilst Brad had been tracking down a couple of invites, he was already working on the next stage. He stood outside the almost complete Orbit Studio Experience, wearing a pair of paint-splattered jeans, a tatty T-shirt, and a grease stained Oakland Athletics baseball cap. He was carrying a large box of light bulbs which were so awkward that he had to hold the delivery note that went with them between his teeth.

"Hi there," he said through his teeth to the guy on the door, who only half looked like a security guard. He stood the box down and removed the note to make it easier to speak.

"I've got an order of light bulbs for you here," he continued. "I've got to drop them to, hold on let me check, to a Mr O'Hanlan. Whereabouts can I find him then?"

"Hold on," replied the guard in a dry tone. He picked up a clipboard to check the day's deliveries. They were all recorded on the sheet, and sure enough there was a delivery of bulbs to Mr O'Hanlan, the foreman. There had to be, Ralph had ordered them from himself on behalf of Orbit two days ago. It had taken less than five minutes on his computer to complete the transaction.

"Okay," said the guard. "Straight down the stairs on the far side."

"Cheers," replied Ralph. "Oh, could I just get a signature on this?" The guard signed the mock up delivery note, and Ralph was on his way. Crossing the room he made a mental note of the floor plan, in case it varied in any way from the specifications he had on his computer. He was relieved to see that it didn't, but you can never tell with builders these days. Ralph clocked an empty display cabinet on the far side. Although nothing was in it, above it was a sign that stated it would soon be full of original movie merchandise from the Bravado Toy & Game Company of Chicago. That must surely be the final resting place of Drax Mantis. Moments later Ralph was in the basement. It had become a makeshift builders yard during the construction work, but at least there was nobody working down there. It was a small area, mainly reserved for storing excess food before it passed to the kitchens. It was also, more importantly, the home of the central fuse box. Ralph dropped the bulbs onto a stack of other boxes. He reached in his pocket and hit a button on a small remote control box he had concealed. This immediately knocked out all of the internal CCTV cameras. The guards in the security control room went into an instant barmy. Ralph had guessed that they would think that this was a technical failure. They would probably put it down to an incompetent electrician, but they might get suspicious, and start searching the building. Ralph knew he was on a clock, and the meter was running. He reached in his pocket again and pulled out two further items. One was a retractable, multi-head screwdriver, no bigger that a marker pen. The other was a tiny remote controlled circuit breaker, no bigger than a matchbox. He clicked the screwdriver out to its full length, and snapped on a Philips head about a centimetre in diameter. With this the metal casing of the fuse box could be easily removed. The fuse box itself was about a metre square, and packed with all of the main wires for the whole building. Ralph, however, knew exactly what he was looking for. It was a single thick red wire on the right hand side which trailed out of the main power switch. The circuit breaker he had built would act as an alternative switch. It was designed so that nothing should actually short out. There would be no bang or explosion, no permanent damage. The circuit breaker slid onto the wire with ease. That was all there was to it. Now Ralph could switch the power on and off in the building from the safety and comfort of his van. What was more, the range of the circuit breaker was so long that he could control it from as far a way as Manchester. That, of course, would not be necessary. With the breaker in place Ralph speedily replaced the panelling. The whole job was achieved in less than five minutes. He flicked the switch in his pocket, and the CCTV cameras ran smoothly again. He had been fast enough to avoid unnecessary attention from the security control room. Ralph returned up the stairs, across the first floor, and back to the main door. He gave a wry smile to the security guard on his way out, and disappeared amongst the shoppers in the street. That part of the mission had been completed successfully. Things were going to plan.

Room 318

Danny Dellapicho's cab pulled in at the Strand Palace Hotel. He gave the driver a modest tip. If the tip was too big or too small the driver would have more reason to remember him. As it was the two men had hardly spoke to each other, and eye contact in the rear view mirror had been minimal. Danny didn't rate the Strand Palace too highly. There were too many of his fellow countrymen residing there, the sort he really didn't like. Too fat, too crude, too loud and too nineteen seventies. Honestly, it was like being on the set of *Charlie's Angels*. He was sure this hotel could easily have featured in an episode at some point along the line. He walked up to the reception desk where he was greeted by a Danish girl called Helga. He knew her name from the badge she wore on her uniform. She was a short, slightly pimply girl with ivory white skin and blonde hair that was just a little over the top in its peroxide content. Still, the uniform smartened her up.

"How are you doing?" he greeted her with the warmest smile and chirpiest American tone he could muster.

"Hello there sir," replied Helga. "How might we be helping you today?"

"Well, honey, I'm just in from California. There's a buddy of mine from Yorkshire staying here. Shucks, we go back a long way. You see, he's getting married next week. It's going to be a huge thing, a big party on a boat on the Thames. The problem is the stag party is tonight, and he don't even know that I'm coming. I haven't seen him in two years. Can you dig that? One of his other buddies, a mutual friend, is also here. He got me involved in this whole thing. Hell, how could I say no? I just booked me a seat to England as fast as I could."

Helga was listening intently, but Danny wasn't finished yet. His performance was quite relaxed for a man who only moments earlier had blown the head off another human being in cold blood.

"See honey," he went on. "This is supposed to be a surprise. I tried to contact our mutual friend to let him know that I was here, but darn me if the old fool hasn't got his mobile phone switched on."

"Would you like me to call his room?" asked Helga.

"I thought about that," replied Danny, "but if our friend, the bride groom to be, is also in the same room right now it's going to spoil the surprise a bit. I mean, you don't fly for twelve hours across the Atlantic in secret only to blow your surprise at the last minute. No, I thought it might be better if I just stroll on up there and really give them a shock! I bet he will have the daftest look when he sees me standing there at the door."

"I'm sorry," said Helga apologetically. "That is against hotel regulations."

"I figured that honey," replied Danny, "but I was hoping for a little compromise. You know it would mean so much to me." He slid his hand across the desk towards her, flashing the corner of a fifty pound note in a subtle manner. Helga was clearly taken aback by this, but fifty quid was fifty quid in anyone's book. This guy seemed reasonable enough. She quickly glanced around her to see if any of her colleagues were paying her any attention. They weren't.

"Take it," whispered Danny. "It's a small price to pay to surprise an old friend. Besides, I'm not asking for a key or anything!" With that Helga's hand reached across to his, and he slid the money into her palm.

"Good girl," Danny went on reassuringly. "I knew I could count on you."

"What is the gentleman's name?" asked Helga, already feeling guilty by her actions.

"The groom is Mr Ralph Lee, and our mutual acquaintance is Mr Brad Clusky. You best give me both numbers, just in case they are in one room or the other."

"They have adjacent rooms," replied Helga, typing the names into her console. "Mr Lee is in room 318 and Mr Clusky is in 319."

"Much obliged, sweetheart," concluded Danny, who was already on his way to the lifts.

In no time at all he was outside room 318. The corridor was empty, so he didn't need to conceal his gun which he now brandished openly in his right hand. The silencer was still in place. He knocked loudly three times, but there was no response. It was possible that Ralph would deliberately not answer the door, but he figured that he was either out or in the shower. Danny pulled a small leather wallet from his pocket, which contained a number of blank white plastic cards, the size and shape of credit cards. There were eight in all. Most hotels these days have a card based locking mechanism on the guest room doors. The Strand Palace was no exception. Danny's eight cards had been perfected by the CIA to open any such door, anywhere in the world. The fifth card in this instance opened the door to room 318, and Danny slipped inside. A quick scam round the room confirmed it was empty, and Danny replaced the gun in its holster. He rapidly assessed his options. It was possible that the two men were in the adjoining room. He could force his way in and kill them both there. It was more probable, however, that neither man was currently in the hotel. This caused further problems, and made the issue of killing Brad and Ralph slightly harder. The obvious option was to wait in Ralph's room for the two of them to return, and shoot them as they come through the door. What, though, if only one came back and was due to meet the other somewhere else at a later point in the evening? If he killed the first at the hotel the other might become suspicious, and blow the whistle on whatever conspiracy it was that the two of them were linked to. That was not an acceptable outcome. No, none of these options were acceptable. Instead Danny decided to track down a point in time where he would have access to both men together. He needed to find a clue in the hotel room which would identify such a time and opportunity. He began to carefully look through Ralph's drawers and closet for a clue, carefully trying not to disturb anything or leave it out of place. The search drew a blank, so he turned his attention to the lap top on the bed. He soon had it powered up with a small mouse plugged in, and was flicking through the various files created by Ralph. There was a fair amount of general crap, but one directory caught his eye. It was simply called "Walter". He hastily doubled clicked on the icon to see what was inside. Surprise was an understatement. The first thing he found was building specifications for a West End restaurant, then a purchase ledger for the Orbit Studio Group. Then a down-loaded personnel file on some bimbo called Dilly Foxtrot. What was it all about? Was it some sick kind of perversion? There had to be more than this! Perseverance paid off. Danny hadn't wanted to be in Ralph's room for more than five minutes, but already it was nearer to ten. The picture, however, was somewhat clearer. These two clowns were planning another job. How stupid was that? Surely they must have realised the USA would not tolerate their failure? Surely they must know they had already been sentenced to death? Despite this they were carrying on regardless, and of all things they were going to hit a restaurant! As Danny scanned through the files the jigsaw was starting to fit together. Danny had worked out that the target was the Orbit Studio Experience, some trendy new burger joint opening in the West End. He knew the date, the opening night. He didn't know the exact reason, but there was no time to sit there and work that out. He still had too many files to look at, and it would take too much time. A maid could come by at any time, and if she did Danny would undoubtedly have to kill her. If Danny killed a maid there was no way that Brad and Ralph would hang around. The lead was too good to throw away.

What Danny guessed, however, was that both men would be at this party. Brad had specifically gone after two tickets, that was clear from Ralph's files. Two men, two tickets. You didn't need a degree in maths to work that out. That was all Danny needed to know. He had a date, a place, and a guarantee that both men would be making an appearance. He thought that the rest would be easy. He thought wrong. If he had spent

143

more time with the lap top he would have found files on Walter Bridgenorth. He would know there was a third man. He would know that Ralph was not going to set foot in that restaurant on that night because he would be in the reconditioned van round the back. In short, Danny had made some assumptions, and that wasn't professional. The consequences of this gap of knowledge would later turn out to be catastrophic. Danny, however, now had a plan. He required no further data, and the opening night was still a few days away. So pleased was he with himself that he decided to enjoy London for a few days. He would get drunk, and sleep with a few easy women, and probably kill them afterwards. It was that thought that reminded Danny of Helga. His next task was to kill her and get back that fifty pound note before she had a chance to circulate it. The risk of the serial number being traced was too great, and besides she had seen far too much of his face. With that thought in mind, Danny straightened the room as he had found it, powered down the lap top, and departed. Five hours later Helga's body was recovered from the Thames by river police. Her neck was broken. The fifty pound note was never seen again.

Jed Largo

FADE IN:

EXT. GLOKORIAN PALACE - NIGHT

Establishing shot of the Glokorian Palace, a majestic gothic palace on a remote, mountainous planet. A number of small space ships circle around.

CUT TO:

INT. GLOKORIAN PALACE: CHAMBER - DAY

The camera pans round a large, seemingly empty, ceremonial chamber. JED LARGO is sneaking about, thinking he is all alone, unaware that DRAX MANTIS is lurking in the shadows.

DRAX MANTIS: So, Largo, at last you have come. I have waited a long time for this day!

Jed spins round, in clear surprise. He pulls out his laser and points it directly at Drax.

DRAX MANTIS: You will need more than that if you bid me harm. Put the gun away, boy.

JED LARGO: If you think that the gun is my only weapon then you would be gravely mistaken.

Jed puts his gun away, as Drax steps from the shadows.

DRAX MANTIS: I am aware of your powers. McTulip has taught you well, but even his powers were no match for mine.

JED LARGO: (*concerned*) You killed McTulip?

DRAX MANTIS: It was easy. For a Skellern Warrior his powers were disappointing. I expected something of a challenge, but the last of the Skellern was no match for my own powers. He died on his knees, begging for my mercy. It was pitiful.

JED LARGO: Fergus may be dead, but the Skellern are not extinct yet.

DRAX MANTIS: You are bold Largo, too bold. Your impatience to challenge me will be the cause of your destruction. It will be a pleasure to kill you, and with you any chance that the Skellern will rise again. Nothing could be more perfect.

JED LARGO: I wouldn't be so keen if I were you. I am more powerful than you realise. I have the power of the Skellern. I share the same knowledge, and the same vision. I am more than equal to you.

DRAX MANTIS: (*laughing*) So you think you have the knowledge, do you? I bet that McTulip never told you about your father?

JED LARGO: I know what happened to my father! I know that you had him tortured and killed. That is why I must destroy you.

DRAX MANTIS: That is what you are supposed to think, but it is not the truth.

JED LARGO: (*sneering*) What do you mean?

DRAX MANTIS: Your father was a gangster and a murderer, a far better man than you will ever be. He killed McTulip's brother, and drove him to join the Skellern order. At first he did not know that he had a son. When he found out he was so ashamed of his actions that he took his own life. It was McTulip that told him of you. It was McTulip that killed him.

JED LARGO: (*in disbelief*) That's not true. That can't be true!

DRAX MANTIS: Search your emotions, boy. You know it to be true. I never killed your father. How could I? He was my greatest asset!

JED LARGO: You can not lie to me, Drax. What of the aliens you sent to kill my mother, how do you explain that?

DRAX MANTIS: (*sneering*) You really are a fool! Your father had your mother slain, for fear of her Skellern sympathies. He hired the alien scum that hunted her down and took her head. The Glokorians had nothing to do with that. You know this to be true.

JED LARGO: (*screaming*) No! I don't believe that! I will never believe that!

DRAX MANTIS: You can hunt down that alien scum if it makes you feel better. Indeed, I hope you do. They are no friends of mine. By killing them you will be taking your first steps as a Glokorian soldier. First, though, you must play witness to the deaths of Lady Carina and Mahnja. As I speak my soldiers are hunting them through this palace. They will soon be dead.

JED LARGO: (*unable to hold back his emotion any longer*) That's where you are wrong Drax! It is you who will soon be dead.

Jed lunges for Drax, who deflects him with an energy bolt from his arm. They struggle, throwing punches at each other and wrestling. The fight carries

147

them across the room, and out through a side door.

CUT TO:

INT. GLOKORIAN PALACE :SERVICE BRIDGE – NIGHT

Beyond the ceremonial chamber, the two struggling characters find themselves on a large metallic service bridge, spanning a vast cavern in the palace the size of a sports stadium. The fight continues until DRAX MANTIS is pushed over the railing, and JED LARGO collapses exhausted. DRAX MANTIS is holding on for his life.

All the Time in the World

Brad Clusky and Ralph Lee found themselves in a traditional pub, somewhere near Euston. It was a typical London local, with a long wooden bar, clusters of round tables with stools, and frosted glass in the windows. Ralph had got the drinks in. He bought two pints of bitter and carried them to the corner booth where Brad sat. Being a Wednesday the bar was relatively empty. A couple of local punters played darts, a lonely businessman was filling up a one armed bandit with his lose change, and a young couple were arguing at the bar. The bar man himself had a TV on behind the counter. The volume was low, he was only looking at the pictures. Other than that the place was empty. Ralph sipped his drink, and fired up a cigarette. "I think things are working out," he said. "Once we've got this nonsense out of the way we can concentrate on getting our arses cleared with the Yanks."

"Yeah," Brad replied tiredly, still suffering from following Dilly around the shops. "I guess so."

"You get the tickets okay?" asked Ralph.

"Sort of."

"What do you mean 'sort of'? I thought you were tailing that babe all day!"

"I was," replied Brad, "but I didn't get the tickets from her. Walter go them."

"Walter? How the hell did he manage that?"

"Believe me, you don't want to know!" The two
men took a drink, and sat back for a second. The
businessman gave up on the one armed bandit, and
tried his luck on the Juke Box. The first track he played
was Louis Armstrong's recording of *We have all the
time in the world*. An unusual choice, but it set the
mood. The effect was instant. Indeed, the couple at the
bar stopped arguing, and began kissing. The
businessman smiled, as if this was the first meaningful
gesture he had ever made.

"So what is this guy like?" asked Ralph.

"Who?"

"Walter. Walter Bridgenorth, the bane of our
lives. You know, he got us in to all this, but I've never
even met him. I just picture him as, I don't know, like
Walter the Softy, from *The Beano*. Do you remember
him? Archrival of Dennis the Menace, but now
updated with an unhealthy appetite for science fiction.
Mr Spock meets Mr Bean. How far out am I?"

"You're close," laughed Brad. "You're real close.
He's a bit like that, but he's clever too. Let's face it,
he's got us round his little finger."

"Correction, he's got *you* round his little finger.
I'm just a passenger on this one. If it was down to me I
would have killed him a week ago."

"Maybe," sighed Brad, "but I think I'm starting to
like him. He's not that much unlike us really!"

"Get out of here," retorted Ralph, sucking on his
cigarette.

"Oh come on Ralph," replied Brad. "I know
you're up for this one. Ever since I told you about this
job you've had a glint in your eye."

"Bullshit!"

"I don't think so," Brad continued. "I mean, what

do we normally do? Our average job normally involves industrial espionage. We steal files, or destroy files, or photograph things that aren't supposed to be photographed, and no-one ever gets to hear about it because nobody knows that any of those files existed in the first place. We like to think that we're Sean Connery and Roger Moore, but we're not. We never play at casinos, we are never chased by guys that look like Odd Job and throw razor rimmed top hats at us, and we never get to shag fantastic looking women who turn out to be Russian spies."

"And the point is?" enquired Ralph.

"The point is that this job is different! This job involves rubbing shoulders with glamorous women and dressing up in dinner jackets. What is more, this job is going to be in the news. Three unknown guys steal a plastic doll, four inches high, at one of London's biggest celebrity galas, in front of television cameras from every major channel and journalists from every single national paper. This will be like the disappearance of Lord Lucan. Everyone will want to know who we are, and why we did it! I know that you are getting off on that thought."

Ralph smiled wryly. Of course it was true. It was as true for Ralph as it was for Brad.

"So was Dilly Foxtrot our own little Pussy Galore?" asked Ralph.

"Uhm," Brad thought, "she had a nice arse. I wouldn't kick her out of bed on a cold night, if you take my meaning."

"A nice arse, eh? Still that's about as close as a guy like you is going to get."

Brad considered this lead as good as any for delivering the news about his dinner date.

"Actually," he said. "I'm having dinner with her tomorrow night."

"What?" said Ralph, his smile dropping instantly.

"I said I'm having dinner with..."

"I heard what you fucking said," fumed Ralph. "Are you nuts? Christ, every time I think you've just done the most stupidest thing in the history of stupidity, you go one better. Do you know how likely it is that you will blow our cover by eating with this chick? How long do you think you can keep a Steven Spielberg impression going for? One glass of wine? Two?"

"Look," said Brad defensively, "she asked me out, not vice versa. It would have looked just as sus if I'd turned her down. You can't just blow out a girl like that. It's not natural."

"You could have said you were gay!"

"Do me a favour."

"Lots of Hollywood stars are gay. She would have been none the wiser."

"Ralph," Brad said impatiently, "I'm having dinner with her tomorrow night. I'll keep my cover. Everything will be fine."

"Well," conceded Ralph, "promise me one thing."

"What?"

"Don't shag her."

"Why not?"

"I can give you two reasons. Firstly, cover or no cover, Warren Kingburger will chop your dick off if he finds out. Secondly, I will be exceptionally jealous, and I might have to kill you for being so fucking smooth."

The two of them regained their sense of humour, and started laughing again. It was enough to put one of the dart players off his shot.

"So," Ralph went on, "you think we're going to be big stars if we pull this off?"

"Absolutely," Brad replied. "We are going to be like the man in black in the TV ads who delivers a box of chocolates 'all because the lady loves Milk Tray'. We are the main event. They'll probably even try and put us on *Oprah*."

"And because of that we have got to be grateful to that little punk for roping us into it?"

"Yeah," said Brad. "Why not?"

"So maybe we should have a toast to our friend Walter," suggested Ralph.

"No," said Brad. "I've got a better idea. Let's toast the big man himself. Charge your glass to the first name in evil, Mr Drax Mantis, without whom Walter Bridgenorth would probably have grown up to be a normal guy and you and I would probably now be in South America getting laid."

"To Drax Mantis," echoed Ralph, still laughing. "Do you know, I've never seen *Galactic Encounter*?" he added.

"No way! Everyone has seen it," replied Brad. "I'm not saying I love it, or anything, but you have to see it. It's a bit like *Apocalypse Now,* or *Pulp Fiction*, or *The Italian Job*. It is mandatory viewing. I can't believe you have never seen it."

"I'm telling you, I haven't. It's not like I never wanted to, I just never got round to it. When it came out the first time I was more into cars and girls than films."

"No change there. You'd better drink up then," Brad added, draining his glass.

"Are you trying to get out of a round?"

"Nope," said Brad. "I'm taking you to the cinema.

It's about time you and Drax became acquainted. It's a good job they've re-released it."

"I'm not going to the cinema," insisted Ralph. "I just want to stay here and enjoy my pint."

"I don't think so buddy," said Brad, standing to leave. "Some things are more important than a few drinks in the pub. Let's just call it operational research!" Ralph realised that Brad was being serious.

"You kill me Brad," he said in defeat. He stood to leave with his partner, downing the last quarter of his pint. "You really kill me," he repeated.

"Let's hope I'm the only one who gets the chance," Brad replied. With that they left the pub and headed for the local cinema.

On the TV screen behind the bar the local news had just come on. Although the volume was low it was still possible to follow the story. The picture showed a computer hardware store off Tottenham Court Road, then a still of a bald man with a goatee beard taken a couple of years ago, then an interview with a student who was a key witness. If only Ralph had stayed in the bar a few moments longer he would have recognised his old friend Buster. If only the volume on the set had been turned up a little higher.

Part Four

Hype and Hypocrisy

Morning

Brad slept late the next day. The night before had turned into quite a session. Both he and Ralph were surprised at how good *Galactic Encounter* still was. For some strange reason they had both imagined it to be much worse. After the film they went back to the pub, then to an Indian restaurant, and then to a nightclub. It had been a long time since they had really had time to enjoy themselves. A night out was a chance to banish the ghosts of the AVREX job once and for all. Ralph disappeared around one in the morning. He had been dancing with some under dressed girl half his age for a while beforehand, and Brad had correctly assumed that he had let her abduct him. He could have scored himself, but he didn't feel like it. He just soaked up the atmosphere, and blew his daily quota of cigarettes several times over. Several hours later he was back at the Strand Palace, naked and asleep in his bed, all by himself. He hadn't ordered a wake-up call, so it was the maid who came at about ten to change the sheets who woke him. The rattle of keys in the door stirred him, then she burst in with her cleaning trolley. Her face was a picture at the sight of Brad in the nude. During the night he had kicked the sheets off, leaving nothing to the imagination. He woke up, and sat bolt upright on the bed.

"Fuck off," he bawled at the maid. She did, very

quickly and in a state of utter embarrassment. Brad slumped back on the bed. His head turned to look at the clock. Was it really that late already? He climbed out of bed and made his way to the bathroom.

Today was a big day. That in itself was no big deal, everyday seemed to be a big day these days. Every day from now on had to be used to perfect the plan. There could be no mistakes like the Gresham Job. This had to be smooth, super smooth. Having said that, things were going well so far. Ralph had procured most of the necessary gear from Buster Urman, and had planted the circuit breaker in the fuse box at the restaurant. Walter, amazingly, had lined up a way in. It was only Brad so far that hadn't really made much of a constructive contribution. Today was the day that was going to change. He looked at himself in the mirror. His hair was sticking out in all directions, and his chin had a thick coating of stubble. Worse still, he seemed to have picked up an exceptionally unpleasant odour. There was a lot of work to be done with a razor, a bar of soap, a hairbrush, and a can of deodorant. What was more he was starving, and had missed the breakfast serving that came with the daily room rate. Indeed, it was going to take at least another hour before he was anything like human, but human he had to be.

The main event of the day was Dilly Foxtrot, or rather dinner with her. He was certain he could get some beneficial information for the job by dining with her, and maybe a few sexual perks as well. That was not the only thing, however, that Brad had to do today. He also had to go and find Walter to take him to an optician in order to buy him a new pair of glasses. There was no way he could turn up at the Orbit Studio Experience with masking tape holding his frames together. Anything that made the two of them stand out had to be erased. After the opticians there was the small matter of buying the appropriate attire for the evening. Dinner jackets, bow ties, cummerbunds, high collar shirts, and Italian shoes were all on the shopping list. An appointment had been booked for Mr. West and Mr. Spencer with one of London's finest gentlemen's tailors. The clothes then had to be passed on to Ralph to be wired up with the appropriate electronics. Brad turned on the shower, and stepped under it. He pondered the agenda for the day. Indeed, there was a lot to do, and half the day was almost gone already. He had his work cut out.

An Inspector Calls

The day had started as slowly for Walter Bridgenorth as it had done for Brad Clusky. As usual, Celluloid Space Cowboy had opened promptly at 9.30 am. As usual there were no customers. As usual Walter went through his daily routine of tidying and organising, before brewing up and settling down with a comic. Oswald Moriarty made his usual appearance, but did not stay long, and left without purchase. He was muttering something about some job interview, or something, and stressing that he couldn't be late. His urgency did not unduly worry Walter as he dunked a digestive into his mug of PG Tips. His thoughts were occupied elsewhere, split more or less evenly between the adventures of *The Laser Ray Gang* (which were unfolding in the comic), and his lunchtime appointment with Brad Clusky in Knightsbridge. Clothes shopping hardly seemed to Walter to be an enthralling aspect of the operation, but Brad had insisted. Still, at least he was getting a new pair of glasses out of it, which would save him a few quid.

Walter wondered if he had got into something deeper than he should. How much did he really know about Brad Clusky? Why had such an obvious menace seemed so keen to help him in what was, after all, nothing more than a flight of fantasy? He shook his head. There was no point in thinking about if, why, or wherefore now. The second that he had attempted to blackmail Brad with that damned photograph was the second he had committed himself to this entire little escapade. There was no pulling out. There was no parachute primed ejector seat. Walter was going to steal Drax Mantis now, whether he wanted to or not. What on earth would his mother say if she found out?

Just then, a doe-eyed woman of maturing years, with greying corkscrew curls and a long tan coloured raincoat entered the shop. She was professional in both her appearance and mannerism, something that immediately caught Walter's attention. She was not, by quite some margin, the typical punter that Walter was used to. Perhaps she was from the Inland Revenue? Walter wondered whether Mr Chang had been making his appropriate tax returns.

"Good morning," said the woman, with a courteous smile, flashing something that looked like a bus pass in front of Walter's face. "I'm Detective Sergeant Mace from the Metropolitan Police. Do you mind if I ask you a few questions?"

Walter froze, midway through dunking his digestive. The result was that the biscuit, saturated, with the lower part falling away, formed a congealed mess in the bottom of the mug.

"This is quite a curious little shop," DS Mace continued, wondering over to examine the comic racks. "Do you get a lot of business?"

"You'd be surprised," Walter replied nervously, anxious to find out what this woman was really after. He placed his comic on the counter, to give her his undivided attention.

"I'm sure I would," Mace smiled. "Do you normally open quite late?"

"I'm sorry?"

"The shop, does it open late in the evening?"

"The opening hours are listed in the window," Walter pointed out.

"What about after hours? Is anybody around then?"

"I am, of course," Walter replied, "I live in the flat upstairs."

"Interesting," said Mace. "And were you at home on Friday the twenty third of last month?"

"Look," sighed Walter, already registering the date in question, "it would help if you told me what all this was about."

"Oh, it's all quite routine," Mace smiled reassuringly. "We are just trying to track the movements of a suspect who was in the vicinity of the High Street on that evening. Caucasian male, aged between thirty and forty. Dark hair, athletic frame, about six foot. Dressed all in black. Combat gear we think. Ring any bells?"

Walter was impressed. It was a good description of Brad on the night he first entered the shop. For some reason, Walter felt his had moving towards the cash register where the photograph of Brad resided.

"What is he supposed to have done?" Walter asked with genuine interest. Perhaps this copper would shed some light on Brad's anonymous past.

"I'm sorry, I'm not at liberty to divulge any information of that nature," Mace apologised. Walter tried hard to mask his disappointment.

"The twenty third," he said, putting on a thoughtful face, "wasn't that the night with all the police cars and the helicopter?" His hand was now dangerously close to the register, and he was fighting with his conscious as to whether or not he should disclose Brad's identity.

The only thing preventing him was the thought of the Drax Mantis action figure with a rocket pack.

"That's right. Do you remember seeing anything? You see, we don't think our man was working alone. We think he had accomplices in the local area who helped him escape."

"I'm sorry," Walter smiled, his hand moving back from the register. "The only thing I can remember about that night was the noise that all your lot were making. I wondered what it was all about."

"I see," said Mace, pulling a business card from her raincoat pocket. "Well, if anything comes to mind, be sure to give us a call." She handed the card to Walter across the counter.

"I will," Walter smiled. Detective Sergeant Mace went to the door, and moved in the direction of the greengrocer next door, no doubt to have the same conversation. Walter flicked the card over between his fingers. He had just dug himself in a little bit deeper. He wondered what the statutory sentence was for the crime of conspiring to pervert the course of justice. And what crimes might follow that? He hit the "no sale" sign on the register, and the cash drawer jumped out. Then he placed DS Mace's card under the same clip that held the Polaroid photograph of Brad. As he slid the drawer shut he let out a sigh of desperation. What on earth was he getting himself involved in?

The Orbit Studio Experience

Warren Kingburger could hardly believe his eyes. His latest masterpiece was finally complete. The London branch of the Orbit Studio Experience was finished. It was both on time and on budget. It had cost fifty million dollars to do it, and over two years of planning and construction. Out of all the other Orbit Studio Experiences that had been constructed so far, this was easily the best. The flagship of the fleet. The bar was now furnished, and Warren Kingburger sat there on a chrome stool, admiring his creation. A somewhat rusty bar man served the first ever drink to him from behind that bar. It was, of course, a Jack Daniels. That was the only way to celebrate, even though it was barely gone ten in the morning. As Kingburger sipped the whisky he struck a match from a specially designed Orbit Studios book of matches and ignited his cigar.

"So, hot stuff," he referred to Dilly Foxtrot sitting next to him. "How about giving an old man a tour of this joint?"

"Of course, Mr Kingburger," Dilly replied. As ever she looked fantastic, this time in a little leopard skin number, sitting with a clipboard on her lap. "Shall we start with the kitchens, the nerve centre of the operation?"

"Fuck the kitchens, baby. I'm sure they are very

important, but I don't plan to be spending much time down there. No, I want to see where it's going to be happening. I want to see the rock and roll. I want to see all the good work that you have been doing for me, sweet thing."

"Well," Dilly responded seductively, "perhaps we should start at the top and work our way down."

"That's more like it, honey," responded Warren in excitement. "You're speaking my language now."

They took the lift to the upper restaurant. Warren took the opportunity in the lift to give Dilly's buttocks an affectionate squeeze. She responded with a minx-like squeal.

"This is the upper restaurant," announced Dilly as the lift doors opened. It was obvious that Kingburger was impressed.

"I'll be a son of a gun," he stated admiringly, for the first time his attention diverted from Dilly's cleavage. He was standing right next to a Mahnja the Smownork original movie costume, mounted on a mannequin.

"You know," he went on, "every time I see this lizard guy it gives me the creeps, and he was one of the good guys!"

"That's not all we have, Mr Kingburger," elaborated Dilly. "If you look to your left you will see an original dinosaur egg from *Dino Island*, and beyond that is the original costume worn by *Cybercop*."

"Fantastic," said Kingburger. "I love this stuff. What about the restaurant? Tell me more about the restaurant."

"Well, sir, this tier has seating for one hundred, and the lower tier seats another one hundred and fifty. We are using the same menu that we recently launched in New Orleans. That means there is a choice of nine starters, thirty two main courses, and twelve desserts. The main courses include a variety of international dishes, along with vegetarian options. We also have twenty customised cocktails, along with a full bar of other beverages including a range of imported American beers."

"I love it," Warren went on, dashing between every exhibit. "I simply love it. It's easily our best yet!"

They descended the stairs to the lower restaurant floor. The staircase was spiral, and was lined with photographs of famous Hollywood moments. Warren paused at a photograph of the director Todd Orchard and himself taken on the set of *Galactic Encounter* in 1979.

"Where did this come from?" he asked, closely inspecting the picture.

"We had it in archives back in LA," replied Dilly, checking her clipboard.

"I hate it," replied Kingburger, still inspecting it. "I hate it. It makes me look fat. I wasn't that fat in 1983. Take it down and have it changed."

"Yes, sir," replied Dilly.

They continued down past many more famous exhibits. There was Jed Largo's original laser gun, an assortment of cowboy paraphernalia from an eighties western that wasn't really a success, and the loin cloth worn by Burns Meredith for his portrayal of *Zayto the Jungle King* in 1968. Kingburger loved it all. He was like a school boy at a fun fair, wanting to go on every ride. His hot breath condensed on the glass of every display cabinet as he pressed his face up close. This was what it was all about to Warren Kingburger. He had lived his life in a private world of fantasy. The films he oversaw at Orbit provided a window on this world, but you could never actually go inside. You could never see these amazing places with your own eyes and, because of that, it was easy not to believe in them. To Kingburger, however, it was all real. The world of Jed Largo and Drax Mantis was as real as Los Angeles or London. Now, after all these years, he was a step closer to sharing that vision with the people who loved his films, the people who had looked through his window and enjoyed the same view. For the first time they would know that Jed Largo had a real laser gun. They would know that dinosaur eggs really did exist on *Dino Island*. They would know that *Cybercop* had a third dimension.

"I love it," he cried out loud. "Miss Foxtrot, you have done a wonderful job. I will be rewarding you personally for your tremendous effort on this project. I would appreciate it if you were available to spend some time with me in Los Angeles after the opening night."

"It would be a pleasure sir," replied Dilly, "but you still haven't seen the museum section downstairs yet. Shall we continue? You will be pleased to know that the Drax Mantis action figure you requested came in this morning. We already have him set up in his own display cabinet."

Warren Kingburger turned slowly at this news. "Amazing," he whispered under his breath. "Truly amazing!" With that he bolted to the stairs. He had meant to check with Dilly that there was a rocket pack, but his excitement got the better of him. He needed to see that exhibit right now. Besides, he knew that Dilly knew that if she had got it wrong it would cost her dearly, and even she wasn't that stupid. There, on the far side of the museum floor, sat the display cabinet he had been looking for. He ran up to it as if it held the secret to life itself, and in his mind the world span for a moment. Sure, he had seen one of these things before. He owned most of them. Yet there was something so perfect, so cool, about four inches of immortal plastic. It represented everything that Orbit stood for. For the children who saw these films in the seventies and eighties the fantasy didn't end when the credits went up. No, with these toys they could take it all home with them. It was such a simple idea, personifying movie characters in plastic so that every kid who saw the film had a souvenir, and everyone that didn't would do anything to get their hands on one. Even now, twenty years later, most of those kids who bought the toys still owned them, even though they were mostly married with children of their own. Warren loved that. He loved the whole magic of cinema. There had never been a day when he regretted jacking in the oil business. This was what it was all about. He stood transfixed on the small plastic man in front of him behind the glass. He ogled at the tiny rocket pack. His grin ran from cheek to cheek, and failed to stop the trickle of saliva running down his lip.

"Have you ever seen anything as beautiful?" he asked Dilly, who had finally caught up behind him.

"Er, well, Mr Kingburger," she replied falsely. "No, I don't believe I have." Inside she couldn't believe what all the fuss was about. For God's sake! It's just a bloody piece of plastic. You could get more satisfaction from a condom, and they are only made of rubber! To be honest she was getting a little bored of the tour, and of Kingburger. An image of Nathan West kept popping into her head. Her mind skipped to a time later that day when she would be dining with him, and then who knows what!

"Yes," Kingburger went on. "In just a few days you're going to see the biggest show business event in London this year. It's going to be an awesome, pumping, power station of a party. I might even wear my yellow suit for a change. In fact, I think I will. What do you reckon baby?"

"Uh?" she said, snapping out of her own private fantasy world. "That would be great," she lied, almost obviously. Did he say yellow? Why on earth wear yellow? A white suit is bad enough, looking like some evangelical maniac! In that moment Dilly questioned why she was even bothering with Kingburger. Why bother with him when there were real men like that Mr West out there. Nathan West, a real dream boat, a real man. Who was to say that Dilly's career couldn't bloom just as well under the stewardship of Nathan West, as opposed to Kingburger. There was no doubt in Dilly's mind. It was time for a change.

The Phone Call

Just as Walter Bridgenorth had done a few days earlier, Danny Dellapicho was now standing across the street from the Orbit Studio Experience. Just like Walter, he was casing the restaurant. Unlike Walter, he had a trained eye, and zoomed in on all of the security systems that were on show. It was obvious that the only safe way in or out was through the front door. That would mean he would have to assume the identity of a party guest. That in itself would probably be easy. Danny could remember when they first opened an Orbit Studio Experience in Washington. The streets had been jammed with movie fans, all hoping to get a glimpse of the big stars. The big stars got driven up to the front door in their limousines. Logistics, however, meant that minor celebrities could only get dropped off in the side streets and had to make the rest of the journey on foot. All Danny had to do was wait around for one such faceless guest. He would request their ticket, or alternatively give them the option of instant death. It was so straightforward. Inside it would just be a case of tracking Brad and Ralph down. As they were doing a job they would probably be easy to find. Perhaps wiring up a bomb in a storeroom, or riding on top of the elevator to photograph an illicit rendezvous between two people who should really know better. Either way once he had them in his sights he would simply blow them away. The confusion and mayhem that followed would make escape easy. Danny was satisfied that the rest of his work in London was a formality. In less than three days it would all be over, and he would be on a plane back to Washington to pick up a juicy, fat bonus cheque. It was time to call in. Ironically, he used the same telephone box that Walter had used to call Brad only a day earlier, to report his encounter with Warren Kingburger. Danny, however, was still blissfully unaware of Walter's existence. Danny unscrewed the mouthpiece on the phone, and replaced it with a special encrypting device. He dialled an international number, somewhere in Washington. The call was answered, but nobody spoke.

"This is 24639," began Danny. "Regarding the two subjects I've been allocated in Area Nineteen. I have received information of a suitable window that will be arising to complete the project. I can confirm that the project will be successfully completed within three days. That's all." With that he hung up, confident that his message had been received by his paymasters. With that matter taken care of, Danny had another task to occupy his day with. He needed a dinner jacket for the opening night. That would normally be a straightforward task, but after the murders the police were bound to ask questions about anyone buying a dinner jacket in London. He considered, just to be on the safe side, that whoever sold him the clothes would have to meet with an unfortunate accident, with a handy electrical domestic appliance. That would probably take a full day's work. Even though Danny had only been in London for less than a week he had already killed thirteen people. After he had dealt with the dinner jacket salesman, there would only be two names left on his list.

Dinner

The day had quickly passed. By the early evening Walter owned a new pair of glasses with designer frames, and both Brad and Walter had been kitted out with snappy evening wear. In total they had spent well over a thousand pounds, wired to a ghost credit card account in Australia by Ralph. Brad had even gone as far as treating himself, and had bought a new suit in which to take Dilly out to dinner. He wanted to look the part, a smooth Hollywood high-flyer with expensive tastes.

Brad arrived early at the Grosvenor House. Dilly was nowhere to be seen, so he resigned himself to an easy lobby chair and a copy of *The Times*. He normally preferred something more easy-going to read, but only broadsheets were on offer. Still, in his new suit, sitting in the hotel lobby and reading a quality paper, he began to feel like a real spy for the first time. He felt like what a spy ought to feel like, dangerous but a little bit sexy.

"You're name is not Brad Clusky," he told himself, "You are Nathan West. Nathan West, secret agent. You are super cool. You are not going to fuck this up. You have dinner, get some more inside information, chat, drink wine, have sex. That's all you have to do."

He was so wrapped up in his personal

conversation that he did not realise that Dilly had arrived in the lobby. He was taken by surprise when he looked up from his paper.

"Hi," she pouted. She looked sensational, in a short designer black dress. It was minimalist in style, exposing her golden arms and a wide arc across the top of her chest. She had her hair pushed back, which exaggerated her cheekbones, and made her look sensational.

"Hi," Brad replied, still trying to take her all in.

"Are you ready?" she asked.

"Sure."

"Lets go then."

Dilly had chosen the restaurant, and had already booked the table. They took a cab to Quaglino's in Bury St James's. In the cab he complemented her on her look, and she admired the cut of his suit. They didn't say much else. Brad felt that Dilly would prefer to make conversation over dinner. Besides, the cab journey was far too short to make any serious attempt to debate anything meaty. Brad had never dined at Quaglino's before, and he didn't really know what he was letting himself in for. For starters, the custom that all guests had to present themselves at the top of the central staircase to the mass of diners below seemed very peculiar. Fortunately Dilly was in a flamboyant mood, and took care of the announcements. Miss Dilly Foxtrot and Mr Nathan West were thus suitably presented. A number of heads turned to observe the couple as they descended. With that minor hurdle out of the way, they were shown to their table. Brad began to relax, and take in the atmosphere. The restaurant itself was essentially a long hall, vast in size, with a ceiling that reminded Brad somewhat of a greenhouse.

The style was hard to place. On one hand it had the decor and demeanour of something you might expect to find in the forties or fifties. Indeed, Brad was convinced that one of the diners on the next table was a direct descendent of Al Capone. At the same time, however, there was something refreshingly modern about it. They ordered. Brad had a steak and Dilly had something French which was quite unpronounceable, topped off with a vintage bottle of red wine.

"So," said Dilly, breaking the ice, "what shall we talk about?"

"I don't know," Brad replied. "What do people normally talk about on first dates?"

"Is this a date then?"

"I suppose so," said Brad. "I hope so."

"I see," smiled Dilly. "So I suppose I should ask what your favourite colour is, or whether you have any pets, or why you are not married."

"Yeah," said Brad. "Those are the sort of superficial questions that people normally start with."

"Superficial?" asked Dilly.

"Yeah. People rather ask those sort of questions rather than asking what sort of things they like to do in bed, which is what they really want to know in the first place."

"Is that what you want to know?"

"Maybe," Brad replied confidentially, "a little later."

The starters arrived, causing the conversation to be momentarily broken off. It cast an awkward silence. After the waiter had retreated again, it was Dilly who broke the deadlock.

"Why don't you ask me something superficial?" she suggested, starting to tackle her salad.

"Okay," Brad replied. "What star sign are you?"

"Sagittarius. How about you?"

"Capricorn."

"Is that compatible?" Dilly asked.

"I have no idea."

"When is your birthday?"

"The seventeenth of January," Brad replied. "I share it with Muhammad Ali, Jim Carrey and Keith Chegwin."

"Who is Keith Chegwin?"

"Uhm," thought Brad. "Actually, there is no reason why you should know who Keith Chegwin is."

"I see," replied Dilly.

"Your turn," said Brad.

"Okay," she said. "Why are superficial questions such a load of shit?"

The comment made them both laugh.

"Maybe you're right," said Brad. "Let's switch the conversation. What is Warren up to this evening?"

"Mr Kingburger," Dilly repeated shyly. "I think he is doing a TV interview."

"Really. I bet he must be dead proud of that restaurant, even if it is a far cry from this place. What is it like inside?"

The conversation shifted to the Orbit Studio Experience, which was exactly what Brad wanted. He needed the low down on how the place was set up. Even though Ralph had down loaded some excellent data on his computer, you couldn't account for human error. It was more than probable that Dilly would have some inside information that would be of use. The time for superficial questions had indeed passed. It was time to get down to business.

Capital Night Out

Dana O'Brien and Marcus Clint were the anchors on the popular cable show *Capital Night Out*, a low budget entertainment set up which emulated trashy society magazines. Cynical observers will note that the channel which broadcasts the show was also part of the Orbit Studio Group. It is no surprise therefore, that in the week running up to the restaurant opening, *Capital Night Out* was broadcasting nightly features on the Orbit Studio Experience. Even if the TV station hadn't been a subsidiary of Orbit, the features were still likely to go ahead. The Orbit Studio Experience opening was going to be one of the big celebrity events of the year, not the sort of thing that *Capital Night Out* would turn its nose up to. Within a matter of days London would be positively brimming with celebrities, especially film stars. Big Hollywood names, who would normally avoid London unless there was a premiere screening of one of their films, had already booked their plane tickets. The opening night was going to be special, and the only way to hear the gossip first would be to tune into *Capital Night Out*.

"Hi there, I'm Marcus Clint," he announced to Camera Four from behind a cheap, imitation pine news desk. Marcus was a tall man in his early fifties with steely grey hair, a gleaming white smile, and a deep suntan that was guaranteed to wash off after three rinses. He wore an expensive Italian suit, and maintained immaculate posture in front of the camera.

"And I'm Dana O'Brien," said his counterpart to the same camera. She was a short, slinky woman, but with a stern demeanour. She was a blazing red head, with cheeks that had been set cosmetically. She oozed her own brand of sex appeal, which was only undermined by the tang of a West Country accent which she was constantly trying to mask. Having said that, she had been voted as the sexiest woman in the world by the men of Cornwall for three years running.

"Welcome to *Capital Night Out*," Marcus went on, "and what a night out we've got planned for all of you at home."

"That's right, Marcus," pouted Dana. "It's the party that everyone has been talking about, and anyone who is anyone is going to be there. We've got more big Hollywood names for you on the show tonight than any blockbuster currently screening in the West End."

"Indeed," smarmed Marcus. "Yes, it's only a few days until the Orbit Studio Experience will be opening for the first time in London. It's billed as the show business event of the year. Following on from the re-release of the legendary *Galactic Encounter* movie trilogy, Orbit has become the hottest ticket in movie circles. Everybody, and I mean everybody, wants a slice of the action."

"Let's go straight over to our roving reporter, Jenny Lovelace, right outside the new restaurant sensation," said Dana. The picture cut to a shot of Jenny Lovelace outside the restaurant. She was a young girl with bounds of energy. Her nose was pierced, as was her belly button which was also on show, and her cropped hair had been bleached white.

"Yo, Dana," cried Jenny. "It's really kicking down here in the city tonight and this place ain't gonna open for a few days yet! This is where the party is at! The crowd outside is already heaving. People are comin' down here to check it out before the big stars fly in. There are even people here with tents and sleeping bags, all hoping to be amongst the first to dine out here." The camera panned to a small party of around twenty odd looking characters in sleeping bags, sitting quietly and politely behind the police railings. A couple of them turned and made gestures to the people watching at home. Some waved, whilst others stuck their tongues out, and others just screamed because it felt good.

"Do ya' feel all right?" Jenny yelled out at the crowd. They positively yelled their approval back at her. "Check it out," Jenny went on. "What a crowd." The picture cut back to the studio.

"Have you seen any big stars down there yet, Jenny?" asked Marcus, knowing full well that his question was loaded. The picture returned to Jenny.

"For sure," she hollered. "As it happens I'm standing next to one of the biggest names in Hollywood. Yes, it is Mr Orbit Studios himself, Warren Kingburger." The picture widened, and Warren Kingburger entered the right of the frame, wearing a sky blue suit and matching Stetson and smoking a large Cuban cigar.

"Mr Kingburger, how are you doin' tonight?" Jenny asked.

"Well, what can I say," replied Kingburger. "This is it. In just a matter of days now we are bringing the hottest venue to London. I can tell you that there are going to be some movie props in there that are worth thousands, and a few stars who are worth millions. No wonder this crowd is going mad. I just hope they can hold out until we actually open the doors."

"But Mr Kingburger," Jenny continued, "considering that you are a multi-millionaire movie mogul, and that you already have joints like this in a number of other top cities, what is the attraction for you personally to be involved in this project?"

"Baby," replied Kingburger in astonishment. "Do you ever see Schwarzenegger deputise cutting the red tape at Planet Hollywood to some junior studio producer? No sugar, that is not how it works. When the champagne needs to be smashed against the ship it is always a job for the main man. At Orbit I am the main man, *numero uno*. My mission in life is to bring the joy of cinema to every man, woman and child on this planet. This week I'm doing it for all you people here in England."

"That's great," replied Jenny, as if she hadn't listened to a single word. "Okay, now it's back over to you guys in the studio." The picture promptly cut back to Dana and Marcus.

"Thanks there Jenny," said Dana. "Coming up on the show we have an exclusive interview with Helena Armstrong, the blonde bombshell star of the hit US show *Coast Guard*. For the first time she is talking frankly about her cosmetic chest implants."

"And, of course," interrupted Marcus, "we have more live coverage from the West End on the imminent opening of the Orbit Studio Experience. Stay with us on *Capital Night Out*. We will be right back after this commercial break."

The commercial break sequence began, followed by a shampoo commercial. In the studio the make up girls had two minutes and forty eight seconds to touch up the faces of Marcus and Dana. They always needed to look good, especially on a week like this when the ratings were bound to be high. The first shows had already gone well, with live reports from the Orbit headquarters in Los Angeles, and interviews with a number of the big stars who would be coming over to England for the opening. At that point, however, neither presenter realised how many times that footage from the climatic show would be repeated on TV networks around the world. They didn't realise they would be breaking a far bigger story than the simple opening of restaurant. Intrigue, suspense, violence and murder were about to replace idle chat and smarmy smiles. It was the sort of material that could really boost the career of a good TV presenter.

Easy Women

Danny Dellapicho sat on his bed in his hotel room, smoking a joint and getting high. He was half watching a CNN report on cable about some volcano that had gone off, killing loads of people on some off-beat island somewhere. Danny got a buzz from that. He laughed out loud at the comparison. Here he was blowing away a handful of people in London, and if he ever got caught it would be big time news. Every network would cover it for weeks. On the other hand you had the wrath of God, personified in a volcano that was killing more people than Danny could ever hope to execute in a life long career in assassination. He knew though that by tomorrow it would be old news and nobody would give a damn. CNN would no doubt be drawn into some sex scandal, or other futile story with sod all significance for everyone. He rested his joint in an ashtray on the bedside, and picked up an ice cold Budweiser sat next to it. Thank God they stocked Bud on this pimple of an island. Danny wasn't ready to submit to warm beer yet, if you could call that brown stuff beer. As far as Danny was concerned it was like drinking bath water. The Bud tasted good though, and slipped down well. There was a knock on the door. Danny looked up without surprise - he was expecting a visitor. He took his gun from the bedside, and slid it under one of the pillows on the bed.

"Who is it?" he asked, climbing off the bed and walking to the door.

"It's, uh, Candy," a harsh female voice replied. "You sent for me."

"Of course," Danny replied, opening the door. Candy walked straight in. Danny had taken the card with Candy's phone number from the phone box he had unknowingly shared with Walter. Candy was, by any man's standard, a bit rough. She was of average height, with hair dyed a strange unnatural red colour. She had poor skin, and her face seemed to have a rough texture. She tried to compensate for this with too much make up. The end result was something more similar to a children's drawing of a face, rather than the real thing. Her figure was equally as questionable. Her chest was at least six inches lower than it should have been, maybe more without a bra. She covered it with a tight sleeveless top which failed to cover the stretch marks on her tummy. On one of her exposed arms she brandished a tattoo of a dragon. It was of very poor quality, and was already fading. Her legs were covered with tight, zebra skin patterned leggings, which clearly showed rolls of fat on her thighs.

"Fucking hell," said Danny. "Not quite like the ad are you?" He picked up his joint and took a puff.

"Thanks a lot," snapped Candy. "You're not such an oil painting yourself."

"Are you clean?"

"I haven't got anything nasty, if that's what you mean. Do you want this or not?"

"How much?"

"One hundred, up front. For that you get the full monty. No funny shit though. Hurt me and I'll cut your bollocks off, and you can't crap on me or anything fucking weird like that. You get one hour."

"Okay," said Danny, who really couldn't be bothered to wait for another girl. "You got a deal." He pulled out a roll of fifty pound notes from his pocket, and threw two on the bed. He sat down next to them, and held out the remainder of his joint to Candy. "Take this," he instructed. She took it from him, and took a drag.

"That's good shit," she sighed, gathering the money. "I just got to make a call then we can get started." She pulled a mobile phone from her bag and dialled a number. Danny waited patiently.

"It's me," said Candy into her phone when the number connected. "I'm here with Mr Davies. He's cool. I'll call again in an hour." She terminated the call without waiting for a reply.

"Your clothes," Danny said, reclining on the bed, "take them off."

Candy obliged the request, peeling off her top and unclipping her bra, allowing her breasts to drift ever further down. She kicked off her shoes, and slipped off her skirt. Finally her knickers slid down her legs, leaving her in all her glory.

"Now take my clothes off," Danny went on. Once again, Candy complied. She started with his belt, pulling it free from his trousers. She unbuttoned his shirt, licking his chest as she went, and then unzipped his fly. As anybody who has ever tried it knows, it is very difficult to undress another person at the best of times, worse still when they are lying on a bed. The initially seductive licking and feeling quickly subsided into something of a struggle. Candy wrestled with Danny's shoelaces, whilst he grappled with his shirt as if it were a strait jacket. Eventually Danny was also naked, but the effort of undressing had done nothing for the passion of the moment. Candy had sensed this, and was eagerly trying to rekindle Danny's biological attention. Soon they were making love. In fairness to Candy she wasn't bad. She was energetic and imaginative, more than most men could probably handle. Danny, however, was more than the typical punter. He was as much a seasoned professional when it came to sex as he was when it came to murder. He had probably slept with more women than Candy had men, and that was saying something. After a poor start, Danny was far from convinced about Candy's performance, and decided to spice things up. As Candy appeared to be reaching a climax, Danny made his move.

"You ever tasted a barrel between your lips, sweet heart?" Danny asked.

"You bet," Candy replied, assuming Danny was speaking in innuendo, "but I'm always hungry for that sort of thing." She caught her breath, as the first ripple of a spasm passed over her.

"Cool," said Danny, pulling his gun from under his pillow, and forcing the barrel in her mouth. "Taste this then, bitch." At the exact moment Candy could no longer hold on, and wailed in orgasm, Danny pulled the trigger and blew her brains out all over the room.

"Fuck," he shouted, at the instant shower of blood he had created. There was blood everywhere. It was up the walls, over the bedside, all over the bed and across the carpet. Everywhere you looked there were fragments of blood and brains. Danny himself was completely covered in the stuff. It had been such a long time since Danny had killed somebody by holding his gun in their mouth that he had forgotten just how messy it could be. He climbed off Candy's corpse, and tried to wipe some of the blood off himself. There was no doubt that the hotel management were going to freak when they discovered this mess. It was time to make a speedy exit, and check into another hotel. There was just enough time to grab a quick shower, and find some clean clothes. He thought for a moment about which hotel he should check into. He was getting fed up of the kind of slums his bosses normally put him up in. He decided instead that it was time to move up-market. An old friend of his back in Washington, and a respectable one at that, had recently taken a holiday in London. He had stayed in some posh hotel, as Danny remembered it. He struggled for a moment to come up with the name before it finally came back to him. It was the Grosvenor House. That sounded like a smart joint, and the sort of place where he should spend his last couple of days in England. He decided that he would check in.

The Kiss

The meal had been going very well. Brad had got some useful information out of his conversation with Dilly so far. He had confirmed that the Drax Mantis action figure was going to be in the display case that Ralph and he had earlier identified. A potential problem was that he would not be alone. Drax was sharing his cabinet with a first edition action figure of Cybercop, in addition to one of Cardinal Fergus McTulip, plus their original boxes behind them. He couldn't, therefore, assume that by removing one doll from the cabinet in the dark he would have the right one. There were some other useful things he had picked up about the security arrangements as well, even though it didn't seem Dilly's speciality area. He now knew that the rear door of the restaurant was fully accessible in order to comply with safety regulations. The head of security, a doddering Glaswegian called McFadden, would patrol that area about every half hour, and Brad already knew the door was covered by CCTV. Despite these obstacles, there was no reason why the rear door could not be accessed as the main escape route. Brad had also learned the agenda for the evening. Fuzzy J, the notorious nightclub disc jockey, would be providing the early evening entertainment. Once things had really got going, it was intended that Warren Kingburger would address the partygoers with

185

a specially prepared speech. After that there would be live entertainment from a number of top bands and pop groups. Well, that was what was supposed to happen. Brad had already mapped out in his head an alternative chain of events. Despite these insights, Brad was finding it hard to concentrate on important matters relating to the plan. The red wine was going straight to his head, and Dilly's looks were as equally intoxicating.

"You seem to want to know a lot about our restaurant?" asked Dilly, sipping her coffee. She signalled to a scantily clad cigarette girl, looking like she had just stepped out of a cheeky picture post card, who strolled over with her tray of cigarettes. Dilly chose a packet of Lucky Strikes. Hardly the most individual of brands, but Dilly didn't mind. As far as she was concerned old habits died hard.

"I find it fascinating," Brad replied. "It makes a change from movies."

"But that's what it is all about," said Dilly, "the movies!" She fired up a Lucky Strike, and offered one to Brad. He took it gratefully and lit up.

"I know it's *about* the movies," said Brad, "but it isn't *actually* the movies, if you take my drift?"

"I guess," Dilly conceded.

"The food was great," said Brad.

"It was very nice."

"How is your coffee?"

"That sounds like a superficial question," Dilly replied, exhaling a cloud of cigarette smoke. "I thought we were past that?"

"I'm sorry. You're right."

"Why don't you ask me if I'd like to be escorted back to my hotel?"

"Huh," Brad said awkwardly. "Oh, yeah, right. Would you like me to do that?"

"I would insist upon it. I've got an ample drinks cabinet in my room. I'm sure I've got something that would suit your palate."

"I'm sure you have," Brad replied. "I'll get the bill." He ushered over the waiter and produced an American Express Gold Card with the name Nathan West on it. Sometimes, the speed with which Ralph could come up with kit like that seemed remarkable even to Brad. The actual account belonged to a leading heart surgeon. Ralph had simply taken a blank Gold Card, of which he had a small supply, recoded it with the surgeon's details, but had embossed the name Nathan West into the plastic. By the time Brad would have finished with it, the heart surgeon would probably need heart surgery himself. The waiter brought over the credit slip, which Brad signed with his newly developed Nathan West signature. He left a twenty pound note as a tip, and the two of them got up to leave. It was a pleasant evening as they stepped from the restaurant, warm enough to walk without the need for a coat, but still with a pleasant breeze in the air. Regrettably the stars had been covered by a thick covering of low cloud, but that wasn't enough to erase the feeling of intimacy between Brad and Dilly. She linked her arm through his, and gently nuzzled her head against his shoulder.

"So," said Brad, not really too sure of what his next move might be, "how many security guys did you say you had hired for this party?"

"Let's not talk shop anymore," Dilly said softly, raising her hand to Brad's cheek. "It was really sweet of you to buy me coffee the other day, and dinner tonight was pretty special."

Brad wasn't so stupid not to realise he was being hit on. He had to think what Nathan West, if the man really were to exist, would do in this situation.

"Is that some kind of line?" he asked dumbly.

"If that's a line," she continued, "are you man enough to cross it?" Her fingers slid across the side of his face, and guided it towards her own until their lips finally met. His arms, with nowhere else to go, eased themselves around her tender frame. Brad had almost forgotten what it was like to kiss a woman, and it tasted good. It tasted very good.

"I've been wondering what that might be like," said Dilly, easing her head away.

"Me too," said Brad. "I certainly could do with that drink now," he added eagerly, looking to hail a cab.

"But I'm not thirsty anymore," she replied, moving to kiss him again. This time they held it a little longer. A taxi pulled up and he wrapped his muscular arm around her. In the back of the cab they would occasionally pause to kiss again, or to share a joke. The whole thing was perfect for Brad, apart from one small detail. Dilly seemed to be falling for Nathan West, as opposed to himself. Still, it was as close as he could afford to become emotionally involved these days. He walked Dilly all the way to the door of her room at the Grosvenor House and, despite Ralph's earlier warning, stayed the night. Ten minutes after they had arrived, a stranger arrived at the hotel reception.

"Hi there," said Danny Dellapicho to the receptionist. "My name is Mr Davies, my plane just got in from Denver. I was wondering if you might have a room for the night?"

The Return of Oswald Moriarty

In the final run up before the opening night of the Orbit Studio Experience, things had become gradually busier at Celluloid Space Cowboy. It seemed to Walter Bridgenorth that he had been on his feet for days. He could hardly remember a week when they had sold so many comics and posters. The re-release of *Galactic Encounter* had been good business. Walter's memories of the original release centred very much around his own desire to own the small action figures that went with the film. Now he was seeing the other side. Dozens and dozens of children were coming into the store, all hungry for merchandise. The new action figures, however, were nowhere near as good as the original set. They had all become victims of the modern era, and seemed to have gone on a course of steroids. All now had bulging biceps, even Lady Carina, to come in line with the other action figure toys available from other films. This angered Walter to an extent. The whole point of Jed Largo was that he wasn't an especially butch character. Walter reluctantly resigned himself to the fact that this was progress. Anyway, the days passed quickly, and soon it was the penultimate day before the Orbit Studio Experience was due to open. Walter's nerves were completely in tatters, especially considering the lack of contact he had received from Brad Clusky over the last couple of days. He had bitten his finger nails down until the ends of his finger hurt. He fidgeted and fretted all day, and was rude to almost every customer. His vague efforts to mask his nerves continually failed. He checked his watch no less frequently than once every two minutes, and ate three packets of digestive biscuits simultaneously in a bid to kill time. Towards the end of the day, just when Walter felt like he was facing an imminent nervous breakdown, things began to quieten down in the shop. That only made things worse. At least serving people took care of some of the time during the day. Long empty periods were just about unbearable. Just as Walter was about to reach the brink of despair, the shop door opened. Walter's elation at the distraction, however, was exceptionally short lived when he realised that the customer in question was none other than Oswald Moriarty.

"Walter," he squawked as he came through the door. "How's it going?"

Walter sank back in his chair, and sighed a depressively deep sigh. "Hi Oswald," was about as much as he could muster.

"Are they new glasses?" Oswald continued. "They're so much smarter than that pair you broke. I see your black eye is better as well."

"I'm feeling much better now, thanks," Walter replied, even though he wasn't completely sure if he was.

"I thought so," Oswald smiled. "Do you want to hear my news?"

"Astound me," Walter invited, already trying to tune out of the conversation. "Oh, but if it is something you have read in *Space World* then don't bother. I have already read this week's copy, several times."

"No, my friend," smarmed Oswald. "Not even *Space World* has got this story yet!"

"So what is it then?"

"I've got a job," Oswald announced, spreading his arms out as if he were some sort of performer taking a bow.

"You," stuttered Walter, "have a job?"

"Yes I do. A real job as well. None of that temporary nonsense. This is permanent employment. Not only that, my job is as cool as yours is. No, it's probably cooler. It's the coolest job in the world. I start tomorrow."

"Is that so," Walter replied, doubting every word. Of course he was pleased that Oswald had a job. Morally that was great for his dear mother's financial burdens, but cynically it was also good for Celluloid Space Cowboy as the profits were bound to gain a positive bump from Oswald's affluence. The coolest job in the world, however, would be to direct the fourth in the series of *Galactic Encounter* films. Since it was simply impossible for Oswald to have a job like that, Walter had already concluded that his new employment was either as a supermarket grocery boy, a kitchen hand, a bathroom attendant in a hotel, or something as equally inconsequential.

"Do you want to know what it is?" Oswald persisted.

"Please, the suspense is killing me."

"Well, I'm going to be..."

Just then the door opened again. A man in dark glasses, an army jacket, jeans and heavy boots walked in. The man had a menacing expression on his face, an ugly snarl that turned the heads of both Walter and Oswald and halted the conversation. The man was Ralph Lee.

The Rendezvous

"Hey you, blondie," Ralph Lee called to Oswald. "Why don't you take your sad shit little frame out of my sight?"

"What the hell do you think you're doing?" Walter shouted back. "We don't tolerate that kind of language in this shop. Would you kindly leave this instant!"

"So you're Walter," Ralph said, turning his attention. "My God. I knew you were a puny little tosser, but I didn't realise how puny."

The familiarity concerned Walter. He didn't feel comfortable that this oversized thug knew his name. Perhaps this guy was a friend of the brute who smashed his glasses at the cinema, back for revenge. Worse still, what if Brad Clusky had suddenly got cold feet about the Drax Mantis scam, and had sent one of his associates round to finish him off? Either way, things looked pretty bad.

"Perhaps it's best if you go," Walter discreetly said to Oswald.

"Are you sure?" Oswald replied. "This dude looks like trouble. He might try and rob you or something."

"Don't worry," assured Walter. "I can take care of him."

Oswald didn't need a second opportunity to get out. Ralph was exactly the sort of guy he didn't want to spend time with. He scampered to the door, and ran away up the street.

"If he comes back," Ralph commanded, "you tell him I was just an irate customer who wanted his money back."

"If he comes back?" questioned Walter. "I take it from that I will still be in one piece to see him come back."

"Jesus," laughed Ralph. "Do you think I've come to rough you up? Oh boy, do me a favour. If I was going to give you a beating I would have done it a long time ago."

"So what do you want then?"

"Me, I'm just the message sender."

"A message from who?"

"Come on Walter, don't fuck me about. You know who we are, and you know what we are about to do."

"I see," Walter replied. He knew now that this guy must have a connection with Brad, although quite what it was he really couldn't be sure of. "So what is the message?" Walter continued.

"Pretty simple really," said Ralph, leaning across the counter to bring his face closer to Walter's. "There's a blue Bedford van parked by the garages in Somerset Road, about ten minutes from here. Get together what you need, and meet us there in one hour. It's time for us to do your little job."

Walter was slightly intimidated by the message. It was so forceful and so up front. The days that had been dragging up until now had suddenly been washed away, and the green light for go was clearly visible. It really was all about to happen. They really were about to do this job. They really were about to steal Drax Mantis. By the time Walter's brain had digested this information, Ralph had already left the shop. Walter really found him rude and abrupt, and hoped that if Brad had him involved in the scam in anyway it would be minimal. He checked the time. It was as near as damn it closing time and, with only about fifty minutes to get ready, it was an easy decision to shut the shop. He locked the door, and took the broom from the cupboard at the far end of the shop. The light switch was right next to it and he killed all the lights but one and began to sweep. Tonight the empty shop had its own special appeal. The Drax Mantis poster on the far wall seemed to have a new expression. Normally he just looked smug, as if to say, "Look at me, I'm Drax Mantis! What the hell are you going to do about it?" Tonight though, the look was different. It was almost as if he was sneering, trying to frighten Walter. He was trying to shake off the all round stereotypical Hollywood bad guy status and replace it with the meaner, darker, murderous personality he was supposed to represent. Walter made eye contact with him, but continued with his chores. After sweeping he straightened all the comics on the shelves. It annoyed him how people picked one out, read it, and then stuffed it back on the shelf with total disregard to alphabetical order. Any decent person would return a *Captain Crimson* comic to its rightful home, and not mix it up with volumes of *Snake Girl*. Still, people like that didn't care about it all as much as Walter did. He looked up at Drax Mantis one more time. The new, menacing stare was still bearing down on him. It didn't intimidate Walter though. Instead he just stared back, with an equally menacing smile, and with a message.

"Okay hot shot," he said to the poster, although it may as well have been to the broom. "Tomorrow night your butt is mine!" With that he switched off the final light, and retired to his little flat upstairs to prepare himself for the task ahead.

Flowers

Warren Kingburger's limousine pulled up outside the Grosvenor House Hotel. He stepped out carrying the biggest bunch of red roses it was physically possible to carry. A couple of women on the pavement sighed at the sight, and secretly wished that one day their own husbands might do something as vaguely romantic. Kingburger strolled past them, and into the hotel lobby. He didn't need to check the room number with reception, he had visited before.

Danny Dellapicho, who had just finished reading a two day old copy of *USA Today* in one of the lobby chairs, was feeling pretty tired. He fired up a cigarette, and decided to call it a day. Tomorrow he had his work cut out. Tomorrow he would take care of Brad Clusky and Ralph Lee. A good night's sleep would help settle his nerves. He got up and headed for the lifts, and arrived just behind Kingburger. The two men stood there side by side waiting for the lift to arrive. When the doors opened it was empty, and Kingburger and Danny were the only two to step inside.

"Which floor?" Danny asked, as he was nearest to the panel. At that point he had not recognised Kingburger from his recent wave of media coverage.

"Ten," Kingburger replied. "And would you please extinguish your cigarette."

"Sorry?" Danny replied, dragging on his cigarette

and selecting the floors.

"Your cigarette. It's a safety hazard. You should put it out."

"Do you hear me complaining about the stench from those flowers?"

"I beg your pardon?"

"Your flowers, they fucking stink. But I ain't complaining!"

"Do you know who I am?" sneered Kingburger, raising his voice.

"I don't know, " replied Danny. "Boss Hogg?"

"What did you say?"

"I said Boss Hogg. You dress like him anyway."

"My name is Warren Kingburger," came the roaring response. It was enough to make the penny drop instantly with Danny. Of course this guy was Kingburger. He had been on the cover of every magazine for months. How the hell could he not recognise him! He must be one of the most famous men in the world. He just didn't look quite the same in the flesh as he did on TV.

"Sure, Mr Kingburger," Danny replied apologetically, dropping his cigarette and stamping it out. "Sorry about that."

"So I should darn well think."

This was an encounter that Danny had not anticipated. Of all the hotels in all the world! The last person he needed a chance encounter with was the guy whose restaurant he was about to turn into a murder scene. The plan had been that nobody would see his face long enough to remember who he was. Just a face in the crowd, that was the idea. Now Warren Kingburger had already had a very good look at his face. Sure, it was a long way from recognising a guy in a lift to associating him with murder twenty four hours later, but it wasn't impossible. All this for a stupid cigarette! Danny decided to make the rest of the journey in silence. Both men got out at the tenth floor. Kingburger turned left towards Dilly's door, and Danny went right towards his own, disappearing down a different corridor. When Kingburger reached Dilly's door he gave a loud knock. He was certain that this bunch of flowers was going to knock her out. The door flung open revealing Dilly in nothing but silky lingerie, barely covering her assets.

"Nathan!" she exclaimed, before she had a chance to think about who might be at the door.

"Nathan?" asked Kingburger, lowering the flowers from in front of him. "Who the fuck is Nathan?"

Dilly instantly realised her blunder. For a moment she had considered that her new lover, Nathan West, had come to surprise her with a monster bunch of flowers, and then make love to her all afternoon. The reality was quite different. The reality was Warren Kingburger.

"Nathan is, er," paused Dilly. "Nathan is my designer. He makes my dresses."

"Your designer, huh?" Kingburger replied, less than convinced. "Do you always open the door to your designer when you are wearing next to nothing?"

"I can assure you he's seen it all before," said Dilly.

"Yeah, I guess he has."

"Are they for me?" Dilly asked, referring to the roses.

"Yeah, they are. A kind of reward, for all the work you've been doing."

"That's very sweet," she said, taking them from

him. "I best put them in some water. Come on in."

The two of them disappeared inside the room. As they did so, Danny Dellapicho poked his head round the corner from where he had been listening. He didn't think the fact that Warren Kingburger was drilling some bird in a hotel would be immediately useful to his impending plan. Then again, you can never have too much background information.

The Plan

"I can't believe she did that!" Ralph questioned, as Brad and he sat in the van waiting for Walter. A light drizzle was falling on the windscreen, and night had already begun to fall.

"I'm telling you," Brad insisted, "she did. Twice!"

"Twice? No way. I don't believe that."

"On my mother's life!"

"That's incredible. I must have slept with dozens of women, and none of them ever did that. Let alone twice!"

"I'm telling you buddy. If I hadn't been there I wouldn't believe it myself. These Hollywood girls are really something else."

Just then there was a tap on the passenger door window, where Brad was sitting. He wound it down to reveal Walter Bridgenorth, fairly damp from the rain.

"Inside," Brad instructed Walter, and climbed over into the back to open the sliding side door. Walter gave a questioning look as the door opened, but climbed in regardless.

"So Mr Universe himself," Ralph teased, "we meet again." He climbed over into the back of the van to join the other two, and slid himself into the control seat in front of his various consoles.

"Who the hell is that guy?" asked Walter, before his attention was diverted by all the computers around him. "What the hell is this stuff?" He was taken by the immense amount of hardware packed into the van. It reminded him a bit of the cockpit of the Centurion Angel.

"I'm your meal ticket, buddy," laughed Ralph, striking a match to light his cigarette.

"Walter," said Brad, squatting on a wheel arch. "This is Ralph. He's our eyes and ears for tomorrow night. Let's say that he's the director of this little epic. Everything that goes on in the restaurant will be controlled from this van by him."

"Can we trust him?" Walter asked with concern.

"He trusts me like he trusted the milk from his mother's titties," Ralph interrupted.

"That is so vulgar," condemned Walter.

"We go back a long way," said Brad. "There have been plenty of times when he's got me out of a tight scrape. We can trust him, no problem."

"Okay," said Walter, slightly unconvinced. "So why am I in the back of a van with more computers than a Dixon's superstore?"

"You need to know the plan, jerk," replied Ralph. It was clear they would not have a constructive working relationship. After all, Ralph blamed Walter for this whole situation in the first place. He turned to one of the consoles and punched up a map on the screen. It was a street map of the immediate area they were in on Somerset Road, and on the map two lights flashed away roughly where the van was parked.

"The suits we will be wearing are wired," explained Brad, pointing to the two tuxedos hung up at the back of the van. "There are micro-sensors stitched into the jacket, the trousers, and the shoes. The electric sensors send a signal directly to Ralph in the van. This will let him know exactly where we are within one metre."

"No kidding!" exclaimed Walter. Ralph hit the keys again, with a wry smile. Immediately a speaker on the control desk repeated Walter's words. "No kidding!"

"What is that?" asked Walter.

Brad picked up a button from the keyboard next to Ralph. "The top button on your jacket is actually a microphone, the same as this one," he elaborated, "It's part of a two way communication system between you and the van. The other part is the earpiece." He pulled out a small earpiece from his pocket. "You put this in your left ear. With that, and the button mike, you will be able to talk to both Ralph and me at any point during the evening, no matter where we are." Walter reluctantly put the gadget in his ear to try it out.

"This is the floor plan," explained Ralph, punching in details of the restaurant into the computer. "The party will mainly be on the ground floor. That is also where the doll is." He used a mouse to draw a circle around the cabinet which housed the Drax Mantis action figure. "You guys go in, and case the joint. If I'm right then there will be eighteen guards on the inside, but only five carrying guns."

"Guns," cried Walter. "Nobody said anything about any guns!"

"What the hell do you expect?" Ralph retorted. "This is no picnic! There is going to be several million pound's worth of Hollywood actors in that building. These days insurance companies insist you take care of assets like that!"

"This is how it breaks down," interrupted Brad. "We case the joint and figure the positions of the guards. These boys are going to be dressed like every other party guest, so we have to be sharp. They should be more interested in the guests than the props though."

"Once we know the lay out," explained Ralph, "we make our move. You, Walter, will create a diversion on the far side of the floor. Brad will manoeuvre into a position next to the cabinet. At that point I'll kill the power. Everything will go dark, and there should be some panic on. Whilst this is going down, Brad gets the doll from the case."

"How do I create a diversion?" asked Walter.

"Whatever," replied Brad. "You could knock a tray of drinks out of the hands of a waiter, or something."

"And how do you break the cabinet?" Walter asked again.

"With these," said Brad, pulling out a gadget from inside his jacket. "Glass cutters. Made of graphite to avoid magnetic detection. They work like a pair of compasses. The sucker clamps on to the glass, whilst the cutter makes a perfect circle around it. The glass just lifts out, and I can reach in for the toy. It's all over in less than a minute."

"While the lights are off," Ralph went on, "you are already heading for the back door. If you have any problems I can direct you from here. The lights go back up after forty five seconds. At that time both of you must be clear of the ground floor, and heading for the service area above the kitchen. When you come through the door the van is there waiting for you. Before they know what's happened we've already taken off."

"That is all there is to it," concluded Brad,

returning the glass cutter to his jacket. "Any questions?"

"Have you still got the tickets?"

"Right here," replied Brad assuringly, indicating to his inside pocket.

"And what happens now?"

"We go back to our hotel," Brad went on. "We have booked you a room there for tonight. We need to go over the plan a few more times so we all know exactly what we are doing."

"Then," interrupted Ralph, "we are going out to find a decent Tandoori. You can't beat a hot curry to calm your nerves before a big job." Walter didn't seem at all convinced by this culinary proposal.

"Any more questions?" asked Brad.

"No," Walter sighed reluctantly, "I don't think there are."

Ralph slipped back into the front seat and turned the ignition. The van moved away in the dark and headed into central London. From here on in there was no turning back.

Part Five

The Big Night

Crowds

Evening fell on London. The encroaching darkness consumed each and every building as the sun began to set. A cool chill to the air began to draw in, and the long shadows of office blocks drew out across the Thames. The suburbs of London began to shut down one by one. The shops closed and the street lights came on. Everything seemed to be coming to a peaceful halt. At the same time as the pace was slowing down in outer London, it was most definitely picking up in inner London. Tube trains delivered droves of teenagers and tourists. Taxis delivered revellers and partygoers. Gradually the pubs, restaurants and clubs began to fill up. A constant thumping base line seemed to be audible no matter where you went, as if it were the very heartbeat of the city. Tonight though, the crowds of Soho had a new attraction to occupy their minds with. Tonight was *the* night. After all the hype and media attention, after all the gossip and glossy photographs, the Orbit Studio Experience was finally about to open. Even though the opening night was by invitation only, it didn't stop the rest of London from wanting to come and have a look. Dozens became hundreds, and hundreds became thousands. It was one of the biggest crowds in central London since the Poll Tax riots. Rarely was such a collection of the greatest living movie stars assembled, and people were prepared to do anything to get a glimpse of a big name. The Orbit Studio Experience looked every bit the part, the big star in its own movie. The neon lighting and designer pillars gave the whole thing a sense of purpose. Not the sort of building you could just walk past without noticing. Visually it was a mish-mash between Buckingham Palace and Stringfellows nightclub. At the same time it had that space age feel to reflect the science fiction flavour of the majority of the Orbit films. It had something to offer everybody, and everybody wanted to go there. At the murder inquiry, which followed the opening night, serious questions were asked about the approach of the Metropolitan Police to crowd control during that evening. It was fair enough to say that nobody quite imagined how many people would turn up, and even the best forecast could not have accurately predicted the incredible numbers that were in attendance. The end result was that only a handful of officers were on duty to patrol the crowd, nowhere near enough to do the job properly. This was okay whilst the crowd were relatively well behaved and orderly, but that was all going to change. It was obvious that things might get out of hand as the first limousines began to pull up. The crowd surged and swelled with each car, putting excessive pressure on the barriers which separated the stars from the fans. Two of the policemen looked nervously at each other, but neither could justify a call for back up at that time. With hindsight they knew they should have swallowed their pride and called for help.

Two streets away the blue Bedford van was moving into position. It pulled up behind the Orbit Studio Experience, a short distance from the back door which was to be the escape route. The side door slid open and two men climbed out. They wore pristine tuxedos, crisp shirts, sharp trousers, and polished shoes. They straightened their jackets, and slid the door of the van shut behind them.

"Check one, two," Brad Clusky said into his button mike, whilst holding his earpiece with one finger.

"Loud and clear," Ralph replied from inside the van. The sound of a small voice in his ear startled Walter at first.

"Check your microphone, Walter," said Brad.

"Huh? Oh, right," Walter replied, bowing his head towards his microphone. "Testing one, two, three. Is that the sort of thing you're after?"

"He's cool," Ralph replied, intended for Brad. "You guys are clear to go inside."

Brad and Walter made their way down a side alley, and across to where the crowd was assembled. They disappeared into it like needles in a haystack, and started to make their way through it towards the main entrance. Meanwhile, on the other side of the crowd, another partygoer had arrived. Danny Dellapicho was ready to deliver the goods.

Jimmy Lambourne

There are two perfect scenarios for killing somebody. The first is where there are no witnesses at all. If no one has seen the crime then it is almost impossible to be convicted of it. The second scenario, oddly, is almost the complete opposite. Situations can arise where there are so many witnesses to a killing that no two people are able to recall the same sequence of events, and invariably some innocent bystander gets sent to prison. With the number of people present tonight, both in the crowd and in the restaurant, Danny Dellapicho was geared up to the latter of these two options.

Danny stood on the corner of the street just down from the Orbit Studio Experience. He dragged hard on his cigarette, but that couldn't match the adrenaline rush that was already starting at the prospect of a kill. Like Walter and Brad he was kitted out with a dinner jacket, but his wasn't wired. He cased the crowd that was building up in front of him. There must have been several thousand people already. Just a wave of confusing shouts and screams. Danny knew he wouldn't be able to make the hit from outside the restaurant. He could, of course, have hired a room across the street and killed Brad and Ralph with a sniper rifle with a telescopic sight. The problem was, however, that despite Danny's accuracy with any firearm, he couldn't account for some airhead running into his trajectory at just the wrong moment. With a high profile kill you only get one chance. You can't afford to blow it by taking the head off some hysterical pleb. No, this kill needed to be at close range, man to man. Bam, bam! Two holes providing perfect ventilation to two separate brains. Danny loved the human brain. It was his favourite human organ because it just looked so good when it was pasted all over a wall. People just go crazy when they see that happen. That was exactly what he was planning for Brad and Ralph. He licked his lips at the memory of Candy's recent demise by the same method. He had picked the street corner where he now stood with great care. In less than five minutes he had established that the big stars who were arriving in limousines had priority access to the red carpet treatment at the main door. The number of guests, as Danny had already ascertained, necessitated that only a limited number of cars could pull up without causing endless congestion. As a result a number of other cars, carrying minor celebrities, journalists, and general free loaders, were dropping off on the street behind him. Those guests had a short walk across to the main door, that was if they could successfully navigate the edge of the crowd. This was a perfect opportunity for Danny. Jimmy Lambourne, an upcoming disc jockey on independent radio, was to be Danny's victim. Of course, Danny didn't know he was a DJ, but it was definitely an asset. Even if the punters knew his voice, how many were likely to know his face? Jimmy stepped out of a black cab, with a shapely young brunette on his arm. He was a short fat guy, with a bushy beard, a large mole on his nose, and yellow teeth from too much smoking. No doubt the housewives at home perceived him as some sort of sex god from the tone of his voice. It would almost certainly be a different story if they saw him in the flesh. The brunette, however, seemed to be an exception. She laughed wildly at one of Jimmy's jokes, as he gave the driver a generous tip.

"Excuse me," said Danny, as they walked towards him, "are you here for tonight's party?"

"Sure am, my man," replied Jimmy. "Are you after an autograph?"

"No sir, I'm part of the security team," Danny explained. "External operations. Can I see your invitations please? There is no cause for alarm. It's just a pre-entry check so we can get you smoothly through the crowd."

"Oh, okay," said Jimmy, pulling out the two tickets from inside his jacket. "Here."

"That's great," said Danny, taking the tickets. He pulled a small ultra-violet torch from his pocket and shone it over the tickets. Of course, it didn't show anything, but that was not the point. It was purely for cosmetic purposes, and Jimmy Lambourne fell for it.

"Well, well," Danny went on. "This is not a good sign."

"What seems to be the problem?" asked Jimmy, whilst his companion seemed to gain some concern at the delay.

"I'm afraid these are fakes, sir. May I ask where you got them?"

"What do you mean?" replied Jimmy in astonishment. "I'm Jimmy Lambourne, top celebrity DJ! I can assure you that these tickets are genuine and were obtained through the appropriate channels."

Danny held one finger to his ear, implying that he

was wearing some sort of earpiece. He tilted his head to speak into his collar, but he was not wearing a microphone.

"Ziggy," he said to himself. "Yeah, it's Mac here. I'm outside. I've got some guy here called Jimmy something. Uh, Jimmy Lambourne. You got that name on the guest list?"

Both Jimmy and his partner went along with this check, even though it was purely a piece of theatre portrayed by Danny. Danny stepped slightly away from them and turned his head, as if further to emphasise the confidentiality of his actions.

"Yeah, Ziggy," he finally said. "Well, is that a fact? Okay, leave it with me. I'll take care of it." He turned back to Jimmy Lambourne. "I'm sorry Mr Lambourne. It appears that you are not on our list! I'm going to have to confiscate these tickets."

"Jimmy, you bastard," shouted the brunette, stomping off across the street.

"Denise," Jimmy called after her, before turning to Danny. "Look mate, you have got to let me in that party. I need this break!"

"I'm sorry," replied Danny. "If your name is not down you can't come in. Those are the rules."

Jimmy would normally have stayed to argue, but tonight he was more concerned with Denise. He was on a promise for the first time in over a year. "Denise," he cried again, running over the street after her. That left the way clear for Danny. In less than five minutes since Jimmy's cab had arrived, he was in possession of his ticket. All he had to do now was enter the party.

A Familiar Face

As Danny was easing his way round the crowd, Brad Clusky and Walter Bridgenorth were already in position to enter. A couple of schoolgirls were hassling Brad for an autograph, convinced he was some minor star. He just told them to fuck off, and eventually they got the message. As they walked along Brad grabbed Walter round the back of the neck and halted his stride.

"Right, mate," he whispered close to Walter's ear. "You are going in first, then I am going to follow. Inside you don't talk to me in person. You don't come anywhere near me. The only way we communicate from now on is through the earpiece and the button mike. Is that clear?" Walter had just enough movement left in his neck to muster a nod.

"Good," Brad continued. "Only speak to guests if they speak to you, and never for longer than thirty seconds. Avoid famous people, or people who look like they might be famous. Any questions?" This time Walter managed a shake of the head. "Right," concluded Brad, "off you go!" With that Walter headed off to the main door to enter the party. As he reached the tuxedo attired security guards he produced his ticket, and Brad followed his progress carefully from afar. There was a pause while the name Mark Spencer was checked against the guest list. The security guard gave a nod, and Walter entered, and in doing so he cleared a line of vision between the next person with a ticket and Brad.

The shock almost sent Brad to an early grave. Surely it wasn't! It couldn't be! What was that guys name? Del Monté? De Niro? No, it was Dellapicho, Danny Dellapicho. Brad quickly turned into the crowd to hide his face, and looked again for the two adolescent autograph hunters. Anything to buy him some cover, at least until he could figure out the significance of who he had seen. He was sure that Danny hadn't seen his face, at least not yet.

"Buddy," he said with some concern into his top button, "are you with me?"

"Right here," replied Ralph from the back of the van.

"Switch to the private channel," Brad ordered. The private channel had been Ralph's idea. It provided a communication link between the two of them which Walter was excluded from. They didn't know whether they would need it or not. As it turned out they did.

"What's the problem?" asked Ralph in confidence.

"Call up the camera covering the main entrance," instructed Brad.

"I'm already linked," replied Ralph, referring to one of the screens in front of him. "Be cool, our man is already inside. He looks a little in awe, but I think he will survive."

"Sod that," shouted Brad. "The guy behind him! He's coming through the door right now. Do you know who that is?"

Ralph enhanced the picture, but couldn't clearly make out this short, stocky, dark haired character. "I don't know," he replied. "I can't get a clear enough view. Is he famous?"

"Of a kind," Brad retorted. "That is fucking Danny Dellapicho!"

"Danny who?" asked Ralph from the back of the van, still not exactly sure of what was going on. "How do you know who he is?"

"Do you remember that job we did back in the service?" Brad asked, still caught up in the crowd outside of the Orbit Studio Experience and trying not to look as if he were talking to himself. "The IRA unit in Eniskillen. We were passed files on a number of US agents who had infiltrated the cell in order to work out their funding links with America. This guy was one of their operatives, I'm sure of it. Access the CIA's intelligence computer in Langley."

"I don't have that sort of software in the van," replied Ralph. "Besides, if I make a hit on Langley they are going to trace it straight to me."

"Ralph, you are in a van in a side street," Brad retorted into his button mike. "Even if the CIA can work out that we have hit them, how long do you suppose it will take them to send a recon team from Virginia to where you're parked up? Just make the fucking link!"

Ralph hit the keys on his keyboard. The modem began to whirr as it made an international call to the United States. Ralph had accessed the CIA at least five times previously, but then each time the job had been planned meticulously. He had set the system up at an office which he had broken into, and hacked in via a modem link through seventeen different international cities. This time he was taking a big risk. He didn't have the specialised hacking gear he would normally use with him. It was a clumsy link, and it was likely that he would hit some form of booby trap in the system at any time. That would automatically cut him off, and leave his signature address on their system. He would have to destroy all of his equipment after tonight, at least fifty thousand pound's worth and none of it insured. All this for four inches of plastic! What the hell were they doing this for?

"Are you in?" asked Brad.

"Yeah," Ralph replied. "But they could bust my ass at any second, so lets make this quick!"

"Okay, you need to access the special agent directories. The name you're looking for is Daniel Dellapicho, D-E-L-L-A-P-I-C-H-O."

"Got him," replied Ralph, after a matter of seconds. "Born in Cleveland, Ohio in 1959. Son of an Italian delicatessen proprietor. Entered the CIA in 1984, and was voluntarily discharged in 1996. Mainly involved in covert overseas operations, very hush hush, and always denied. Operational experience in whole load of unpleasant places. We've got Cuba, Afghanistan, Iran, Northern Ireland, East Germany, South Africa and Colombia. He's certainly well travelled."

"What about after '96?" Brad asked frantically.

"Well," replied Ralph. "He's still on the payroll, but I've got nothing listed on duties. Could be some unofficial covert work."

"I bet," muttered Brad.

"Shit," interjected Ralph in a panic. "They've got me. The link's gone, and I reckon they've traced us." The screen instantly went dead.

"Don't worry about it," assured Brad.

"I'm not worried about it," said Ralph, stubbing out one cigarette and automatically lighting another.

"I'm worried about the fact that there is an ex-CIA, psychotic, murdering machine inside that building. Since there is a high likelihood that he is there to turn you and I into fish food, may I suggest that we abort this mission. I for one have no desire to sustain damage of a permanent nature for the sake of a your anorak friend's desire to own some stupid toy!"

"We can't do that," Brad responded.

"Why the hell not?"

"Walter still has the photo," continued Brad. "He could still tell the police what he knows, and MI6 would have us clipped automatically."

"So, we have a choice of being killed by the CIA or MI6," laughed Ralph. "That makes me feel so-o-o much better."

"Not necessarily," said Brad. "Firstly, we don't know that Dellapicho is here for us. It's not like this job is high profile. The only three people that know about it are you, Walter and me. It's not like somebody has made an illegal entry on to your system to work out our movements."

As Brad was saying this, Ralph was already running a systems check. When the results flicked across the screen he could hardly believe his carelessness, and it felt like someone had pushed their fist into his guts and twisted them upside down.

"Someone has got into the system," Ralph reported with shame.

"What? When?"

"A week ago. They scanned about half of the Orbit files I created. God knows how much they know."

"How?" questioned Brad.

"I don't know, I just don't know."

"So he is here for us," sighed Brad.

"It looks that way," Ralph replied.

"Well that only gives us one choice," Brad announced. "We still go in and we still do the job, but we watch this guy at all times. We make sure he doesn't get near us. Somehow, when the shit hits the fan, we make sure this guy is in the frame. I want every security guard in the building to be on to him."

"Nice idea Romeo," said Ralph, "but how the hell do we pull it off?"

"Leave it to me," Brad assured. He began to make his way towards the main door into the restaurant. The goal posts had definitely just been moved. Things were getting interesting.

The Place to be Seen

As parties went, this one was certainly living up to its billing. The whole place was already packed with what appeared to be the entire network fraternity of Hollywood. The men, for the most part, met the dress code and were suitably presentable in their dinner jackets. There was, of course, the odd exception. The latest teenage boy group to dominate the pop charts, curiously originating from Scunthorpe, were making a statement by wearing exceptionally baggy and obviously uncomfortable trousers and equally ill-fitting tight shirts in loud colours. A few other male stars were out to be noticed, and had taken exception to the dress code. No one, however, was really bothered by this. Most of the other men were secretly quite jealous. At the end of the day they were the ones who were blatantly over dressed for what was, essentially, a posh version of McDonalds.

The women, on the other hand, were not deterred by such thoughts. Apart from one saggy, over the hill fashion designer who was obviously past it and had let everything go to seed, the rest of the women had some enchanting appeal in one way or other. For those who had the appropriate figure, sun tan, silicon and credit cards, there were some spectacular dresses to match. Off the shoulder, on the shoulder, strapless, short, long, transparent, flowing, and revealing, they were all there.

For those of more conventional shapes and sizes, the minimalist look was quite popular. A number of girls wore simple two piece black suits, whilst a number of others wore sensible but flattering dresses. That's not to say these girls were in a different league, far from it. What they lacked in curves they made up for in dazzling whit, inspired conversation, and the kind of smiles that some guys just die for. For every girl that had turned up alone, there was an eager entourage of potential suitors on her scent. Of course, it takes more than just a glittery cast list to make a party kick. There are a few other essential ingredients, and this party had them all. Firstly it had the music. The DJ, Fuzzy J, was providing the warm up act, although a live soul band was due to follow after Warren Kingburger's speech. Fuzzy J had acquired his unusual name for reasons best known only to himself. He was a popular figure at a number of Soho night spots. Tonight, however, he had been briefed directly by Kingburger, and was only allowed to play tunes with some form of science fiction connection, tenuous or otherwise. For that reason the guests were subjected to the likes of *Starman* by David Bowie, a dance remix of Kate Bush's cover of *Rocket Man*, and Babylon Zoo's *Spaceman*. Several party guests commented on the fact that every science fiction record seemed to end with the word "man", and that there should be more songs about space women. In between the tracks Fuzzy J would subject the crowd to his own special brand of patter. "Yo! This is goin' out to all you party groovers out there. Fuzzy J has got all of the smoothest sci-fi flavas comin' at ya tonight. Be wild. Be outrageous. Get on that dance floor and show me what's goin' down!" Roughly translated, he was implying that everyone should have a jolly pleasant evening, and possibly even enjoy a wee disco dance, whilst he played a number of popular records. Most of the guests, however, required no translation and were eagerly complying by cavorting their bodies in a variety of unsavoury manners. Then there was the food. Needless to say, the guests this evening were not being subjected to Drax Mantis Burgers with fries, Skellern Fillet Sandwiches or Jed Largo Chicken Buckets. The tone was a little more sophisticated. For starters there was a wide range of entrées being served by the waiters and waitresses donned in their *Galactic Encounter* costumes. Champagne was also available in countless glasses. In addition, on the restaurant floors upstairs there was a lavish and flamboyant buffet laid out. Just about everything you could imagine to eat was there for the guests. The final ingredient to the outlandish display was the essence of the Orbit Studio Group. The mixture of memorabilia, nostalgia, atmosphere and magic gave the impression that the guests were actually part of some big screen production. There were countless photographs, costumes, and props. Things that everyone who had ever been to the cinema would instantly recognise. Things that, at least for two golden hours on celluloid, belonged to one of the great names of Hollywood. Things that linked the greatest actors and actresses that had ever lived. On paper, it was destined to be the greatest party that ever happened. The ingredients were all there. Between them, Warren Kingburger and Dilly Foxtrot had covered everything. No detail had been left unchecked. What could possibly go wrong?

The Entrance

Danny Dellapicho handed over his ticket to the security guard.

"Jimmy Lambourne?" the guard asked.

"Yeah," said Danny, attempting a poor English accent just to be safe. "That's me."

"I listen to your show all the time," the guard continued. "You know, my sister told me that you had a beard, but I told her that wasn't so. I mean, you don't sound like you've got a beard on the radio, do you?"

"I guess not," replied Danny. The answer provoked a reserved response from the guard.

"Something wrong with your voice, Mr Lambourne?" the guard asked. "You don't sound right!"

"That's always the thing with radio," replied Danny, quickly improvising. "It has a funny way of making you sound a little different."

"I guess so," said the guard with a smile of newfound assurance. "Well, sir. I mustn't be keeping you. You best get in there and enjoy the party."

Danny gave a final smile as he walked in. Where did they hire that guard? It didn't matter now anyway. A better guard, however, might have searched Danny and found the gun that he was concealing, strapped to his left calf muscle. He may even have found the thin steel chain that was clipped into Danny's inside right leg. That was purely an insurance measure. If Brad and Ralph were to escape then it would almost certainly be by the back door. If, however, that door was chained it would scupper their plans, and leave them at the mercy of a bullet.

Brad, watching from a safe distance, had monitored Danny's progress as he disappeared inside the Orbit Studio Experience.

"Is he safely inside?" Brad asked Ralph through his microphone.

"He's away to the left, scanning the bar," Ralph replied. "You should be safe to move in now."

With that Brad spruced up his jacket, straightened his bow tie and his hair, and headed for the main entrance. The same guard that had dealt with Danny was now dealing with him.

"Evening sir," the guard began. "May I see your invitation please?"

"There you go," said Brad handing it over.

"Nathan West, heh? I don't know that name. Guess you ain't too famous?"

"No, not yet."

"I tell you why buddy," the guard continued. "It's your name. Famous folk like to keep their names snappy. You see, James Dean was known as Jimmy Dean. You don't ever hear nobody refer to Burt Reynolds as Albert Reynolds. It ain't cool."

"Sorry," interrupted Brad. "If this isn't leading anywhere I'd really like to go inside and join the party."

"The point, my man, is this. If you turn Nathan West into a snappy name you end up with Nat West, and you sound like a frigging bank. That ain't cool either."

"Nat West," repeated Brad. The penny dropped. Nathan West and Mark Spencer. Nat West and Marks & Spencer. So bloody obvious that even the security guard had worked it out. How on earth had he let Walter persuade him to be known as Nat West? He felt like a total prat.

"You think about that, Mr West," the guard added handing back Brad's ticket. "You have a nice night now."

Brad entered the party whilst enduring an identity crisis with a high street bank. In addition, he now had to contend with the fact that there was also a highly trained killer in the room who would certainly take the first opportunity to wipe him out. Surely, things couldn't get any worse.

Breaking Up

Several women, mainly actresses, were all trying to steal the limelight of the evening from each other. The rivalry over who had the best dress was intense. None of them, however, were in the same league as Dilly Foxtrot. She was wearing a strapless crimson red dress. Her hair flowed gallantly, and her make up was precise. Heavy, expensive earrings hung from each lobe, and complemented an equally stunning necklace. She didn't need such trinkets though. Her figure was enough to turn every male head in the room. Dilly, however, wasn't her usual self. Ever since that night with Nathan West she had found it hard to concentrate on the restaurant. He had been so gentle, so easy going. She could talk about anything with him, books, television, travel, or whatever. He was laid back in a way that made Warren Kingburger seem very rigid. He was both well dressed and well spoken, a perfect gentleman and a perfect lover. The images of that night danced around her mind, refusing to leave even when ordered. Warren Kingburger, although unsure of the reason, had noticed this change in Dilly. It was obvious that something was wrong when he had taken the roses to her on the previous evening. She had not been so forthcoming to his advances, and didn't seem as enthusiastic about the restaurant as she used to be. Maybe it was time to get rid of her. This was always the way with these young girls. At first they are hungry for everything, eager for a chance to live life in the fast lane and sleep with a movie studio boss. Then, after a while, they think they know it all. They think they can make it on their own two feet. Of course, none of them ever do. They all seem to end up on the giant scrap heap of bimbo failures.

"Things are going well," Dilly said, walking up to Kingburger with a glass of Jack Daniels, and a glass of champagne for herself. As he had promised before, he was wearing his yellow suit, complete with matching shirt, tie and Stetson.

"Do you mean with the restaurant, or with us?" Kingburger questioned, accepting the Jack Daniels.

"I meant with the restaurant," Dilly added. "It looks really good, and I think the guests really like it. They certainly seem to be looking at the exhibits far more than I imagined."

"It's great isn't it," Kingburger added, half heartedly. "The cream of the movie world here, under one roof. Here to admire my fantasy world. I can't help but feel proud about that."

"You should be proud. I know if it belonged to me I would be proud of it."

There was a silent pause. An awkward pause, the type that always come up in awkward conversations. At any time either of them could have drifted off to mingle with the party guests, but neither did. In the end it was Kingburger who broke the silence.

"I've been thinking Dilly," he began grimly. "Perhaps when we get back to Los Angeles we might find you a different role in the organisation."

Dilly didn't answer at first. She just looked down into her drink. By rolling her wrist she was managing to send a wave around the edge of the glass on the surface of the champagne.

"Okay," she finally said. She didn't say anything else. There was nothing else to say. She knew there wasn't going to be another job with the Orbit group. That was just Kingburger's means of pulling the plug. Still, she wasn't that bothered. If she had been then Kingburger would probably have never had to resort to this.

"I should attend to the guests," said Kingburger, slightly dejected. He moved away from her to a group of celebrities nearby. She swallowed hard, and a slight tear welled in her eye. She wondered if she had done the right thing, allowing Kingburger so decisively to cut her out of his life. For a moment she felt very alone. Then, from the corner of her eye, she noticed a familiar face. It was Nathan West. Suddenly she felt a warm glow again, deep inside. Seeing Nathan was a reassurance. Maybe he would take care of her. Maybe he was exactly what she needed.

Contact Lost

Walter could not believe his eyes. He was there, inside. He was at the actual opening night of the Orbit Studio Experience. That in itself was the coolest thing that had ever happened to him. Whereas most of the guests were talking politely in small groups, or dancing to the assortment of tunes provided by Fuzzy J, Walter was rapidly visiting as many of the display cases as he could. He was anxious to take it all in, especially before they got down to business. The attraction for Walter, however, did not end with the stars. It wasn't just the razzmatazz of the event. To Walter what really counted was what it all represented. This was the epitome of science fiction. This was as close as the world of *Galactic Encounter* would ever come to being a real place. He could see Jed's laser with his own eyes. The models of ships that seemed so big on the screen were equally as impressive in miniature. All of the intricate details were still there. Walter was indeed in his own private heaven. Ralph Lee was following Walter's progress with some amusement. He had three monitors in the van linked to the CCTV system. Brad and Danny were on the other two screens, each making their way through the crowd of faces. Two men with very different agendas for the evening, both trying to get the desired result. If Ralph was being honest with himself, he should have been giving Danny his one hundred percent undivided attention at that point. Danny Dellapicho was the most obvious threat to the mission, and needed close observation. Ralph's attention, however, was being drawn by the antics of Walter, especially considering that he was about to be approached by a very attractive young lady. "Check out three o'clock, little guy," said a voice in Walter's head. It took him a couple of seconds to work out that it was Ralph, but even then he had no idea what he was on about. That was until he turned to face the girl that Ralph was referring to. She was a young girl, in her early twenties, wearing an identical costume to Lady Carina in *Revenge of the Skellern Warrior*. It was the skimpy little bikini number, the one she wore in the dessert scene, but even the real Carina hadn't filled it as well as this girl. Neither did the real Carina have a tray of champagne on offer.

"Glass of champagne, sir?" she pouted.

"Uh," stuttered Walter, "er, yeah. I mean yes. Yes, er, that would be very nice. Thank you."

"Woo-hah," screamed Ralph in Walter's ear. "Don't you worry about Brad, my friend. This fox is yours for the taking."

"She's not a fox," said Walter. "It's just a costume."

"I'm sorry?" said the waitress. Walter had not realised that she was party to only half of this secret conversation.

"Oh," Walter said to her apologetically and with an element of sarcasm, "I didn't mean anything. I'm just a deluded science fiction fan. A nerd, even. It's probably best to avoid me."

"At last," Ralph interjected rudely. "I think you are finally starting to get it!"

The waitress smiled politely, and went on her way. Walter just sipped contentedly on his champagne. The night was still young, perhaps he would get another crack at it later.

At that point, Brad joined the conversation from the other side of the room.

"What are you guys up to?" he expertly whispered into his button mike. "Where the hell is Dellapicho?"

"Uh, he's...," paused Ralph, scanning the monitors in the back of the van. "Fuck! I've lost him."

"Don't make me nervous out here," Brad replied, avidly scanning the crowd in the party. This was the last thing he wanted. Stuck in a crowded room where anyone could be Danny Dellapicho. He could be dead even before he heard the gun go off. Or maybe it wasn't going to be a gun. Maybe he was holding a syringe with a lethal injection. Brad probably wouldn't even feel it. He would probably just slump into a corner. It would easily be mistaken as fainting from claustrophobia, or something like that. Danny would be on a plane out of the country before the doctors worked out it was murder. Brad rapidly darted his eyes over the room, trying to work out where Dellapicho might have gone. As he did so his eyes met contact with Dilly Foxtrot. Once he met her eyes it was fairly hard to pull them away, impending doom or not. The dress was perfect on her, she looked sensational.

"Nathan," came her approaching voice. "Nathan, is that you?" Her presence only made Brad more nervous. He would have to act normally with her to avoid her suspicions, but in concentrating on her he was dropping his guard to attack.

"Nathan, it is you," she smiled. "It's so good to see you again."

"Uh, yeah," Brad replied.

"And how is Arnie?"

"Who? Oh, Schwarzenegger. He's cool," Brad assured.

"Couldn't make it tonight, huh?"

"Well," Brad went on, "you know how it is with Planet Hollywood and everything. Plus there's the new movie. We are a bit behind the schedule, losing a million dollars a week. The big guys in LA are after me big time at the minute. If there were any here tonight I'm sure you like to know where they are." The last part of that was meant for Ralph, and Ralph knew it.

"I really enjoyed the other night," Dilly said. "I was wondering if you might like to do it again sometime?"

Ralph Lee, still desperately searching the monitors in an effort to locate Danny Dellapicho, took a new found interest at the way the conversation between Brad and Dilly was developing. He was kind of smug at the thought that he knew Brad would have to be relatively open with Dilly, but at the same time a little paranoid with the thought that Ralph was not only listening in, but was also recording the conversation for future entertainment value.

"Is she talking about doing dinner again or doing that sex thing again?" Ralph whispered into Brad's ear.

"That would be nice," Brad said, answering Dilly's question and ignoring Ralph completely "Wouldn't Mr Kingburger take exception to that though?"

"I don't think Mr Kingburger and I will be seeing that much more of each other anymore," she replied.

"I see," said Brad who had been expecting a different answer. Dilly titled her head forward and delicately kissed Brad on the cheek. He didn't know why he returned the kiss, he just knew it felt right. His arms slipped around her and their lips met. Neither were too sure how long the kiss would last.

"That is so sweet," added Ralph, taking the piss out of his colleague. He was about to light up a cigarette when he noticed something on one of the other screens. It was enough for him to drop the cigarette, and break up Brad's romantic interlude.

"Major red fucking alert," screamed Ralph into his headset. "Nutter psycho bastard coming right at you at ten o'clock. He has you my man, he fucking has you!"

"Where?" said Brad, in panic.

"Where what?" said Dilly.

Mahnja the Smownork

As Brad swung round he saw Danny Dellapicho, about ten yards away, and looking straight at him. Danny had the wry smile of a hunter, who had his prey in his sights for the first time. He stood his ground as he gave Brad the once over. He wasn't attacking though, at least not yet. He didn't care about Brad's look of recognition either, he would soon be dead. In the few seconds that Ralph had lost track of Danny, he had managed to chain up the back door. Now there was only one way out, and Danny would have the front door covered with his gun.

"Where what?" Dilly asked again.

"Uhm," said Brad, finding obvious difficulty to concentrate on all the things going on around him. "Where would you like to go next time?"

"How about my hotel a little later?" Dilly suggested seductively, kissing him again.

"Christ man," Ralph balled into Brad's ear. "You are about to get your fucking head blown off! Do you think you can leave the girl alone for two seconds and do something more constructive about your self preservation?"

"Sure," Brad replied, to both Dilly and Ralph at the same time. "Sure I'll come back to your hotel. I'd love to. I need to network a little first though. I've got a suggestion for you in the mean time. It might be the start of a good career move. See that guy just there?"

"That little guy, the greasy one?" asked Dilly.

"That's the chap," Brad confirmed. "His name is Danny Dellapicho. He's the number two at Twentieth Century Fox, and I happen to know he is looking for a female lead for his new Mel Gibson picture. I've read the script and I just know it's you. Why don't you just go over there and have a chat with him. He's a bit shy though, and he gets angry real quick. He likes to dance, but never asks. Just bully him a little, he'll soon come round."

"Okay, Nathan," said Dilly, "If you're sure. I'll catch you later." She kissed Brad one more time, and pushed through the crowd towards the smirking assassin.

"Very smart," complimented Ralph. "Very smart indeed."

"Where are you Walter?" Brad asked his button mike, as Dilly moved away.

"I'm right here, at the back still," Walter replied. "What the hell is going on with you two? Why aren't we getting on with this?"

"Stay calm," instructed Brad, "I'm on my way. There's going to be a change of plan."

The next few moments were relatively chaotic. Fuzzy J had decided to spice up the beat with an acid dance tune, which was a bit too much for most of the dancers. An Austrian footballer who played for Everton had thrown up over a 1967 movie costume, insured for quarter of a million dollars. Danny Dellapicho, however, was oblivious to this. He was more concerned, although not exactly pleased, about his impending meeting with Dilly Foxtrot.

"Are you Danny Dellapicho?" she asked.

"How the fuck do you know my name?" he snapped. This was bad news. He had already recognised her as the girl at the hotel with Warren Kingburger, and it was clear that she had a thing for Brad Clusky too. There were far too many links for Danny's liking. Maybe he would have to kill a few more people than just Brad and Ralph in order to protect his identity.

He could see Brad Clusky disappearing into the crowd, and wanted to follow. The fact that this bitch knew his name, however, meant that he had to take care of her first.

"Don't be shy now," she continued. "I know that you are one of the big names at Fox. I'm Dilly. Dilly Foxtrot. Hey, we've both got a foxy connection. That's cute isn't it?"

"Look bitch," Danny said aggressively. "I don't know who you are, and I don't know how you know my fucking name, but if you don't back off right now I'll swear I'll snap your neck where you stand."

"I guess you didn't get where you are today by your manners," slammed Dilly. "I hear you've got a new script, with Mel Gibson in the lead."

"I don't know what you are talking about. I really don't have time for this."

"Maybe we should have a dance," suggested Dilly. "It will help you calm down a bit." She grabbed his arm and pulled him onto the almost deserted dance floor. Normally Danny would have just walked away, but he was aware that the sudden arrival of the two of them on the dance floor had generated a great deal of interest from the surrounding crowd. Reluctantly he attempted to dance with her.

Brad meanwhile had reached Walter at the back of

Jim Carley

the room.

"I thought we weren't supposed to talk?" Walter said on his arrival.

"I told you," said Brad. "I'm changing the plan." As he said that a waiter dressed as Mahnja the Smownork walked by with a tray of drinks.

"Excuse me," Brad said to him, grabbing him by the shoulder. "Do you have a phone?"

"Walter?" said the plastic clad incumbent in the Mahnja suit. "Walter is that you?"

"Do I know you?" Walter replied, with some confusion.

"It's me," said Mahnja lifting up his mask. "It's Oswald. Oswald Moriarty."

Brad turned to Walter for some form of explanation, although Walter's mouth was already agape with abject horror.

A Change of Clothes

"I told you that I got a new job," said Oswald. "At least I tried to tell you. Did that thug hurt you at all back at the shop?"

"Er, no," said Walter, still not able to comprehend the fact that Oswald Moriarty was at the restaurant. "It was nothing. He just wanted a refund."

"Is that all?" sighed Oswald. "What an arrogant bastard." If Oswald had known however, that Ralph was listening in to every word he probably wouldn't have been so rude. "Anyway," Oswald went on, "enough of all that. How the hell did you manage to get invited to this party?"

"It's a long story," Walter replied.

"Excuse me," interrupted Brad. "I asked you where I might find a phone?"

"Oh sure," said Oswald. "There's a pay phone near the main door."

"Come on mate," Brad sighed, pushing a twenty pound note into one of the flaps in the costume. "Do I look like the kind of git who carries shrapnel about? You must have a phone out the back."

"Right, I get it" replied Oswald. "If you're with Walter you must be okay. Follow me." Brad grabbed Walter as they followed Oswald in his lizard suit to the back of the restaurant. They went through a side door and out into a small stock room. It was full of cans, packets and other containers of non perishable foods, all stacked on pallets. A single light bulb hung down from the ceiling.

"What's going on?" Walter whispered to Brad.

"Shut it!" was the only response he received.

"Here's the phone," said Oswald, pointing to a grubby grey plastic phone mounted on a wall. "It's nine for an outside line. You'd better be quick as well. It's my job if anyone finds you guys out here."

"That's cool," said Brad, and as he said it he punched Oswald so hard in the head that he crashed backwards into a stack of bean cans. His tray of drinks smashed on the floor, sending splinters of glass flying. The blow had rendered him instantly unconscious.

"What the hell are you doing?" screamed Walter.

"Are you okay?" added Ralph, who could no longer see them, but was startled by the noise of the crashing cans and smashing glass.

"Everything is fine," assured Brad.

"Why did you just belt him?" Walter asked insistently.

"Why didn't you tell us you knew somebody on the payroll?" Brad asked back.

"I didn't know he was here! Honestly!"

"How do you know him?"

"He's a local. He comes to the shop a lot. That is no reason to beat his brains out though!"

"Listen Walter, this is going to be a bit hard for you to understand," Brad began. "There is a guy out there who wants to kill Ralph and me. We didn't know he was there before, but we know now. I'm pretty certain he doesn't know who you are, so you're safe. Ralph is in the van, so Ralph is safe. I'm standing out there though, like a sitting duck. A couple of moments ago he almost had a clear opportunity to finish me off. That's not going to happen again. In addition to that, the last thing we need right now is a witness who knows who you are!"

"That's no reason to go round beating up other people," lectured Walter. "Anyway, I thought this wasn't a violent mission!"

"In case you haven't worked it out," Brad went on, "this friend of yours has just provided me with a disguise. I'm going to take the transmitter out of my jacket and somehow fix it to this lizard suit. It looks about the right size. Once I'm in the suit we go back to the original plan, just that I'm a waiter now, and not Nathan West. That reminds me, I've worked out your drop of inspiration behind our names. Your lucky I've just belted the crap out of one guy, otherwise you might have got that."

"What about Oswald? We can't leave him here," Walter protested.

"We have to," Brad ordered. "Besides, I didn't hit him that hard. He should wake up shortly after all this is over. In the mean time I need your help. You strip him down and hide him behind those boxes while I un-stitch my transmitter. The quicker we get this done the quicker we can get out of here."

"Do I have to undress him?" Walter pleaded. "I mean, I know this guy."

"Just remember who we are doing this for," shouted Brad. "Now skin that lizard, and no more protests!"

The last ten minutes had certainly been chaotic, but at the end of it all the advantage had gone back to Brad and Walter. It wasn't over yet though. Danny Dellapicho still had a few cards to play, and then of course there was the impact that Warren Kingburger would have.

Miami

Danny Dellapicho was furious. He pushed past guests, causing them to stumble and spill their drinks. He searched every floor meticulously, twice over, in an effort to make eye contact with Brad again. How could he have been so stupid? Moments earlier he could have killed him. He only needed to have pulled his gun and pointed. Bang! It was that easy. The blonde girl called Dilly Tango, or whatever her name was, was the one to blame. The simple fact that she knew Danny's name had put her on death row. It wasn't all her fault though. The real reason he had not killed Brad already was that he had not yet seen Ralph. He could only kill them when they were both together. To have killed Brad when he first had the chance would have been too risky. There would be mass confusion and panic at the sight of a gun, let alone the blast. If all hell broke loose with only one man dead the other would certainly get away. There was no way that could be allowed to happen. If only he knew, however, that Ralph was nowhere near the scene but safely tucked away in the control van, he would not have bothered with any of this. He would have slunk away and waited for the next opportunity, and there would have been a next opportunity. Danny was ignorant to Ralph's absence though, and his obsession to kill was starting to get the better of him. The heat of all those gyrating bodies was

starting to take its toll. If there was any air conditioning
he couldn't feel it. Just heat, muggy saturating heat.
His shirt was beginning to stick to his back, and beads
of sweat were forming on his brow. The noise of the
music was getting too much as well. Endless thudding,
tuneless crap. He looked hard at Fuzzy J the DJ with
daggers in his eyes. He too had unknowingly signed up
to the death list due to his poor taste in music. The
droning noise pulsated through Danny's head and was
threatening to ignite the part of his brain that controlled
his killer instinct. The disco lights dazzled Danny's
eyes, and there was the stench of all that food and
alcohol. The air was so thick with smoke from cigars
and marijuana joints that it was choking him. To make
it worse, all around him were images of aliens and
weird creatures, taken from some childhood nightmare
he could barely remember. He tried to remember if he
had ever been in operation in conditions such as this.
As a special operative with the CIA he had been
exposed to a load of weird shit. American society was
like that. He remembered his first case, when he had
been trailing a serial killer in Miami. This guy was a
total screwball. He worked for a car cleaning company,
vacuuming the inside of cars, but he just hated leopard
skin seats. It turns out his mama had leopard skin seats
in her Cadillac. She was having a thing with her
husbands business partner, and one day the little boy
caught them screwing on those leopard skin seats.
Twenty years later he was vacuuming seats just like the
one his mama was getting laid on. That made him
pissed, real pissed. As far as he was concerned any
woman who had seats like that was fair game. He just
took their address from the invoice ledger, and went
round to their house. He killed eight women in all,

each with a vacuum cleaner, and only after inflicting the sins of his mama upon them. Every single body was found spread eagled on the back seat of their car. The CIA became involved after the third victim was killed, the mistress of a Senator. A theory developed, although it turned out to be false, that the first two killings were just a cover for the third. The possibility had to be considered that the killer actually had political motives, rather than just being a head case. As a result, Danny was paired up with a couple of agents from the FBI to bring this guy down. It took Danny three months to figure the connection, and work out who his man was. The political angle had long since been discounted, but Danny was in too deep to give up on this one. He tracked the killer to some form of drinking den in downtown Miami. It was full of junkies, crack pots, mobsters, and pimps. It was not the sort of place you just walked into. The music was loud, and thumping, just like here. The air was thick with all sorts of chemicals, and it was hot enough to suffocate just from walking. It was much like Danny was feeling right now, here at this science fiction orgy. Back then in Miami his plan had worked though, even though he was lucky to walk out alive. The man he was after was buying crack out in the toilets. Danny, dressed in regular clothes like every other guy in the joint, found him there. He was stoned out of his face, the post mortem proved that. He couldn't have hurt a fly, even if he wanted to. That didn't stop Danny shooting him twenty eight times, decapitating him in the process. He was the first man that Danny ever killed, the first time he got that ultimate rush. That night proved to the CIA just what sort of a ruthless killing machine they had employed, and they liked what they saw. Within twenty four hours Danny was on a plane headed for Eastern Europe, where it was felt his skills would be better employed on business of a more unofficial nature. The events of that night were all coming back rapidly to Danny now. He could feel the adrenaline building up inside him to an unbearable extent. He needed to kill as much as he needed the air that he breathed. The word execute was tattooed across the back of his eyes, and the only colour he could see now was red. The same red as the gushing blood which covered those toilet walls fifteen years earlier in Miami. He needed that fix again, he needed it now. He could feel his hand reaching down his trouser leg, towards the gun holster on his calf. He imagined the feeling of the metal in his hand, his finger against the trigger. He imagined the sight of Brad's body buckling, as his chest exploded with bullets. He imagined the smell of gunpowder, and the blast of the shot. He imagined the satisfaction of it all. Just then, as Danny was reaching breaking point, the music stopped and the lights went up. Danny's hand immediately pulled away from the direction of the gun. He was startled, like a vampire meeting daylight. The speakers crackled, and there was the enhanced metallic sound of a man's breath now filling the restaurant.

"Howdy, y'all," bellowed the voice. "I'd like to introduce myself. My name is Warren Kingburger, and I am your host for the evening."

The Black Out

Needless to say, the Mahnja suit was a little too small for Brad Clusky. It was tight across the shoulders, and made it difficult to move. The transmitter was safely stuffed into the lining, and Ralph was happy that he could track the lizard suit as easily as he could track the dinner jacket. The only other modification was that the button mike was now lodged in the front of the Mahnja mask. Oswald, still out stone cold, had been tucked away behind a freezer in the corner. Ralph had suggested that they hide him in the freezer, but that idea was quickly discounted by Walter. Brad slipped the glass-cutters into Mahnja's utility belt, and the plan was ready to proceed again. They edged their way back out of the stock room and into the party. The aim was not to get noticed, but they failed instantly.

"Oi! Oswald," shouted another waiter, this time in a Fergus McTulip costume with a false beard. "Where the hell have you been?"

It took Brad a moment to work out that he now had to answer to the name Oswald rather than Nathan, or indeed Mahnja. His best defence in this situation was to assume that the suit would prevent him saying anything that could be understood. Instead he just shrugged.

"I've told you before about sloping off," shouted

Fergus. "Now take this tray of drinks, and get back to work." He passed Brad a tray of drinks, and pointed to some guests whose glasses were empty. He then headed off back towards the kitchen.

"Okay, boys," Brad said to his mike, whilst discarding the drinks on a small display cabinet. "Are you all with me? Let's get this finished!"

Just then the music stopped.

"Howdy y'all," came a voice from the speakers. "I'd like to introduce myself. My name is Warren Kingburger, and I am your host for the evening."

The crowd went silent. Fuzzy J was standing back from his turntables, and had passed the microphone over to Warren Kingburger. The big man just stood there on the platform above the awaiting masses. He basked in the glory of his own success. In his yellow suit he looked like a bloated grapefruit. He fired up a cigar before he continued.

"Is everybody having a good time?" he shouted. The crowd shouted back in the affirmative. "That's great," he continued. "I'd like to tell you a little story tonight. I'd like to tell you the story of this great restaurant we are celebrating."

As the speech began, the crowd was oblivious to Walter Bridgenorth making his way though them. "Keep going Walter," Brad instructed. "Head for that waiter dressed as McTulip. That bastard could do with being brought down a peg or two."

"As you know," Warren Kingburger continued, "when I was young I wasn't destined for the movies. My daddy was an oil man, and I was supposed to be an oil man just like him. Well, I managed to *slick* my way out of that one." He laughed loudly at his little joke, and the crowd replied politely.

Jim Carley

"Okay," said Ralph from the back of the van. "We are looking good." He tracked the events using every piece of hardware available to him. On different screens he could see Kingburger, Brad, Walter and Dellapicho. He kept his team constantly updated of the positions of all the key players. He was also managing to direct Walter to a position, an elevated platform at one side, where he thought his disruption would have maximum impact.

"Well, I never fancied oil," Kingburger went on. "About twenty years ago I was shown a movie script. I'd never thought much about movies before, but this script really got to me. I tell you that I was so into it that I sold the oil company and used some of the money to back this project. A lot of people laughed at me at the time, but that film was *Galactic Encounter,* the biggest box office smash in history."

Brad was edging his way round the room. He could just see the glass cabinet he was aiming for through the eye slits in his latex mask. He could also see Danny Dellapicho, standing on the stairway to the next floor. He was like a hawk surveying the crowd. He had obviously figured out that Brad had not tried to escape, but would he figure out that he was now wearing a lizard suit as a disguise?

"The rest, as they say," Kingburger went on, "is history. Characters were created in that film that are still household names today. Who could forget the bravery of Jed Largo, or not have sympathy for his long suffering side kick Mahnja? Who could not be enchanted by the beautiful Lady Carina, or be intrigued by the wisdom of Fergus McTulip? And who, most of all, could not have felt their flesh tingle every time they saw the awesome Drax Mantis?"

246

Brad was close to the cabinet now. He looked down upon it, a simple glass case. The cutters would make a clean hole in it, and it would be easy to reach inside and steal the action figure. Although there were three figures in the case, Brad easily recognised Drax Mantis. For the first time Brad now found himself with the one thing that had dominated his life since that awful night at the Gresham Corporation. It was very much what he expected really. Four inches of black plastic. It had little arms and little legs. It also had a little black helmet and a little laser gun. Most importantly though, it had a little rocket pack. This was what they had come for. This was what it was all about.

"Yes, my friends," said Kingburger. "Twenty years ago we created a legend that lives on today. It was only fitting that, to mark this special twentieth birthday, we re-released the entire trilogy of *Galactic Encounter*. That wasn't enough though. I wanted to share this special anniversary with my friends. The best way to do that was to have a party, and the best place to have a party is where the movie is so close you feel you are part of it."

Brad's hand reached inside his utility belt and pulled out the glasscutter. "I'm ready," he whispered into his button microphone. Walter stretched his neck on the other side of the room to get a glance of his plastic clad companion. He then drew nearer to the waiter in the Fergus McTulip costume. That was his target, although he wasn't sure what to do when he got to him. The waiter, however, answered that question for him.

"Would you like a drink, sir?" the waiter asked.

"Uhm," replied Walter in surprise.

"Perhaps a gin and tonic?"

"Keep it together," Brad whispered in his ear from the other side of the room.

"A gin and tonic would be fine," Walter finally said, with a deep breath. The waiter passed him the drink from his tray.

"So, my friends," Kingburger continued over the loud speakers. "It only remains for me to invite you to make a toast." He reached across to grab a neat Jack Daniels from the Lady Carina waitress.

"I'm cutting the power in ten seconds," instructed Ralph from the back of the van. Walter panicked at the time scale, but knew he had to act fast. Brad stuck the cutters to the glass, and prepared to cut.

"Ten, nine..." began Ralph with the countdown.

Just then Danny Dellapicho saw the guy in the lizard suit behaving suspiciously. He knew at once that it had to be Brad.

"Eight, seven..."

"A toast," repeated Kingburger, raising his glass. "To the Orbit Studio Experience. Down the hatch!"

"Six, five..."

As Walter was about to knock the tray of drinks out of the waiter's hands, Fergus McTulip walked away to serve drinks to those desperate to join in the toast.

"Four..."

"Down the hatch," the crowd shouted out, and poured alcohol down their throats.

"Three..."

"I can't do it," Walter shouted into his microphone. As he said it Oswald burst out of the stockroom, wearing absolutely nothing and nursing a bump on his head.

"Two..."

"Who the hell has got my costume?" Oswald shouted, and as he did it every head in the room turned to stare at him.

"One," Ralph concluded into the ears of Brad and Walter. The whole building went dark and silent as Ralph cut the power.

A New Beginning

FADE IN:

<u>INT. GLOKORIAN PALACE: SERVICE BRIDGE - NIGHT</u>

The scene is a bridge over a power canal where we left DRAX MANTIS and JED LARGO. The battle between them is over. JED LARGO is stretched out on the deck, with one arm hanging over the edge. DRAX MANTIS is holding on to his arm, about to fall a hundred feet to certain electrocution amongst the power cables below.

JED LARGO: It's over Drax. My powers have beaten you, but I can't let you die without mercy. Let me pull you up.

DRAX MANTIS: Never, Largo. You may have beaten me in battle, but I will never surrender to you. Release your grip and let me die.

JED LARGO: (*struggling to hold on to DRAX'S weight*) I don't want you to surrender. I don't care. The Glokorian Territories are in ruin anyway. Whatever happens now you are not going to prove anything. Why not let me help you?

DRAX MANTIS: No, I will not yield to you. I would rather die. At least that is honourable.

JED LARGO: I can sense your emotions, Drax. I know you don't want to die. I feel your relief at the end of all this hate. There is good in you. I know it. I know you want me to help you, to help you discover the man you used to be, rather than the creature you have become.

CUT TO:

LADY CARINA and MAHNJA bursting through a side door onto the bridge, laser rifles at the ready, they have just finished off a unit of Glokorian marines.

LADY CARINA: (*taking aim at DRAX*) Jed, look out. Let me blast that monster!

JED LARGO: No, wait. I don't want you to kill him. I'm trying to save him.

DRAX MANTIS: End it Carina! If you have the guts to kill me, that is!

MAHNJA: (*also taking aim*) Graaarr, raaoo, erraaghh!

CUT TO:

Close up of JED LARGO.

JED LARGO: No, don't kill him. I mean it.

CUT TO:

LADY CARINA and MAHNJA, reluctantly lowering their weapons. The camera pans back to JED LARGO.

JED LARGO: You see Drax? They aren't going to kill you. Nobody is going to kill you. Face it, you may as well let me pull you up.

DRAX MANTIS: What for? So they can put me up in front of some form of show trial? Either way I die. At least this way I go with dignity.

JED LARGO: (*Really starting to strain under the weight*) There won't be a trial. Nobody needs to know you survived if you don't want them to. You have my guarantee on that.

DRAX MANTIS says nothing, but looks regretfully at the drop below him, and then hopefully back at JED.

JED LARGO: Mahnja, help me pull him up.

The Smownork discards his rifle and helps pull DRAX MANTIS onto the bridge. Carina, still untrusting of DRAX, keeps her laser at the ready. DRAX says nothing, but allows Jed and Mahnja to pull him to safety.

JED LARGO: It's time for a new beginning Drax. It's time for peace now.

DRAX MANTIS: What makes you so sure you can trust me?

JED LARGO: I'm prepared to take a chance on that. Just the same as you are going to have to take a chance on trusting me.

JED LARGO holds out a hand to DRAX, who reluctantly takes it, but there is something in his eyes that suggests it's not over yet.

Panic

Forty five seconds later the lights went back up. In the interim all hell had broken out. Women were screaming, as bodies tripped over each other. The security team were going bananas. On the first floor a major star had tripped in the darkness and had smashed into one of the major exhibits. Chairs flew, and plates of food were knocked to the floor from the tables. Those security guards carrying guns had them pulled, but could not see anything to fire at. Then the lights went up. Initially they blinded everybody's eyes, as they had only just adjusted to the darkness. Soon after, the bedlam that had ruled in the darkness began to take over once again. Two security guards immediately jumped on Oswald, and dragged him out back. They then proceeded to give him another beating just in case he turned out to be some sort of subversive. They only stopped when he was unconscious again. In the main room Warren Kingburger still had the microphone, and intended to use it wisely.

"Everybody stay calm," he instructed the crowd, but the sight of the guards with guns had accelerated the panic in some of the guests. More and more of them had decided to head for the main door. There was no order to their rush, it was everyone for themselves. The weak and the elderly had already begun to fall underfoot.

Dilly Foxtrot pulled herself from the crowd, her dress was torn and almost in tatters. She was not, however, as distressed as the rest of the guests. She was more concerned with finding the pervert who had taken the liberty of fondling her breasts during the black out. That would have to wait though. Right now she was trying to reach Kingburger. She knew that if tonight turned to shit she would never be able to work in the movies again. Kingburger was one of the few people who had any chance of saving the proceedings from certain doom.

"Dilly," said Kingburger, aside from the microphone and momentarily forgetting their differences, "where the hell have you been?"

"I'm sorry, Mr Kingburger," she apologised. "I have no idea what is going on. It must have been a power fault or something. We've got to get those guards to put their guns away, or this is just going to get way out of hand."

"Everybody," Kingburger said, ignoring Dilly and returning his attention to the crowd. "Please be calm. The men with guns that you can see are security officers. They will not harm you. They are purely here for your well-being." His words were falling on deaf ears. The panic just escalated at an alarming rate.

"Okay, guards," Kingburger tried again, with a different target audience. "Please put your guns away, and secure the exhibits. I want to know if anything is damaged or missing."

"Damaged or missing?" Dilly shouted. "Is that all you damn well care about? There are people here getting hurt! They should be your first concern you stupid prick."

"Listen sweetheart," Kingburger snapped back

away from the microphone. "You of all people should know how much all this stuff is worth. Do you think a restaurant like this could bounce back if this stuff is looted or smashed? This is already going to create a shit load of bad publicity. The share price will sink like a lead balloon! And who do you suggest I should blame for all this, huh?"

"Fuck you, Warren," she retorted.

"You're fired, you insolent bitch," Kingburger replied.

"You can't fire me, you dick, because I already quit. Oh, and by the way, when I told you that you were good in bed it was a lie. I'm afraid that you are the worse shag I've ever had. I only did it for the job."

"Hah," laughed Warren, "you didn't think I hired you for your brains did you?"

The tiff could have blown out of hand like the chaos all around, but it was stopped by the emergence of a distressed security guard pulling himself from the crowd.

"Mr. Kingburger," he cried.

"What the hell do you want? Can't you see I'm busy here?" slammed Kingburger.

"There's been a theft," the guard wheezed, trying to recover his breath. "One of the exhibits."

"What!" screamed Kingburger. "Which one?"

"One of the action figures. Drax Mantis I think."

"With a rocket pack?"

"Yeah, that's the one!"

"My God," sighed Kingburger, grasping the microphone again.

"What about these people," Dilly interjected. "Aren't you going to help them?" Once again, though, Kingburger was following his own agenda.

"Attention all guards," he called out over the intercom across the room. "There has been a theft of one of the key exhibits. A Drax Mantis action figure has been removed. This must be recovered at all costs. It is highly likely the perpetrator is still on the premises."

"For Christ's sake," Dilly cursed. She turned her back and left Kingburger to it. As far as she was concerned she wished she had never got mixed up in this. As for Kingburger, well that was surely a case of her ambition getting in the way of her dignity and self respect. There was no way that was going to happen again. There was no time to regret it now though. She had to help these people out of the building, before someone got seriously hurt. Little did she know that someone was about to get seriously hurt in a permanently dead sort of way, and that person was Fuzzy J the disc jockey.

Five Minutes

Danny Dellapicho had been stunned by the blackout. A big guy standing behind him at the time had violently pushed him aside causing him to fall. Although he wasn't seriously hurt it was enough to knock him off the scent of the guy in that lizard suit. When he managed to stand again all hell had broken out, and the lizard suit was nowhere to be seen. Whatever Brad Clusky and Ralph Lee had been perpetrating, the odds were that they had now carried it out. Nobody as yet, though, knew what that perpetration might be.

"Attention all guards," came the voice of Warren Kingburger over the speakers. "There has been a theft of one of the key exhibits. A Drax Mantis action figure has been removed. This must be recovered at all costs. It is highly likely the perpetrator is still on the premises."

Danny shrugged at the thought. A toy! Surely two ex-SAS men wouldn't be sodding about trying to steal a toy. Danny was offended at the thought. Surely the White House wouldn't send him across the Atlantic for professional teddy bear kidnappers, or guys that have a bad reputation for cheating at Monopoly. No, that couldn't be it. They must have been here for something else, an assassination perhaps. He tried to figure out his next move. For one thing, he knew that if he was going to make the kill he had to make it fast, or else he might not get the chance. If Brad and Ralph were following normal logic then they would be heading for the back door. If they were there they would be cornered. That was where Danny had to get to, and he had to get there fast. Like everything else that night though, getting to the back door wasn't going to be straightforward. For starters, there was the Oswald factor. At that time the guards were still working on the theory that poor old Oswald had a hand in the chaos that had erupted in the restaurant. They also thought that it was unlikely he was working alone. For that reason the guards were desperately trying to secure the far end of the ground floor that lead to the back door, just in case some of Oswald's associates might be lurking back there. This put a big dent in Danny's plans. He cursed the guards. Surely, for safety reasons it made sense to allow people out the back way, rather than allow the present crush at the front door. At the same time Danny was relieved. If the guards had sent a large number of guests towards the back door they would only have been stopped by the chain he had wrapped around the door bars. That would have just created another crush, and might have given Brad and Ralph enough of an edge to escape. Still, there was no easy way of reaching the back door to find out whether or not Brad and Ralph were down there. With each passing moment the guards were establishing greater command of the crowd. It no longer seemed like a mass panic. It was now more like a badly organised evacuation. The guards were successfully keeping everyone away from the back, and steering them towards the front.

"Excuse me," Danny said to one of the guards. "I need to get back there. I think my wife was over in that direction before the black out."

"I'm sorry, sir," said the guard. "This is now a restricted area. We have reason to believe there are suspects in this area whom we need to question. Please make your way out of the front door."

"But my wife," pleaded Danny. "You don't understand!"

"I'm sorry sir. If your wife is back there I'm sure we will find her and bring her to safety. You can't stay in this area. For your own safety, I must ask you to make your way to the front door."

Danny contemplated breaking this guys neck and pushing him inside. It was too risky though. There were too many people around, too many guards looking for an excuse to beat the shit out of someone. Reluctantly he found himself heading for the front door. His mind was desperately trying to think of an alternative way of reaching the back of the restaurant, but there was no obvious route. He had to make the kill though, it had to be tonight. He had never failed his Government before, and he wasn't about to start now. As thoughts of desperation began to crowd his head, he found himself drifting back to that night in Miami. That night he had been the one in control. He had been the one who had orchestrated the violence. That was how he worked best. Somehow he needed to do the same here. He needed to take control, if he didn't he would soon be out on the street and it would all be over. Once again he found his hand reaching for his gun, but this time there was nothing stopping him from unclipping it. His hand slipped around it, and guided it from its holster. Already he felt far more powerful holding his weapon, but just holding it wasn't going to be enough. He needed to use it, to take control. If he could not reach Brad and Ralph, then he would use his power to bring them before him. He climbed onto a table at a corner booth near the bar, which had a good vantage point across the entire ground floor. Nobody had really noticed at that point, but that changed when he let off the first bullet. He aimed at one of the main speakers next to Fuzzy J's turntables. The speaker exploded from the impact of the bullet. As the bullet passed through the speaker it went on to lodge itself in Fuzzy J's abdomen, killing him instantly. His heavy body crashed down on his CD player. A guard turned round quickly to return fire, blowing four holes in the wall in a straight line. His inaccuracy cost him dearly though. It took Danny only one shot, straight through the side of the guard's head. His head exploded across the wall behind him. Danny got a kick out of that. Exploding brains. You just can't beat it. In that instant the entire crowd had been silenced. No one was panicking any more, but instead they stood in silent horror at these two very public executions. The remaining guards that had previously put their guns away had them drawn again, all pointed at the gunman standing on the table. Danny, however, now had the power that he craved for. The advantage had returned to him. "I don't think you boys want to chance it do you?" Danny challenged the guards. The headless body of their ex-colleague had already scared them senseless. None of them were paid enough for this sort of shit. Reluctantly, one by one, they lowered their weapons. They stayed alert and vigilant though. With a man down they wouldn't need much of an opportunity to seek revenge. "Listen up everybody," he shouted. "If you want to live you do exactly as I say. I don't want to kill anybody unless I have to, but if I have to I won't think twice about it."

The crowd did not verbally respond, but he could tell they were happy to comply with his rules.

"Okay," he went on, "I only want two things, then we can all get out of here. Firstly, I want Mr. Kingburger, and his lovely associate Miss Foxtrot, to step over here and join me at this table. You see, I like to keep a very good insurance policy in situations such as this."

Warren Kingburger placed the microphone down on the turntable. His eyes, however, were not on Danny Dellapicho, but instead focused on the dead body of Fuzzy J lying next to him. Fuzzy J's mouth lay wide open, and the puddle of blood around him was gradually getting bigger. The hole in his stomach seemed immense, big enough to put a fist into. His eyes were fixed at a single point on the ceiling, his pupils already dilating. More blood seemed to well in his mouth and spill over his lips, running down the side of his cheek. Kingburger was equally enthralled and disturbed by this sight. In all his movies he must have killed off thousands of characters. Of those a fair percentage had been shot. He recalled a scene where Cybercop must have fired at least fifty rounds into one of his victims. There was blood everywhere, but it was nothing like this.

"Mr Kingburger," shouted Danny. "Are you fucking ignoring me? Do I need to kill some more of your guests to get your attention?"

Kingburger turned to face him. He recognised him at once as the man in the lift at the Grosvenor House. Surely this was an over reaction to being asked to put your cigarette out? Dilly had already moved over to the table and sat down on the upholstered bench that bordered one side of the table. Her face was level with one of Danny's ankles.

"Get your fat butt over here," insisted Danny. Kingburger reluctantly moved away from Fuzzy J's body towards Danny and Dilly through the diminished crowd of guests who were still in the restaurant. He took a seat next to Dilly.

"Okay," Danny went on. "That's cool. I'd like you two where I can keep an eye on you. Right, let's talk about the second thing I want. What I want is two guys. One is called Brad Clusky and the other is Ralph Lee. They are the two men who sabotaged your evening. I want them, and I want them fast. For every five minutes I have to wait before they show up, I'm going to kill one of you lovely people. So, you see, it is in everybody's interest that I find these guys, and I find them quickly."

Dilly Foxtrot and Warren Kingburger looked ominously at each other. They had no idea who the gunman was, but they knew he meant business.

Part Six

Plan B

The Chain

"Shit," cried Brad, as he tried to force the chain. "There's no way this chain is going to break!" There was no way round it. The chain on the back door was not going to move. Brad, however, was not completely stressed by this. After all, everything else had gone horribly wrong tonight, so another problem wasn't really that much of a big deal. He was stuck in a dark corridor wearing a lizard suit. On one side of him there was a chained door, and somewhere in the restaurant behind him there was a crazed gunman. These were exactly the sort of situations that Brad thrived on, or at least he seemed to.

"Can I see it?" asked Walter, referring to the newly acquired Drax Mantis action figure.

"If you ask me that one more time," Brad replied, "I'm going to punch you."

"It's just that ...," Walter tried to continue.

"It's just nothing," slammed Brad. "In case you hadn't noticed, our one and only escape route has been blocked. If we don't figure out a way round this pretty soon we are fucked. It is not going to take those guards upstairs too long to work out that their Drax doll is missing, and it's going to take them less time to search this place afterwards. If they find us down here it's curtains for sure."

Brad pulled off his Mahnja mask in despair, but

soon had to pick it up again to recover his microphone in order that he could stay in contact with Ralph.

"It must have been Dellapicho," Ralph reported into his headset.

"Of course it was bloody Dellapicho," Brad shouted back at his microphone, which he was now holding. "If you, and all your fancy gadgets, had been watching him, like you were supposed to be doing, perhaps we wouldn't be in this bloody mess!"

"Keep your cool, buddy," Ralph retorted. "At this moment in time I'm probably the only person that can get you guys out of there in one piece!"

"What's the problem?" Walter jumped in. "If we can't get out the back, why don't we just go out the front?"

"Oh, I like that," replied Ralph in laughter. He clicked on his mouse button to call up the images from the CCTV on the ground floor. "Shall I tell you what is going down in the main arena? Our boy Dellapicho has just blown the DJ's guts out and the head off one of the security guards!"

"Are they dead?" Walter asked in astonishment.

"Of course they're dead," Ralph replied.

"My God," said Walter, slumping to his knees. He was silent for a moment before he could speak again. "Those poor men. It's all my fault. All I wanted was Drax Mantis. I didn't think that anyone would die. I never thought that. We have to give ourselves up. That's what we have to do. We have to give up!"

"Listen to me," said Brad, slumping down beside Walter. "It's a pisser. It's a big pisser. That DJ was an ordinary guy, and now he's dead. The guard was probably an average guy as well. That isn't your fault though. This guy Dellapicho, he's only after Ralph and

Jim Carley

I. Sooner or later, somewhere, he was always going to find us. The chances are that somebody would end up dead. Today it was the DJ and the guard, but it could quite easily have been someone else on another day. Either way, that isn't your fault, it's mine.

"We can't let this get to us. We've come too far for that. We've got what we came for! Now, all we have to do is escape. Every second we spend not trying to achieve that is a second nearer were are to joining the DJ. We just need to keep going for a bit longer. Are you with me?"

Walter's eyes had reddened. He was instantly nauseous and still felt like there was blood on his hands. Those poor men, just trying to make a living. Despite this, Walter could see the point of some of the things Brad was saying. He knew that time was running out. He knew they had to escape or possibly face death themselves, they were the only two choices. He tried to think what Jed Largo might do in these circumstances, but Jed Largo seemed a very long way away now.

"It gets worse," interrupted Ralph, who was also listening in on the frequency of the security guards' radios. "I think our boy is going nuts! He is really mouthing off. He reckons he's going to kill someone every five minutes unless you and I show. If he isn't bluffing, you have got about three and a half minutes to save someone else's life."

Brad sighed, and looked at Walter. Walter was predictably disturbed by this development, but there was a new hope in his eyes.

"Let's finish this," he said firmly. Brad smiled, and slapped his shoulder. Three and half minutes can be a long time in show business.

"It's time for Plan B," announced Brad.

"What's Plan B?" asked Ralph over his microphone.

"Good question," Brad replied. "I'll tell you just as soon as I've figured it out."

Jenny Lovelace

"We interrupt that report on the story on the latest children's TV presenter accused of drug taking to bring you urgent news from the West End" said Dana O'Brien to Camera Two. She wasn't very good at improvisation when the director abandoned the script, and tried to turn *Capital Night Out* from the trashy magazine show that it was into a hardhitting news documentary. The camera had cut back to her earlier than expected, mid way through having her make up touched up. The result was that she now had far more blusher on one cheek compared to the other. It looked like someone had just slapped her round the face. Marcus Clint, however, was more experienced in these situations. In his early career he had been a journalist on a regional news programme, and could always keep his cool in front of the camera. During one famous report he managed to keep a level head, and deliver his live report on the subject of cruelty in zoos, whilst a large gorilla was trying to mate with him.

"Yes, Dana," he said, taking over. "*Capital Night Out* is able to bring you exclusive pictures from the opening party at the Orbit Studio Experience. I regret to tell you, however, that it is not the great party we were all hoping it would be. Only moments ago a mass evacuation of the new multi-million pound restaurant was ordered after an electrical disturbance caused some form of blackout. The blackout resulted in scenes of panic and hysteria. Then, literally seconds ago, a series of gun shots were heard inside the building."

"Yes, Marcus," interrupted Dana, regaining her composure. "We do not yet know who, if anyone, has been injured in this incident. Fears are growing though for the safety of some of the big Hollywood stars still inside, now at the mercy of a deranged gunman. As we speak, the police are dispatching every available officer to the West End, including an armed unit. We have been told by a source at Scotland Yard that extreme force will be used if necessary to guarantee the safety of those still inside."

The director switched over to Camera Five, giving Marcus the chance to have the last word.

"Without further delay," he said in his most news-like manner, "we can now go live to the West End where our roving reporter, Jenny Lovelace, is waiting to give us the latest update on this horrific incident."

The picture cut to a jolty image from the pavement outside the Orbit Studio Experience. Even though the cameraman was having problems focusing and keeping his camera steady, his pictures were destined to be used by ITN, the BBC, and CNN. He was filming a destitute scene. All around people were screaming and running in panic in all directions. There was no longer a separation between the stars and their adoring public. The barriers and red carpet had been swept away. Everybody was equal now, all desperately trying to get away from the restaurant. Word of mouth had ensured that everybody knew there was a mad man inside with a gun, and nobody wanted to hang about to meet him. Jenny Lovelace was having an identity crisis. The dizzy, bimbo-esque, side of her "in front of the camera" personality was urging her to run with the others. Another side of her, perhaps the ambitious, career advancement side, was urging her to stay and deliver the greatest performance of her quasi-journalistic career. As she moved into the frame of the picture it was obvious that she was possessed with terror, brought about by the unfolding events.

"There are no words," she began, attempting a far more serious tone than she had used on earlier broadcasts, "to describe the scenes we are witnessing tonight. It seems like only moments ago we were raving it up at the party of the year. This happening scene, however, has descended into some seriously bad vibes. As I speak, the gunman, who is reported to have already murdered at least one party dude, is believed to be still inside holding quite a few hostages. One eyewitness said to me that they believed the gunman to be the popular radio presenter Jimmy Lambourne, who is known to have been on tonight's guest list. I mean, who would have thought? Jimmy Lambourne! He always sounds like such a puppy on the radio. Now though, it seems like he's the next Hannibal Lecter. Way out!"

Back in the studio the programme's lawyer was almost having a coronary. Jenny Lovelace had unwittingly just ended her career by implying that Jimmy Lambourne had any involvement in the murder of Fuzzy J and the security guard. She had based her accusation on the strength of an identification made by the other security guard who had checked Jimmy's invitation when Danny Dellapicho had entered the party. Although, months later, Jimmy managed to successfully sue the programme, his career was also effectively over. Meanwhile, the plug had been pulled on Jenny's exclusive before she provided any further cause for litigation.

"Weh, hey, hey," reported Marcus to Camera Three, taking over from Jenny. "You have to hand it to our Jenny, she is one live wire! Of course, those reports on Jimmy Lambourne's involvement are as yet unfounded. Stick with us on *Capital Night Out* and we will be the first to let you know the latest developments from the West End."

"That's right, Marcus," Dana came in, "and I can confirm now that this programme is being extended to cover the events as they unfold. I'm afraid to say that the scheduled late night international darts programme that was due to follow this show has now been postponed."

The coverage did indeed continue, late into the night. The footage obtained that night by Jenny Lovelace's cameraman was to become legendary.

The Chapel Bell

In the dark corridor by the back door, time seemed to be zooming by. Three and half minutes seemed like it should be a long time. Most of the classic rock songs that had ever been recorded must have been about three and a half minutes and, when you think about it in those terms, it seems like an incredibly long time. Brad knew for a fact that the song *The Chapel Bell* by legendary rock star Solomon Sweet (from album *Two in the Bush*) was exactly three minutes and thirty seven seconds long. He knew this because he once had a sexual experience whilst playing that album which had been initiated when the song began and climaxed almost exactly at the point it finished. Brad had found the whole thing so unusual that he felt obliged to check the length of the song on the sleeve afterwards. Three minutes and thirty seven seconds, it wasn't easily forgotten. Recalling the song was quite a relief for Brad, as it gave him two further options for keeping track of time rather than guessing or checking his watch. He could either try to recall the exact actions which compiled that particular sexual experience (this idea was quickly discounted, as he was sure he would use too much artistic licence and make things last longer than the reality), or the other, and far more sensible, option was simply to sing along to the song in his head.

Baby don't cry
I'm back here tonight
Ask me questions
But don't ask me why
Just stay with me tonight

At the point where Solomon's words "don't ask me why" went through Brad's head, his brain started systematically spurting out new options for their escape.

"Ralph," he said, standing again with a newfound ferocity. "Is there any chance you can ram this door with the van from the other side?"

"Negative," Ralph replied. "It's a really bad angle. I reckon it would do more damage to the van than it would to the door."

"Then Walter is right," Brad went on. "We have to go out through the front."

"Are you crazy?" cried Ralph. "I have a live link up with that room. I can see what this guy is doing. I'm telling you he has lost it completely. He is standing on a table waving a gun at anything that moves. He's got Kingburger and Foxtrot sat right next to him, ready to blow them away at a moments notice. If he gets one look at you it's over."

"No, I don't think so," replied Brad. "He wouldn't kill me by myself. He needs to kill us both if the Gresham job is going to be tidied up."

"The Gresham Corporation," blurted Walter. "You were behind that? That's how you came to be in my shop?"

"It's a long story," Brad replied.

"I read about that in the paper," Walter went on.

"Why would you want to rob that? It's just an insurance company."

"I can assure you it's not an insurance company," said Brad.

"So what is it?" asked Walter.

Still night calling out....Listen to the Chapel Bell
Tell me what it's all about...Listen to the Chapel Bell

"Never mind about that now," Brad replied. "We don't have enough time. Let's just say that the Gresham job is why this guy wants us dead. If he kills me though, he's risking that Ralph will blow the whistle."

"So why is he here then?" asked Ralph.

"He must think you are both here, on the inside," suggested Walter.

"Why would he think that?" added Brad.

"Because he only accessed half of my Walter files," deduced Ralph, now frantically running a systems search to assess how much Dellapicho really knew about the job. "He knows we needed two tickets to get inside, but he didn't know that one was for Walter. He never opened the reconnaissance files relating to the van. He doesn't know I'm out here!"

"I think Mr. Dellapicho might have just given us a way out," Brad smiled. "How long have we got?"

Talking slow
Not sure of which way to go
Ask me questions
But you will never know
Just stay with me tonight

"If he keeps to his pledge," Ralph reported, "somebody is going to die in less than a minute."

Brad looked around the corridor leading to the rear door for something he could use against Dellapicho. He saw what he needed on a catering trolley which had been abandoned down there, a nine inch carving knife with a razor sharp blade.

"Listen up, guys," he instructed. "I've got a new plan. Ralph, I want you waiting by the front door with the engine running as soon as you can."

"I'm on my way," Ralph replied, already moving to the driver's seat.

"Walter," Brad went on, "I need your help in a big way."

"Okay," Walter replied. "What are we going to do?"

In the back of Brad's head, *The Chapel Bell* was already beginning to fade out.

Hostages

"Time's up," shouted Dellapicho at his terrified congregation. He still controlled the room from his position on the table. Five minutes exactly had passed since he made his original threat. "Anybody out there want to die?"

Nothing had changed in the previous five minutes. Around forty guests were still trapped in the restaurant with Dellapicho. Most had now resorted to taking seats on chairs, tables, or on the floor. It was difficult to remain rigid at the prospect of such violence, it was easier to drift downwards and wait for fate to play its hand. The only people still standing, with the exception of Danny, were the four armed security guards who were still contemplating their options. They still managed to keep their guns on Danny, but gravity was starting to make their arms ache, and accuracy was no longer a certainty.

"For God's sake," said Dilly, at Danny's feet, "what's the point? These people, Brad and Roy..."

"Ralph," corrected Danny. "The fat one is called Ralph."

"Brad and Ralph," Dilly continued. "Nobody here knows who they are."

"Ha," jeered Danny. "You bare faced lying bitch! You know who Brad is. He's the one that put you on to me!"

"I don't know what you are talking about!"

"No," continued Danny menacingly. "Well, if you can't remember you are no use to me. Perhaps I should kill you first!" He took aim, with his barrel only inches from Dilly's face. Remarkably, however, she didn't flinch at all. This whole experience seemed to be making her stronger.

"Hold on a God damn moment," interjected Warren Kingburger from the seat next to Dilly. "Who the hell do you think you are? You can't just go round killing people because they haven't heard of other people. If Dilly says she doesn't know these boys then she doesn't know them. I should know, I introduced her to everyone she knows. The only famous Brads and Ralphs I introduced her to were Brad Pitt and Ralph Lauren. Now, I don't think they were the names you were looking for."

"Steady, old man," said Danny, taking his aim off Dilly. "I know that you are keen on this here lady, seeing as you are porking her in a posh hotel and everything, but you don't want to make me angry. Maybe I might kill you next."

"You are hardly likely to do that," Kingburger replied.

"Why's that?" asked Danny.

"Because I'm your star hostage, you idiot," Kingburger replied, with ice cool delivery. He hadn't got to where he was today by pussy footing about. "You've already let all of the other big stars escape. No disrespect to these others, but they hardly carry the same clout. In no time at all this building is going to be surrounded by armed cops. The only way they are likely to let you escape is if you still have one big hit hostage, and that's me. Now, on my calculations you still have about forty hostages. If you kill one every five minutes, that gives me over three hours before my time is up. That's a fair old while, so I'm going to have a cigar and a Jack Daniels while you work out your new strategy here."

Danny almost killed Kingburger for his impertinence, but he decided that he had a point. He couldn't really kill him, at least not yet. Kingburger pulled his cigar case from his jacket, and lit up. "Are there any waiters left in the house?" Kingburger called. "Christ, I'm dry."

"No drinks," ordered Danny, "the bar is closed. You need to concentrate on the big issue here. Two guys, one fit and one fat, looking shifty. I know they're here, and I want them. I get them, everybody else walks. Well, not quite everybody, one of you guys is already on borrowed time. If I say I'm going to kill somebody after five minutes, then I kill somebody. I'm nothing if not a man of my word."

One or two guests were getting visually anxious. Most, however, were trying to cover their terror rather than risk a reprisal. Danny traced an outline of the group with the barrel of his gun. It was a bit like being given a box of chocolates, and not knowing which one to eat first. Maybe he would kill the toffee supreme, the body building wrestler cowering in the corner. Alternatively there was the strawberry cream, the petite red headed tennis star. Then there was the chocolate fudge, the stand up comic who got most of his laughs from looking dumb. So many to choose from.

"I still don't see the point of this," repeated Dilly, her hair crumpling over her brow. Her make up was smeared and she was beginning to look like she had just gone ten rounds with Mike Tyson. "We've told you we don't know these people. Maybe I did speak to one earlier, but I don't remember him. You can kill us all and it won't change anything. We don't know! The chances are they have already crept out the back and are well clear of here!"

"They didn't get out the back," Danny replied.

"How the hell do you know that?"

"I chained the back door," slammed Danny. "Nobody gets out the back, so if any of you were thinking about it I would reconsider big time."

"So, everybody dies, whatever happens," concluded Dilly.

"If you want it that way," Danny responded. "I'm getting tired with this, and I'm getting tired with you, blue eyes. You've got one hell of a mouth on you. Time to eat lead, baby."

"You're full of shit," Dilly replied, but Danny was raising his gun once again to take aim at her head. He eased back the trigger, and prepared to shoot.

"Hold it right there," shouted a voice from the other side of the room. Danny was so startled that his concentration broke. He let off a bullet, but rather than shooting Dilly he managed instead to shoot Warren Kingburger. Dilly screamed loudly, initially in reaction at how close she had come to death, but then at the atrocity of seeing Kingburger injured. His body slumped forward on to her lap, knocking his Stetson to the floor. It was a good job she was wearing red, because blood was everywhere.

"Shit," cursed Danny at his error, but he had already spun round to greet the voice that had broken his concentration. His trigger finger was poised to fire again. When he saw the voice belonged to Brad Clusky he almost fired on instinct, but there was something else he hadn't reckoned on. Brad, still in the tatters of his Mahnja costume, had a hostage too. The trajectory between Danny's gun and Brad's body was blocked by another guy. Brad was standing close behind him, holding him with one hand in a tight arm lock. The other hand was free to hold the blade of a sharp carving knife close to his throat. Brad knew the scene. He knew Dellapicho wouldn't shoot, at least not yet. The best way to beat shock tactics is to have a bigger shock up your own sleeve. Walter, on witnessing first hand the shooting of Warren Kingburger, was filled with terror making him a first class candidate as a false hostage. With a wry smile, and a smug voice, Brad opened the negotiations on his own terms. "Anybody want to bargain?"

The Carving Knife

Danny had not banked on Brad revealing himself so easily. He had presented himself without significant force or coercion. Sure, Danny had threatened to kill off a number of hostages but, if Brad was as super cool as his file said he was, then a few dead bodies would not rest heavily on his conscious. No, ex- SAS guys don't just give up. It's not their style. In addition to that, Brad must surely know that taking a hostage in a situation like this does not guarantee survival by any stretch of the imagination. If Danny didn't Brad him out of total disregard, then you could bet your bottom dollar that some wise ass cop outside would be waiting to blow his brains out. Walter, meanwhile, was wondering how he had been drawn into all this. When Brad had suggested that he hold a carving knife against his throat whilst using him as a human shield against a trigger-happy maniac he had laughed out loud. That was before he realised that Brad wasn't joking. A short argument followed, which nobody had time for. Walter took the line that Brad was becoming deranged, and submitting to negative evil messages inside his brain that were urging him to become like Danny. Brad claimed that this line of argument was in fact "bollocks" and told Walter that if he didn't agree he would slice his jugular there and then. It was a brutal and out of character tactic, but the last thing Brad wanted was to endure another one of Walter's tantrums. Needless to say, Walter retracted his earlier comment, and gladly complied with Brad's suggestion. So there he was, standing in the remains of what was the ground floor of the Orbit Studio Experience. He could feel the cold metal of the knife's blade against his throat as Brad held him firmly from behind. To his left were the forty bewildered party guests, each with a look that suggested that Walter was about to meet an untimely demise. To his right Danny Dellapicho was standing on the table, looking cock sure of himself. At his feet in the seats were Dilly Foxtrot, and Warren Kingburger, who was slowly bleeding to death. The four armed security guards were now completely bewildered. Two of them kept their attention on Danny, but the other two had switched to monitor Brad.

In recognition that the guards were still carrying guns, and that they represented a further wild card in the already precarious deck, Brad wanted to address them first.

"Tell me boys," said Brad, referring to the guards. "Who do you think is in the most danger here? You've got a bad shit situation. Far worse than anything you guys have probably ever seen before, that's for sure. Anybody ever pointed a gun at you before and meant it, huh?"

The guards looked sheepishly at each other, but none of them answered. Danny, for the time being was prepared to let Brad have the stage. Dilly was speechless. She didn't know what was doing her head in the most; the fact that Kingburger had been shot, or the fact that Nathan West was holding a knife against another man's throat.

"So nobody has ever seen any action before," Brad went on. "That's bad news, boys. That's really bad news. You see, I'm not your problem here. There is only one of me with a knife, to four of you with guns. It's not even an issue. Now, our friend on the table over there is quite another story. He has already shot three people and, if you ask me, if he starts to get jumpy I reckon the next four people he is going to go for are the four people causing him the biggest threat."

"Actually," added Danny, addressing the guards in the same way that Brad did, "as much as I am looking forward to blowing that piece of shit away, I have to admit he has a point. I would kill you next, if I had to."

"You see," said Brad, "you're stuffed. Now I know you think you are doing the noble thing by hanging back here to protect these people, but I can assure you they don't need protecting any more. He has no interest in killing them. He only wants to kill my associate and me. I would suggest then that the four of you take your guns and get out of here right now. There's no point taking a risk. As we speak there are dozens of armed policemen on their way here to take care of business. You've done your bit, it's time to go home."

Three of the guards looked at each other, as if seeking each other's approval to do a runner. The guys in the lizard suit had a point. The decision seemed to be taken almost immediately.

"You can't leave us," screamed one of the female guests. "They'll kill us for sure if you go."

"Shut it, bitch," barked Danny, as the three guards moved towards the door. One guard remained, maybe he could still take this maniac down single handedly?

"So what's your fucking problem?" Danny

shouted at the remaining guard.

"I can't let you get away with this," the guard replied nervously.

"Fine," replied Danny. He fired his gun so casually that he didn't even appear to be aiming. The guard's chest exploded, and his body flew across the room smashing into a table. Walter flinched again at being exposed to such violence, to the extent that he almost forgot he had a knife pushed against his throat.

"Well that's taken care of that," said Danny. Brad had also wanted the guards to leave, to avoid unnecessary accidents. Regrettably, however, that was exactly what they had ended up with, an unnecessary accident. There always seems to be one "have a go" hero who thinks he can sort out the bad guys. On this occasion though, the hero was out of his depth, and was now dead. Brad checked Walter's pulse from the grip he had round his wrist to see how he was handling things. He wasn't too sure how he might be taking these unexpected events. If he flipped out it would be a perfectly normal reaction. The only problem with such a reaction is that it would have probably got him killed on the spot, and Brad with him.

"It's just you and me now, home boy," Danny went on, waving his gun at brad. "Let's talk about your buddy Mr Lee, and where he might be hiding."

The Earpiece

It was almost like a scene from a seventies disaster movie, when finally all the main characters are brought together. The audience in the theatre would already be guessing the odds on who was likely to survive. Danny, the bad guy, had a zero survival factor. Kingburger had already been shot and was on his way out, and Dilly also looked pretty vulnerable. Brad was in the role of Steve McQueen, so he was bound to make it to the sequel. As for Walter though, things looked grim. Throughout the plot he had established himself as a sad little runt, commanding a lot of audience sympathy, but just a lost cause at heart. That was the worse sort of character to play, bound to be killed off in the closing scenes. As the seconds passed Walter resigned himself to the fact that he was about to die. His quest for Drax Mantis had been an honourable one, almost as if it was straight from the script of *Galactic Encounter*. He realised, however, that he was no Jed Largo. No, the stage was almost empty for Walter, and the curtain was about to come down.

"This is how it is going to be," Brad began, barking orders at Danny. "Me and my hostage here are getting out of here, through the front door. If anybody tries to stop me then I slit this guy's throat, understand?"

"What the hell makes you think I give a fuck

285

about him?" laughed Danny, lining up his barrel with Walter.

"I don't suppose you do," replied Brad, "but others will, and that might keep me alive!"

"Hold on a second," interrupted Dilly, finally finding her voice. "In case you hadn't noticed there's a man dying here." She indicated to Kingburger. "And besides, that guy isn't called Brad or Ralph! He is Nathan West, the top Hollywood producer, you jerk!"

"Do you mind?" slammed Danny. "I'm trying to have a conversation here. This guy needs to know how he is going to die. Now, as I was saying..."

"But you've got the wrong man," Dilly persisted. "I don't know what he is doing with that knife, but I don't think anyone here is thinking rationally."

"Listen lady," Danny shouted. "This guy here is called Brad Clusky, not Nathan, or any bloody other stupid name. He is Brad Clusky, ex-SAS killer and first class scum bag."

Brad's heart sank as he heard the words. It was not the fact that Dilly was discovering the truth for the first time. It was the fact that forty people, most of whom he had never met before, now knew both his name, his face, and his ex-occupation. Coupling that with the fact that he had seemingly just taken a hostage at knife point at a murder scene, the odds were on that word was about to get out and in no time MI5 and MI6 would be launching a man hunt to bring him down. Worse still, there was a chance that Warren Kingburger would recognise Walter as the guy he gave two tickets to. If he remembered that he might also remember that the second ticket was for Nathan West, and what he was seeing now was anything but a hostage situation. It was that thought that made Brad slightly relieved that

Kingburger had been shot. Maybe it would cloud his memory enough to make him forget the names Nathan West and Mark Spencer.

"Nathan," said Dilly soulfully. "Is it true? Is your name really Brad? Are you really a secret agent or something?"

"I'm sorry Dilly," Brad replied. "It's true."

"You bastard," she shouted back, "and to think I had sex with you!"

"Whoa there," interjected Kingburger, lifting his head in obvious agony. Blood trickled down from the corner of his mouth. "What the hell do you mean by that? Is this the same Nathan who is supposed to be your fucking designer? You had sex with this guy? And when, may I ask, were you going to tell me about this, you slut!"

"Shut the fuck up," roared Danny. Kingburger's head slumped over again, and this time came to a rest on the edge of the table. "All of you, just shut the fuck up!" Danny went on. "I'm trying to kill somebody here. I don't need your constant bickering in my ears all the time. Christ, I'm losing my thread. Where was I? Oh yeah, lover boy here was going to tell me why I shouldn't end his life and that of his pathetic little hostage. Well come on Bradley, you got five seconds to convince me!"

"It's simple," Brad replied, still holding the knife with precise steadiness against Walter's throat. "You kill me, Ralph escapes. If Ralph escapes he blows the whistle on the whole deal. The job we did that went wrong becomes public knowledge. That won't make your President very popular with my Prime Minister!"

"But Ralph is still in the building," Danny replied, sliding himself down to sit on the edge of the table.

"All I have to do is torture a few people, perhaps yourself, until he comes out. It isn't that complicated."

"You're wrong," Brad replied. "I know what you did, but I'm one step ahead. About a week ago you broke into our hotel room, and accessed files on a lap top, correct?"

"Ouch," Danny replied in jest, "you are sharp. I was hoping you wouldn't find out about that. I guess I better give myself up."

"Trouble is," Brad went on, "you were either pushed for time or just plain bored. You didn't open all the files you needed to see, and that's not professional."

"This is shit," sighed Danny. "I saw enough on the lap top. You were planning to get two tickets for this gig, not one. You work together, so he must be here. It's black and white, buddy. I think your five seconds are up!"

Danny took careful aim, once again, at a point on Walter where he felt certain one bullet would pass straight through him and kill Brad as well.

"The second ticket was a contingency," Brad called. "Ralph is here, but he's in an operations van out back. Somewhere you can't reach him!"

"Prove it," demanded Danny, beginning to squeeze his trigger.

"No problem," said Brad. "But I'm going to need some help."

"You're out of luck," said Danny.

"Miss Bourgromenko," said Brad to Ingrid Bourgromenko, who was curled up on the floor under a nearby table, "would you come over here please."

It was the same Ingrid Bourgromenko who weeks ago, just before the Gresham job, Brad had listed as one of the best looking women on TV. That conversation seemed surreal now. He never imagined that he would ever meet Ingrid, let alone under these circumstances. The only reason he picked her was because she was one of the few hostages left that he actually recognised. Ingrid Bourgromenko was a young girl from Albania, who had become a well-known weather girl on breakfast television. Her peculiar accent, and uniquely strange good looks, had made her a household name. She was wearing a long silver dress, which didn't quite match the curve of her body, and Doctor Marten boots. Her pitch black hair was tied back in bunches, and her make up was smudged where she had been crying after witnessing the stream of murders. When Brad requested her company, her fear grew even more intense. She looked over to Danny as if seeking consent to move across the room, although she would have preferred to have stayed under the table.

"Well go on then," Danny shouted at her. "But this better prove something Brad, or the rest of the world will hold you personally responsible for Miss Bourgromenko's untimely demise."

Ingrid didn't like the sound of that. She had no plans of making tonight her last night on earth. Even though she didn't care much about sunny spells, heavy drizzle, and foggy patches, she wanted to carry on talking about them on television for some time yet. She nervously climbed out from under the table, and walked over to where Brad and Walter were standing. Walter was especially curious at this development. There was no mention of this when they were talking by the back door. It was, however, just another part of Plan B, which Brad was making up as he went along.

Jim Carley

"What," Ingrid began in trepidation, "what is it that you are wanting me for you to do?"

"Don't be nervous," said Brad. "I know you're scared, but nobody wants to hurt you. All I need is an extra hand, you see my other two are tied up with this guy."

"Cut the crap," said Danny. "I'm not a patient man. Let's get this charade over with."

"My ear," Brad said to Ingrid, completely ignoring Danny's taunts. "I want you to reach up to my ear, and take out the little black earpiece that is in there."

The request under any other circumstances would have seemed abnormal. In a world of abnormality though, it seemed more normal than not. Even Danny was curious at how this part of the proceedings was developing. Ingrid reached up to Danny's ear, and pulled out his earpiece.

"Good girl," said Brad. "That's very good. Now, if you don't mind excusing the wax, I want you to put it in your ear and tell me what you can hear."

Ingrid looked at Brad in curiosity at the request, but lifted the earpiece towards her own ear. Danny lifted his gun again, preparing himself to blow Brad, Walter and Ingrid away if this little scam fell through, which he expected it to. Ingrid fitted the earpiece neatly into her ear and, as soon as she did, her eyes opened in amazement.

"Noises I hear!" she exclaimed, turning to Danny. "The sound of a car I recognise, on a road, and a voice. Somebody is talking to me in a car."

"Actually it's a van," Brad pointed out. He was reading Danny's expression as he finally began to accept that Ralph wasn't in the building.

"He's not here is he?" said Danny, although the

290

question was rhetoric.

"And I am hearing also…." Ingrid went on.

"Oh, shut the fuck up," Danny interrupted in a blaze. "And take that fucking thing out of your ear." He was that close to putting a bullet in her. Ingrid reluctantly complied, and scurried off back under her table.

"I don't get it," said Danny. "If Ralph is outside in a van, why in God's name did you get two tickets for tonight's party? Unless…"

Not for the first time that evening, Danny was completely confused. His mind wandered off in an effort to explain the irrationality in a plan that required two tickets for only one operative on the inside. He scratched his head for a moment in confusion, allowing his gun to drop by his side. It was a mistake he wouldn't normally make. It was a mistake he wasn't going to get away with. In that second when his concentration had been broken, Warren Kingburger was starting to get his strength back. Almost effortlessly he reached across the table and grabbed Danny's gun from him.

The Law

Whilst all the confusion had been raging inside the Orbit Studio Experience, Ralph Lee was having an equally colourful time outside in the van. As the crow flies, the distance between the back of the Orbit Studio Experience and the front is literally a matter of metres. To drive it, however, is quite another story. The Victorian layout of the roads in London made any seemingly speedy manoeuvre a lengthy affair. Ralph had slid the van into reverse in order to back down the side street he was in. There was no room to turn around. He had cursed at this in the first instance. He should have thought about that before the job started, and parked the van accordingly. It was too late to worry about that now though. Brad needed him at the front of the restaurant, and he needed him there fast. The van spun out on to Shaftesbury Avenue, causing a motorcycle to slide out of control and through a shop window. A double decker night bus also had to swerve to avoid Ralph. He gunned the engine, spun the wheels, and completed an immaculate hand brake turn which pointed him in the direction of High Holborn.

"Shit," he cursed, it wasn't the direction he wanted. There was no way he could turn round either without causing more mayhem and destruction. His route from there had just become more difficult and complicated. At High Holborn he met the first of several sets of red lights, each eating into his time. His fingers drummed on the steering wheel in agitation. As soon as the lights turned to amber the van lurched forward, cutting up a black cab, and edging off onto Endell Street. That, however, was still taking him further away from Brad rather than nearer. At the end of Endell Street he cut back onto Long Acre, and finally he was heading in the right direction again. It was at that point that he started paying attention again to the various conversations he was overhearing in his headset which he still wore. Even he had no idea why Brad would want to involve somebody like Ingrid Bourgromenko in all this. As far as Ralph was concerned too many people were already involved, and things were too complicated. When Ingrid finally put the earpiece on though, Ralph knew he had to do something that would at least convince her that he was not in the restaurant. That was the only way that Brad and Walter would get out alive. He revved the engine when he felt sure she was wearing the earpiece. That seemed to work well. Then he started talking, the first things that came into his head.

"Ingrid. Ingrid please listen to me. You don't know who I am, but I don't want you or anybody else to get hurt. My name is Ralph I need you to tell the man with the gun that I am not in the restaurant. You can hear my van. You know that I must be outside, so tell him that."

Brad had chosen Ingrid well. He guessed that she would be convinced by Ralph, even if he had been standing in the next room. This little episode did, however, raise another problem. Although Ralph could still hear Brad, he could no longer talk to him. The only person left in the room who Ralph could communicate with was Walter, and he was the only person who couldn't talk because he still had a knife to his throat. As the van moved along the top of Covent Garden, Ralph found he was facing even more difficulties. He was moving back towards the crowded part of the West End, which had initially been taken over by all the razzmatazz surrounding the opening of the restaurant and then sent into hyper-drive by the sound of gun shots. As the van moved towards Leicester Square things became more and more hopeless. The chaotic crowd became deeper and more unruly almost by the yard. Ralph seemed to be the only person trying to get into Leicester Square, whilst everybody else was getting out. To make things worse, as the van sluggishly moved forward, a policeman emerged from the crowd and beckoned Ralph to stop. There was nowhere to escape, the crowd was too thick. Ralph reluctantly pulled down his window to greet the officer, confident that at that stage his own hand in all this chaos had not been recognised.

"Good evening, sir," said the police officer, a wrinkly man in his mid forties.

"Hi," Ralph replied.

"Do you mind telling me where you are headed this evening?"

"I've got a delivery," said Ralph. "Leicester Square." He switched off his headset. The last thing he wanted was for Walter to start worrying about the additional distraction. He had enough to deal with inside the restaurant.

"At this time of night?" the officer went on.

"I don't choose the hours."

"And do you always wear a personal stereo when you drive?"

"It's not a personal stereo," explained Ralph. "It's a headset. I'm a courier. Besides, I switched it off."

"I see," said the officer. "Listen sir, I'm afraid there seems to have been some sort of incident near Leicester Square this evening. I really don't think you are going to make it."

"Incident?" Ralph asked, playing ignorant. "What incident?"

"I really can't say, sir," the officer went on. "All I can suggest is that you try and turn back."

"Turn back?" laughed Ralph. "That is hardly very realistic with these crowds, is it?"

"I suppose not," the officer replied glumly. "You might try and reach as far as Charing Cross Road, then. At least from there you have a slight chance of heading north or south away from this area. At least until the crowds die down and we can fully analyse the situation."

"Okay," said Ralph. "I'll try." He put the van back in gear, and fired up a cigarette from the box he kept on the dashboard. He pulled away from the policeman, and further into the crowd. He laughed at how straight forward the encounter had been, and at the fact that the police really did have no idea as to what was going on. He switched the headset back on, and made contact with Walter.

"Walter," he said reassuringly, "I know you can hear me. From now on it is me and you, okay. Don't try and say anything because I know you can't. Just hang in there. I need about another five minutes and I'll be there. Oh, and if you can think of a way of passing that message on to Brad, without the pair of you getting killed, I'd be real grateful."

The Recovery

"Jesus, Warren," cried Dilly, "what the hell are you doing?"

Warren Kingburger was in obvious pain, holding his side with his left hand where his bullet wound was. The blood pumped out like a gushing river, staining his suit and the seat he was sitting on. He was visibly weakening by the second, he had lost too much blood to be completely in control of his senses. Having said that, he now had the gun, and with that asset anything was possible.

"Man," hollered Danny, "you better give me that gun back right now or I swear I'm gonna waste you!"

"Shut up and sit down," Kingburger said in pain, pointing the gun directly at Danny. "If you think, son, that I don't know how to handle this thing then you are gravely mistaken. Believe me, I don't need even half an excuse to put a bullet in you."

Danny reluctantly took a seat opposite Kingburger and Dilly.

"Keep those hands on the table," Kingburger added.

Walter almost felt like asking Brad whether or not Plan B had just changed any further, but he concluded instead that Plan B had probably had been abandoned ages ago, and they were probably already up to Plan X. Brad himself was feeling edgy. He was starting to feel confident with Danny as his opponent, but Kingburger was much more of a wild card. Danny was a military man and would have played by military rules. He wouldn't have taken unnecessary chances, even if he was a loud mouthed bastard. Kingburger, however, was an injured man incapable of thinking straight. With him in the hot seat there was no guarantee that the body count wouldn't raise any higher. Brad decided it was high time Walter and he pulled out, before things got any weirder. He took a chance, and began to nudge Walter towards the door, taking advantage of the change in the balance of power in the room.

"Hold it," called Kingburger, pointing the gun towards Brad. "I'm not finished with you yet, boy. You stay exactly where you are. The only people who are going to move are the hostages. They leave the building right now, agreed?"

"Fine," replied Brad. "All apart from this one," he indicated to Walter.

"We'll come back to him," Kingburger replied. "How about you, butt head?" he said to Danny. "Are you cool for these people to leave?"

"I'm cool," Danny replied, but his eyes gave away the fact that he was anxiously looking for a way to get his gun back.

"Right," Kingburger went on to the remainder of the guests, "I want you people to move out of here quickly and quietly. Straight to the front door, nice and slow."

The remainder of the guests began to pick themselves up from where they had collapsed around the room. Ingrid Bourgromenko crawled out from under her table, and joined the others. They all stood slowly, and shakily, the trauma of the experience already beginning to sink in. Visually they were similar to a line of troops on the Somme. They were exhausted, bedraggled, and wasted. Soon they would be free though, and it was that thought that saw them all safely through the door. After around five minutes the last of the hostages were gone. Only five people were left in the building now. Kingburger sat at the corner table, brandishing the gun at Danny opposite, with Dilly by his side. Dilly thought about leaving with the other hostages, but stayed put. She knew that she needed to look after Kingburger, despite all the things they had said to each other. Besides, she wanted to know how all this was going to end, and the best way to see that was on the inside. Brad and Walter stood a short distance away from the other three, the knife still poised at Walter's throat. Brad was wondering how long he could keep his arm there without it going to sleep, and possibly ripping out Walter's throat by accident in the process. Walter, however, out of the remaining five was perhaps in the best position. Other than Brad, nobody really knew who he was. Brad had already thought of that, and was trying to think of how that fact could be an asset.

"I've had a bad night, fellas," said Kingburger, in pain. "Tonight was supposed to be a milestone for me, but instead it has been a pile of shit. My restaurant was going to be a huge sensation, before you guys saw to it that it had the shit kicked out of it. I've got three dead bodies over there, blown to hell. My girl here has been having sex with some sort of terrorist. On top of all that, some bastard has stolen my top exhibit, Drax Mantis. You can call me stupid if you want, but I can't see any reason why any of you guys, with the exception of our last hostage friend, should get out of here alive tonight."

"What are you saying?" asked Dilly in confusion.

"God, you're stupid," Danny replied. "He's saying that he's got a good reason to kill all of us. That includes you for not being more careful as to who you sleep with. He's gonna waste us all and say it was an accident. Pretty easy to get away with if you have been shot and aren't totally in control of your senses."

"That would be your style," laughed Kingburger, "but not mine. No, everybody will get out of here alive, unless they do something really stupid! All I want is a few answers."

"That depends on the questions," said Danny.

"Well, why don't I start with you," Kingburger went on. "Who the hell are you, and why did you kill all these people?"

"You expect an answer to that?" Danny replied.

"His name is Dellapicho," Brad interrupted, "Danny Dellapicho. He used to be a special operative with the CIA, before they realised his true potential as an assassin."

"Watch your mouth Clusky," warned Danny. "You're already wearing dead man's clothes, don't give me an excuse to torture you too."

"And he's here to kill you, right?" Kingburger asked Brad.

"That's right."

"For what?"

"I can't tell you that, sir," Brad replied. "I gave an oath."

"I see," replied Kingburger. "Does it have anything to do with my restaurant?"

"No, sir, it doesn't," Brad answered.

"So why are you here?"

"I'm doing a job," said Brad. "It's how I make a living!"

"Are you going to cut that boy's throat?"

"If I have to. If circumstances give me no choice," Brad lied.

"I see," repeated Kingburger, "and have you ever slept with Dilly?"

"Yes, sir," Brad replied, "but I never meant to hurt her, or you for that matter. Things just seemed to get a little out of hand."

"You're damn right they did," interrupted Dilly. "If I'd known that you were some seedy low life scum you would never have got to first base!"

"Shut up," muttered Kingburger to Dilly. "The fact of the matter is that if this man actually was the character he was portraying, you would have slept with him without remorse. That hardly makes you an innocent party in all this."

"It was my fault, sir," Brad went on. "I take full responsibility for sleeping with your girlfriend." That didn't come out quite as Brad would have wanted it to, but he felt that Dilly's reputation might just survive this one. What was making his dialogue more convincing was the inclusion of the word "sir" when referring to Kingburger. Brad wasn't sure why he had adopted this practice, but it seemed to be going down well even if it appeared that Kingburger might die from his injury at any second.

"So why did you need to approach her in the first place?" Kingburger asked, turning his attention back to Brad.

"I needed to be at this party tonight," Brad answered. "I needed Dilly to get me tickets for tonight."

"That's a lie," Dilly interjected. "I never gave that

man tickets!"

"That's true," added Brad, "she didn't."

"She must have done," said Danny. "I saw it on his computer files!"

"If Dilly didn't give you tickets," continued Kingburger, "how did you get in?"

"If I told you that," said Brad, "you wouldn't believe me."

"Wait a second," interrupted Danny. "Now, before you stole my gun off me I was having an important thought about this. You really know how to fuck up a guy's concentration, do you know that?"

"This job you're doing," Kingburger continued in conversation with Brad, ignoring Danny's interruption, "did you come here to steal Drax Mantis?"

"Yes," replied Brad. "Yes, I did."

"Why?" asked Kingburger. "Why the hell would you go to such elaborate lengths to do something like that? Was it worth it? I mean, there are three dead men over there! Was it worth stealing a toy for that?"

Kingburger coughed violently at the end of the question. His pain was obviously increasing. Dilly eased her arm round him to comfort him, her hand ran through the little remaining hair that he still had on his head.

"Believe me Mr Kingburger," said Brad. "If this had gone to plan nobody would have died. Mr Dellapicho killed the DJ and the security guards. That was his choice, not mine"

"Is there anything I can say to make you give yourself up?" Kingburger enquired. He had recovered from his coughing fit, and was now trying to focus his aim as carefully as he could on Brad. "You do realise the police will stop you, if I fail."

"I've come too far, Mr Kingburger," Brad responded. "I'm walking out the front door right now, no surrender." Brad nudged Walter again, and they began to slowly walk towards the door.

"Or else your hostage dies?" asked Kingburger.

"That's right," said Brad.

"Listen, buddy," Danny said to Kingburger. "If this guy walks out of here alive a lot of your fellow countrymen in Washington are gonna be real pissed. In addition, the chances are they will send someone to clip me for screwing up! Do you want to think about that for a second? Do you want that on your conscience?"

"Why don't you just shut up," Kingburger replied. "You're a murderer plain and simple, and you're going to jail. Just be thankful this isn't Texas, or you might be facing the chair!"

"Please, Mr Kingburger," blurted Walter, joining the conversation for the first time. "It's me, Mark Spencer. The guy who stood about outside your restaurant, remember? You gave me my ticket, you personally! I would never have come if you hadn't invited me, and I'm too young to die. Please do what this guy says, don't give him an excuse to kill me. If I have to go with him then so be it. Maybe it will give me a chance to live. Maybe I will get to see my mum again!" At that point he inadvertently burst into tears. Brad couldn't tell if they were real or not, but they were certainly doing the trick.

"Okay," Kingburger responded. "It looks like you're out of here, Mr Clusky. If you don't want to surrender, then you better take your chances with the police outside."

"Are you nuts?" hollered Dilly. "You can't just let

that man escape!"

Escape, however, was exactly what Kingburger let Brad do. Brad and Walter edged slowly to the door, the knife still jammed against Walter's throat. Danny sighed in failure as he watched them go. Even with Kingburger's weakened condition, however, it was too risky to try and steal the gun back. He had failed, and he knew he must face the consequences. The thoughts of certain doom, however, never had the opportunity to take hold. They were washed away in an instant by sudden realisation, and the penny finally dropping.

"That's it," he cried. "I've worked it out." At that point though, it was already too late. Brad and Walter had already disappeared into the shrill of noise outside.

The Crowd

"Christ," said Walter, "are you going to take that bloody thing out of my neck, and let go of me?"

"Not yet," said Brad, "we still have an audience." Indeed, there was quite an audience, an audience of several thousand. Not only were there the remains of the panic-stricken crowd and a few disorientated celebrities, but there was also an audience of millions linked in through *Capital Night Out*, whose cameras were still rolling. Luck was still on Brad's and Ralph's side though. The sheer number of people in the crowd meant that the people were having trouble dispersing. Leicester Square tube station had been closed due to the volume of people, leaving no other real courses of escape. Instead the crowd just milled around, some screaming and others subdued, just waiting for someone in authority to tell them what to do. The crowd plugged up the streets, bringing the West End to a standstill. Police patrol cars couldn't get anywhere near. A few policemen had arrived on foot, but had no idea what they were supposed to be doing. Some tried to hopelessly control the crowd, whilst others looked in trepidation at the Orbit Studio Experience, uncertain whether or not to venture inside and tackle the gunman. The crack armed policed team who had been sent to take care of the mysterious gunman were the only ones who had got through, but they were now at the back of the restaurant where Ralph had been parked. They were a safe distance away from Brad and Walter, and posed no real threat to them.

The blue van swung out from a side street, and into the crowd. Ralph needed to get through these people, and fast, before a police presence could really establish itself. The sound of police sirens could already be heard just a few streets away. The van was hard to manoeuvre with so many people. Ralph was convinced he was going to hit someone. He blasted the horn, and rolled down his window to swear at the masses.

"Get your fat arses out of my way," he shouted to a group of girls. They gave him the two finger sign, but moved anyway. The van, despite the number of people, made rapid progress through the crowd. People just seemed to move out of the way at the last minute, before ending up with flat feet or broken shins. Although progress was faster than could be expected, it was still slow enough to allow a couple of policemen to move in on Brad and Walter as they stood at the main door.

"Back off," shouted Brad, "or this guy gets it!"

"Take it easy, mate," said the shorter of the two policemen, slightly confused as to why Brad was wearing a lizard suit. He came to the conclusion that this man was obviously disturbed, and should be approached with extreme caution. "Just let that guy go, and we can talk about this."

"You think I'm nuts?" asked Brad.

"I never said that," said the policeman, spreading his arms in a symbolic fashion as if he was calming Brad in some way. Just then, the van at long last emerged from the crowd. The side door slid open.

"Don't get in that van," shouted the policeman.

"Anybody need a lift?" asked Ralph, poking his

head out of the window.

"Listen up, copper," Brad said, turning to the policeman. "I'm getting in this van, and I'm taking this hostage with me. If I see or hear a police patrol anywhere near me, then this guy has his insides rearranged and his body gets thrown out the back door." Brad was so convincing in his description that even Walter was getting worried.

"Don't worry," assured the policeman, "there's no need to hurt him."

With that Brad pushed Walter into the van, and jumped in behind him.

"Be seeing you, boys," he called out to the police, slamming the door shut behind him. Ralph hit the gas, and the van sped away.

The policemen looked at each other in disarray.

"Bastard," said the tall one, "I hope he gets his head blown off." His colleague, however, was already one step in front. He was already on his radio back to base.

"This is Tango Delta to Alpha Yankee, are you receiving, over?"

"Receiving you Tango Delta," crackled the radio, "go ahead."

"Yeah," the policeman went on, "I've got two suspects in a blue Bedford van, no plates, heading north from Leicester Square. They are armed and dangerous, one has a knife and they might have guns as well. They have a hostage, repeat, they have a hostage, and they are threatening to kill him."

"Roger that, Tango Delta," the radio crackled again.

"If you want my opinion, for what it's worth," the policeman went on, "I think we might need a helicopter."

The Fourth Kill

The police team at the back door of the Orbit Studio Experience were ready to move. They were kitted out in black suits, with the word "POLICE" in big white letters across their backs. The only other thing that gave away their identities were their baseball caps, with their distinctive checker board rims, and the large automatic machine guns they were carrying. There were eight of them in all, and they were here on business. A small metal battering ram caved the back door in, sending Danny's chain flying. The eight men eagerly piled inside.

Now only three people remained on the ground floor, sitting round a table at one side. Danny Dellapicho seemed to be having some form of spasm, as his brain finally worked out a credible explanation as to why Brad and Ralph had two tickets, but why Ralph wasn't in the restaurant. Kingburger wasn't especially impressed by this outburst. As far as he was concerned Danny Dellapicho didn't give his would-be-victims the slightest bit of credit. They were far too shrewd and smart, even for an experienced killer. Although he hadn't yet mentioned it, Kingburger had worked out several minutes earlier what Danny had just realised. Between the time he had been shot and when he was strong enough to talk again, Kingburger's mind had been methodically analysing the events of the evening. He knew there was something odd about the names Mark Spencer and Nathan West when Walter had originally given them to him. Although he hadn't thought about it since then, he never forgot a name. Now the jigsaw was complete. Mark Spencer, or whoever he was, was the third man. The third man that Dellapicho had missed. If Kingburger had thought that Mark Spencer was really in danger he would never have let Brad leave with him. He recognised, though, that if these guys wanted Drax Mantis so badly they were prepared to go to these lengths, then maybe they should get to keep him.

"Don't you see?" shouted Danny. "Don't you see what you've just done? You should never have let those guys go!"

"Because of the third man?" asked Kingburger, coughing violently again. Blood began to well in the back of his throat. His body seemed to sink lower in the seat, but he still managed to keep the gun on Danny. Dilly drew closer to him to comfort him.

"You knew?" asked Danny, in surprise. "How could you know?"

"Know what?" Dilly asked in confusion. "What are you on about, a third man?"

"I think Mr Dellapicho knows all to well," Kingburger said with a smile.

"But I don't get it," Dilly went on. "Tell me."

Another surge of pain swept through Kingburger. This time he needed both hands to nurse his side, dropping the gun to the table. Danny was on it like a cat jumps on a mouse. He spun it round and turned it on Kingburger and Dilly.

"Well well," Danny grinned. "This is just the break that I've been waiting for." He stood from the table and edged away slightly in the direction of the main door. "I guess I better be heading off now," he went on. "There is every chance that I might catch up with those boys, and give them what's been coming to them. As for you guys, well I guess it's time for you to check out too."

"You're going to kill us?" Dilly shrieked. "What the hell for?"

"He's not going to kill us," whispered Kingburger, still just able to manage speech.

"What makes you feel so sure, Boss Hogg?" laughed Danny, waving the gun at his two captives.

At that second the armed police unit crashed into the room. The eight officers piled in, automatic machine guns at the ready. They poised themselves to fire, rapidly spreading out across the room and taking cover behind pillars and display cabinets. Danny was totally taken aback.

"Shit," he murmured, as the police marksmen moved in faster than a swarm of bees.

"Put the gun down," barked one of the officers. Danny just froze. If anything his grip on the gun seemed to tighten, and his aim stiffen on Kingburger and Dilly. Dilly buried her head into Kingburger's shoulder, who was now on the verge of unconsciousness. Unfortunately for Danny, he wasn't going to get a second warning. A blaze of machine gun fire rang out across the room, each bullet ripping into Danny's torso. Blood splashed everywhere as his body was lifted up into the air from the force of the impact, his own gun spinning harmlessly out of his hand. When his body finally came down again it crashed into the glass cabinet that had previously been the home of the Drax Mantis action figure. The glass splintered as the body finally came to a rest, several shards impaling Danny.

Moments later the place was crawling with police, and paramedics were desperately trying to save Warren Kingburger's life. For Dilly Foxtrot, however, the worst of it was over. In a few hours time the whole thing would have become a mere tabloid sensation, and all she would have to worry about would be her nightmares.

The Police

"Thank God for that," cried Walter, finally relieved at having the carving knife removed from his neck. "You know I think you drew blood. Why did you have to press so hard? Couldn't you have just waved it about and pretended that you might stab me with it?"

"Have you never heard of authenticity?" asked Brad, who was already easing himself into Ralph's control seat in the back of the van.

"Still," said Walter, nursing the scratch on his neck, "it hardly matters now. We've got away with it, although I never wanted anybody to get hurt. You've got to believe that. I've got to be honest I never thought it would be anything like this."

"I told you before," said Brad, "that wasn't your fault. That guy wanted to kill us, not you, and he didn't care how many other people he had to hurt in the process. You can't account for people like that."

"Do you think he's going to chase us?" Walter went on.

"I tell you this, Walter," Brad answered, "if that guy gets out of that restaurant without a bullet in him he's a better man than I am."

"Can I see Drax now?" Walter asked. "Is that okay, since we are in the clear now!"

"Get out of the fucking way," hollered Ralph up front to some people trying to cross the road in front of the van.

"We haven't got away with anything yet," Brad pointed out to Walter, sliding on a headset and logging into the system.

"What do you mean?" asked Walter. "I heard what you said to the police back there. You said if they chase us then you are going to kill me, as it were. No police chief in his right mind is going to want that sort of blood on his hands!"

"You're a bit behind the times," said Ralph from the front. "Most of the coppers I've ever met tend to want to shoot first and ask questions later. If some poor innocent bastard gets shot along the way then so be it. Then again, you're not some poor innocent bastard. You're in this up to your neck!"

"Okay," said Brad, linking up with the main police computer at Scotland Yard. Despite the movement of the van, the satellite dish on the roof was still working, and allowed a link up over a cellular phone line. Brad didn't know as much as Ralph about computers, but he knew enough to carry out a simple hacking job, such as getting into Scotland Yard. "It look's like we've got ourselves some serious heat. I'm counting over forty police patrols on this one."

"Forty!" Ralph shouted back in astonishment. "Are you serious?"

"Certainly am. Most of those seem destined for the restaurant though. I reckon we are going to have to deal with about fifteen cars!"

"Oh my God," said Walter, slapping his brow with his hand. "Just as soon as I'm convinced things are not going to get any worse, they get worse. Do you realise that so far today I have been wired up like Christmas tree lights, forced to strip a man naked and hide him in a mountain of bean cans, watched three men be executed, and then had a knife stuck in my throat for what seemed like forever? Now, after all that, I find that I am in a beat up van trying to outrun fifteen police cars across North London. I don't believe it, I just don't believe it!"

Back at the Orbit Studio Experience the street was now full of police cars. Armed officers were moving in on the restaurant itself, whilst others were going straight through to pursue the van. The West End, normally lit up by the neon lights of nightclubs, was now providing a spectacular light show comprising of dozens of police cars, a constant strobe of blue and red. In addition to the police cars, a significant number of fire trucks and ambulances had also now broken through the barricade of the crowd, and behind them came an endless stream of news vans with reporters. Anybody and everybody was trying to get to Leicester Square to be a part of these obscene events.

"They are on the scene back there," Brad reported to his two companions. "It looks like Dellapicho is dead, and it sounds as if Kingburger is in a pretty bad way."

"What about the girl?" asked Ralph.

"They're not saying anything about her," Brad explained. "She must be okay."

"Maybe you should watch out for those maintenance payments then," joked Ralph.

"For sure," Brad replied laughing. His laughter was cut short, however, when he realised from the screen in front of him that a helicopter had been scrambled. "Shit," he cursed. "It looks like we are going to have some company. They've scrambled a chopper to come after us!"

"Great," Ralph replied, "another helicopter is all

we need. Maybe this is going to be our last waltz after all!"

"If I remember right," interrupted Walter, "you two don't have a very good record at escaping from helicopter chases. Am I right?"

"Shut up," said Brad. He was really getting tired of Walter, "Just shut up!"

The Helicopter

The police helicopter soared above some of the most famous landmarks in London. It whirred its way past Big Ben as it struck midnight, onwards to Nelson's Column and Trafalgar Square, and finally to Soho. The crowd below were still causing gridlock, but the police were starting to establish themselves. Irate cab drivers were instantly defused, and lines of people were being directed towards Covent Garden, Piccadilly Circus and Tottenham Court Road in an effort to unplug the streets. The people looked peculiar to the helicopter crew. It was almost as if they were ants and the Orbit Studio Experience was their ant hill. The spectators were the worker ants, wondering around aimlessly, relatively uncertain of their position in the grand scheme of things. The police were the soldier ants, dark and forceful, barking orders at the workers. As for the queen, well maybe she was the knock out blonde in the red blood stained dress. There was no time to stop there though, there were suspects to be caught and questioned. If the squad cars were going to pull that off they would need all the help in the air they could get. Experience had taught them how easy it was to lose suspect vehicles on dark streets. They had no intention of letting that happen tonight. They headed north, constantly north, on the trail of the blue van.

"They are giving out an ETA of five minutes on

us," reported Brad, as he tuned in to a police frequency on the receiver equipment in front of him. "They're moving really fast!"

"What's the big deal?" asked Walter. "I mean, they are up there and we are down here. Even if they catch up with us there's nothing they can do about it!"

"You don't get it, do you?" Brad sighed. "If the helicopter catches up with us they can monitor our movements. They can direct every police car in London to our position. In short, if they pin point us then we are screwed!"

"I see," Walter pondered. "I hadn't thought of it like that."

Despite their predicament, the van was making good progress. By the time the helicopter was first scrambled, the van was already past Euston and heading through Camden. The lateness of the hour favoured Ralph and his erratic driving style. There were few other cars about, and those that did get in the way were easily negotiated at speeds of eighty and ninety miles per hour. There were no grounds for complacency though. Whatever speed they managed the helicopter could match it, and then some. What's more, the helicopter didn't have any obstacles such as other cars or red lights to worry about.

"Don't you think we are going a little fast?" Walter asked Ralph. "I'm sure this road has a forty mile per hour limit!"

"If you don't want to spend the rest of the night in a cell," Ralph bawled, "you'd best leave the driving to me!"

At that point the first police car screeched out from a side street behind them. The driver struggled to correct the steering, pulling the car heavily across the road and on to the trail of the van. The blue light on the roof flashed violently, and the siren was at top volume.

"Shit," cried Brad, "where did he come from?"

"Don't worry," assured Ralph. "I can take this one."

"The others can't be too far behind," Brad went on.

"Don't worry," repeated Ralph. With that he inadvertently changed carriageways, on to the right hand lane. The force was enough to knock Brad out of his chair. Oncoming cars swerved to avoid him, with one almost smashing headlong into the police car.

"Bloody hell," screamed Walter. "Are you trying to kill somebody?"

"Just hang on," ordered Ralph, pumping the gears and pedalling the gas. The steering wheel spun violently from side to side. "I nearly had him then, but this time he won't be so lucky!" The van abruptly spun into a left hand turn from the right lane, at almost ninety degrees. It lined up precisely with a side street and disappeared down it. Throughout the manoeuvre Ralph never dropped below sixty. The police car tried to copy him, but ended up losing control in a spin. By the time it came to a rest it had already smashed through the front window of a Post Office and become embedded in the counter.

"Yee hah," cried Ralph. "That got him!"

"I can't believe you did that," Walter shouted. "You might have killed those officers."

"Relax," Brad replied, picking himself up off the floor of the van. "At that speed they probably only got a few bumps and bruises. Think of it like the *A-Team* - nobody ever really gets hurt!" The van cruised out of the end of the side street, and back on to a major road.

"You don't know that for sure," Walter went on.

"Trust me," Brad replied, checking his headset. "I've been in enough smashes to know!"

"Maybe, if we crash," Walter went on, "you might find it a new kind of experience altogether. Perhaps you'll be wondering what you did with your legs?"

"Give it a rest," Ralph butted in. "I promise you we are not going to crash."

"We haven't got time to worry about that anyway," said Brad, checking the console screen again. "We've got more squad cars coming in fast, and that isn't far behind them."

"We are going to have to go to ground," Ralph suggested, implying they should try and hide rather than escape.

"How?" asked Brad. "Even if they can't see us, that engine is so hot it will be giving off a thermal image like *The Towering Inferno*."

"Are we near Finsbury Park?" Ralph asked.

"This is not the time for sight seeing," Brad shouted.

"Yes," Walter came in. "It's up on the left there somewhere!"

"I thought so," Ralph replied.

"Does anybody want to tell me what the hell we are talking about?" shouted Brad.

"I've got an idea," Ralph replied. "It's almost as daft as beating up a guy in a lizard suit and pinching his costume, but it just might work. I used to see a girl from round here, and if I remember right..."

"You better remember fast," Brad butted in. "We have got two squad cars literally in the next street, and that helicopter will be beaming a spot light on us in less than sixty seconds."

Meat

Ralph spun the wheel again, without changing gear, and the van spun off on to what appeared to be a small industrial estate.

"This is the place," he beamed. "Do either of you guys remember the space chase scene in *Galactic Encounter*?"

"What are you doing?" Walter screamed again. He felt like all he had ever done in his life was accuse Ralph of doing stupid things, but each accusation seemed perfectly justified. "This is a no through road. If they find us down here then it's curtains for sure."

"Bear with me," Ralph replied. "I think you're going to like this!"

Behind them a police car zoomed across the end of the road, losing their trail by assuming they were still heading out of London. At that moment only Ralph knew exactly where they were heading. Above them the incoming roar of the helicopter was becoming increasingly audible.

The van wove its way around the different business units. There was a plumbing centre, a graphic design studio, and a lawnmower warehouse, to name but a few of the businesses that had ended up down there. The estate was seemingly deserted at the lateness of the hour. Normally you would expect to find a beat up Ford Escort, parked up and being used as a vending stand for the local drug dealers or a Jaguar with some business man inside, sorting out a local prostitute. There was none of that tonight though. The coast was perfectly clear.

The van continued to jerk sharply, with Walter and Brad giving up any chance of ending up anywhere else but on the floor. Then Ralph saw what he was looking for. The sign that marked the last business unit told him he was where he wanted to be.

"W.G. Caruthers and Son," muttered Ralph, reading the sign as the van rapidly approached it. "Cash and Carry Butchers and Meat Merchant!"

"Butchers?" questioned Walter.

"Meat Merchant?" echoed Brad.

"Hold on," shouted Ralph. "This might hurt just a little."

With that he put his foot to the floor, and accelerated into the biggest building belonging to W.G. Caruthers and Son. It was a fairly large warehouse, with thin corrugated walls. The van hit the wall head on, smashing a large panel and sending fragments of plaster in all directions like lethal missiles. In the back of the van there was chaos. Brad and Walter were slung around like stuffed toys, and hurled to the floor again by the force of the impact. Walter's new glasses went flying, and were smashed to pieces. As if that wasn't bad enough, the various monitors and hardware in the van began to dislodge themselves and started falling on top of the pair of them. Needless to say their screams said it all.

"Hang in there fellas," said Ralph, who was already suffering from whiplash. "This isn't over yet!"

The van was now hurtling across the darkness of the warehouse, smashing into various machines used to dismember the carcasses of frozen cattle and package them into handy size chunks ready for the oven. Ralph was only just maintaining control, guiding the van towards a large metal box in the corner, the size of a small house. The box wasn't really a box though, it was in fact W.G.'s main carcass freezer. The van careered through the side of the freezer, impacting on the far wall and coming to a rest. The internal red lights inside the freezer came on, flooding the van with crimson. There was a moment's silence before Ralph's plan finally came to fruition. With the structural stability of the freezer in tatters, the beams holding up the menagerie of frozen carcasses collapsed, bringing down at least thirty frozen animals of various descriptions on top of the van. The murmuring noises coming from Brad and Walter in the back told Ralph that they had survived.

"Walter," Ralph called, slumping back in his seat and nursing a cut on his face where the windscreen had caved in.

"Yes," replied a voice from somewhere in the back of the van.

"You know I said we wouldn't crash," Ralph went on.

"I remember," the voice said again.

"Well," said Ralph. "I lied."

The Press Conference

Dilly Foxtrot looked as if she hadn't slept. Her red dress was smeared with grime, stained with blood, and torn in several places. Her eyelids were heavy, and her whole face seemed to sag. Five hours had passed since she had walked out of the Orbit Studio Experience after witnessing Danny Dellapicho's demise. Since then she had been interviewed by a plethora of policemen about the events of the evening. After a while it seemed like it was the same questions again and again and again. She had intended to travel with Warren Kingburger to the hospital. She had been with him almost constantly since the police and paramedics had arrived. In no time at all they had him strapped to a stretcher, and heading for the back of an ambulance. She would have climbed in with him if he personally hadn't stopped her.

"Don't come with me," he managed to whisper to her as they carried him away.

"Why not?" she asked. "You need somebody to be with you."

"No," he replied. "What I need is for somebody to take care of things here. Somebody smart. Somebody with their head screwed on."

"But Warren," she went on. It felt strange now to call him Warren, when she was used to addressing him in public as Mr Kingburger.

"But nothing," Kingburger replied. "I need you to face the music for me."

"But," she hesitated, "but I love you." It was the first time she had ever said it, to anyone.

"I know you do, kid," he replied, reaching his hand out to take hers. "I love you too. That's why I need you to take care of things. I wouldn't trust anybody else." They smiled at each other, and she bent over to kiss his cheek.

"Take care, Mr Big," she whispered. "Don't go dying on me now!"

"Count on it," he said as he was finally lifted into the ambulance. The doors closed, the blue light began to flash, and the siren shrieked as the ambulance pulled away.

The police had given a statement to the press at three in the morning. Dilly, wishing to live up to Kingburger's expectations, thought it was necessary that Orbit made its own response. She assembled what was left of her staff, and set them to the task. Her aim was to hold a press conference before the breakfast television news broadcast. If possible, she would even get into the late editions of the morning papers. To the credit of her staff the press conference was put together in two hours. At five o'clock exactly Dilly Foxtrot walked into a medium sized conference room in a Central London hotel. She had not bothered to change her clothes. She wanted the world to see what that evening had taken out of her. Designer suits and haircuts were the very last things on her mind. There must have been a hundred journalists in the room, sat down in rows. Each held a camera, or a dictaphone, or a note pad. At the back of the room the various TV cameramen were lined up. The faces in the room all turned to look at Dilly as she walked in. Each was startled in some way to see such a glamorous woman looking so washed out. The pause was only momentary however, and was rapidly followed by an arsenal of camera flashes exploding in her face. The flashes didn't bother her though, she had already lived enough shocks for one night. She made her way through the room of reporters, to a small desk at the front of the room set out with a cluster of microphones and a glass of water. The water she ignored, choosing instead to fire up a cigarette which she had pinched from a porter in the corridor. She took a seat, and surveyed her audience. How very different they all were to the audience of party animals that Warren Kingburger had addressed only hours earlier.

"Good morning ladies and gentleman," she began, "and thank you for joining me at this very early hour of the morning. I would like to give you my account of the events that occurred last night at the Orbit Studio Experience, at our restaurant." she gave special emphasis to the word "our", because for the first time she felt as if some part of it belonged to her personally.

"During the opening gala we hosted last night, a gun man managed to infiltrate the building. We are co-operating with the police on this matter, and consequently I cannot divulge any information relating to his identity. The police have allowed me to confirm though, that this man was responsible for the deaths of three innocent people at our party. We are truly sorry for that, and at this moment in time our thoughts and condolences go out to the families of those that died. I can also tell you that Warren Kingburger, the proprietor of the Orbit Studio Group, was injured during the events. I am told by the hospital, though, that the operation he has just undergone appears to have been very successful."

"What about the knifeman and the blue van?" asked a reporter from *The Sun*.

"There are other suspects," Dilly went on, "but they are still at large."

"Are they also involved in the murders?" another reporter asked.

"No," replied Dilly. "I do not believe so."

"There is an allegation that the other men were involved in some sort of robbery," said a female journalist, "is that true?"

"We will be carrying out a full inventory of our exhibits just as soon as the police have concluded their forensic examination."

"Do they have a hostage?"

"A man was seen being held by the suspects at knife point, but there is no indication that they are still detaining him. We are not sure who he was, and the police cannot confirm at this time whether or not he is now safe."

"Miss Foxtrot," came another questioning voice. "Can you tell us how these additional suspects managed to escape?"

"As your colleague mentioned earlier," said Dilly, "they had a van. That was how they escaped. There was a police chase, but it failed to stop them. I understand from the police that the vehicle was recovered from a meat merchants on a trading estate in North London about an hour ago, following an explosion."

"Very unusual," *The Sun* man said. "Why would they go to a meat merchants?"

"Well," replied Dilly, inhaling her cigarette, "I'm

no expert on these things, but I gather there was a helicopter involved. This is a wild stab in the dark, but I reckon they were copying a scene from *Galactic Encounter*, the space chase scene."

This was the part of the police statement which she knew was wrong, and she knew that Kingburger would know that it was wrong. Jthe police statement made no attempt to explain the link between *Galactic Encounter* and the escape but to Dilly it was obvious. For the past few months she had ate, slept and drunk *Galactic Encounter*. It was now time for her to show the world that she actually knew a little bit about it.

"You see," Dilly begun, "Drax Mantis is in his Cybercopter, circling Leibfield Space Port on the trail of Jed Largo and his companions. Jed is wise to this though, and knows Drax is coming. Also, as this isn't the first run-in Jed has had with Drax, they have a bit of an idea as to what kind of hardware he's packing on the Cybercopter."

"Is this relevant?" asked a young girl.

"Bear with me, toots," Dilly replied, "I'm about to fill in the gaps that the police have left out. You see, Jed knows that if Drax sees his cruiser then he would have no problem in blowing him to shit, if you would excuse my language. Jed thus needs to get under cover. Drax is a bad ass dude though, and he has thermal imaging cameras on board, so he can trace the thermal image of the cruisers engine even if it is parked up out of sight. Now, Jed Largo is a smart boy, and speeds off to this chemical factory he knows of downtown where they've got a chiller big enough to hold a space station. They hide in there whilst Drax is totally flummoxed up above. Cool idea, huh! And that is exactly what those boys last night did."

"Hold on a moment," said a well spoken society reporter. "Are you saying that the suspects in question outsmarted the police by hiding their van in a meat merchant's freezer?"

"I'm not saying anything," Dilly replied evasively, "but you have to admit that if you bury a van under half a ton of frozen cattle, it's hardly likely to show up on a thermal image camera."

"Are you suggesting," the same reporter went on, "that the conduct of the police was lacking professional integrity last night?"

"No comment!"

"Do you blame them for the death of the three men?"

"No comment!"

"Are you suggesting that the police should have been more aware with the script of this film, *Galactic Encounter* did you say it was called?"

"No comment!"

"One last question," said the man from *The Sun*. "Did Jed Largo get away with it?"

"Yeah," Dilly replied with a smile. "That is what I love about the movies, the good guys always win. It's just a shame it's not always like that in real life."

W.G. Caruthers & Son

"Of all the people to remember a scene out of *Galactic Encounter*," said Brad, "I never thought it would be you."

"You were the one who took me to see it," Ralph replied.

"Lucky I did," said Brad.

The three men had pulled themselves out of what was left of the van. It was covered in an assortment of frozen bodies, mainly pork and beef, which were now rapidly defrosting. It was abundantly clear that this was going to be the van's final resting place. It was an eerie sight, the van embedded in a tomb of meat, illuminated by the red lighting. Walter Bridgenorth sat down on a wrecked mincing machine outside the freezer, nursing a nasty bump on his head which had left him mildly concussed. "I never knew they even had meat merchants in London," he said. "How did you know this was here?"

"I tried to tell you earlier," explained Ralph. "I used to see a girl from around here. She still lived with her parents, so we used to drive down here late at night to get our kicks. I never thought I'd end up back here though. Fate moves in mysterious ways!" He lit up a slightly bent cigarette and offered one to Brad who took it.

"I think I've earned this," he said, lighting up. The

three of them just sat there in the vast emptiness of the warehouse, slumped over various machines used to dismember cows and pigs. The machines were all neatly laid out in lines, apart from the ones that had been on the trajectory of the van as it had careered through the wall, leaving a trail of destruction in its path. Ralph walked over to the wall where there was a line of coat hooks. He took a white boiler suit off one of the pegs and carried it back over to the other two.

"Here," he said, throwing the boiler suit at Brad. "You'd best change out of that daft looking lizard suit."

"Thanks," said Brad. "Hey, do you hear that?"

"I can't hear anything," Ralph replied.

"Exactly," said Brad. "No sirens. No helicopter. I think we're in the clear!"

"I think he might be right," added Walter.

"Well, we'd best get on with things," said Ralph. "Morning is on its way, and I bet the guys who work here start early. I'm going to sneak around outside and line us up with some wheels. Brad, you'd best set the charges in the van, after you've got changed. Walter can probably help with that. I'll see you in a while." Ralph strutted out of the big hole the van had left in the wall, and left the other two by themselves. It was the first time Brad and Walter had really been alone since they entered the Orbit Studio Experience several hours earlier. They both knew that a short while later they would probably never see each other again.

"Quite a ride, eh?" Brad grinned, inhaling heavily on his cigarette.

"I suppose you could say that," Walter smiled back.

Brad stripped off the Mahnja suit. He still had his

dinner shirt on underneath, and he pulled the boiler suit over the top. Where the Mahnja suit had been too small, the boiler suit was too big, making him look a bit like a kid who had been trying on his dad's clothes.

"I'm sorry," said Walter apologetically.

"What the hell are you sorry for?" Brad replied.

"I'm sorry it went wrong," Walter went on. "I'm sorry that those people got killed. I'm sorry that your van got bust up. I'm sorry that Oswald got the shit kicked out of him. I'm sorry that the guy who owns this place is going to have to start paying higher insurance premiums. I'm sorry all round, I suppose."

"Hey," said Brad, "I'm not going to have this conversation again. We've been through this enough times."

"You know," Walter went on, "when you first came in my shop I didn't offer you my sympathy, I just saw you as an opportunity to get something I wanted. What I wanted was a toy, pure and simple. Okay, maybe it was a rare toy, but it was still a toy. Nothing but a piece of plastic! Look at me, for Christ's sake, I'm twenty six years old. I should be thinking about careers, and families, and mortgages. I shouldn't be thinking about sodding toys."

"Is that so," said Brad, opening one of the pockets on Mahja's utility belt and pulling out a small black plastic figure. "So you won't be wanting this then?" He passed the figure across to Walter, who held out his hand to receive it.

Brad walked off towards the van, leaving Walter to have a moment alone. Walter just sat there in silent awe. In his hands he held a Drax Mantis action figure with a rocket pack, the rarest toy in the entire *Galactic Encounter* range. It was a unique feeling, after all they had gone through. After all the danger and the drama, the clashes and the close calls, Walter finally had what he had wanted all his life. He felt like Edmund Hillary at the summit of Everest. He had everything now. He had his dream. To anyone else this pathetic piece of plastic would look like any other high street toy, but to Walter it was the equivalent of the Holy Grail. He knew, at that precise moment, that he would never be able to let that toy out of his care. It became his everything, his purpose of life, his entire sense of being.

"Whatever happened to..."

Brad Clusky felt something unusual, something he wasn't used to. It was a strange feeling that rippled across his skin, and chased up his spine causing him to shiver. He couldn't quite place it, though. It was a strange cocktail of pride, pleasure, nausea and nostalgia. This job had been a whole new experience for him. In all his days of being a control freak, he had gained a certain satisfaction at being in a world of chaos, at least for a few days. His mind was telling him that he should be furious with himself. The whole thing had been so unprofessional. It should have been clean and simple, but instead it had three dead bodies and enough media hype to totally eclipse what had happened at the Gresham Corporation. It was not the sort of thing that a professional like Brad should wish to be associated with. At the same time, however, it had been a very special experience. It had been wild and reckless, intense and dangerous, romantic and intriguing. It had a little bit of everything. All the wrong sort of treats that guys like Brad were never supposed to have. He looked over to Walter, sitting there on a bust up mincing machine, wearing a torn tuxedo he would never have otherwise been able to afford, and completely captivated by a small piece of black plastic. He admitted to himself that there was something pretty cool about that. Simple, yes.

Disturbing, definitely. Cool, absolutely. He walked back over to his entranced partner.

"You okay?" he asked.

"Yeah," Walter replied. "I'm fine." Brad sat down next to him on the mincing machine, and looked on compassionately at the small plastic figure.

"So, whatever happened to Drax Mantis?" he asked.

"What do you mean?" Walter replied.

"Well," Brad went on, "I reckon I can admit this now. I only ever saw the first film."

"You saw *The Glokorian Revenge* with me."

"Well, sure, I was in the cinema, but we were hardly watching the film. The last thing I can remember about Drax was that he was seriously getting his arsed kicked by Jed what's-his-face at the end of the first film."

"You really want me to give you a synopsis of the second two films? I wouldn't have thought that was a suitable subject after having just escaped from the police and sitting in a pile of dead cows, would you?"

"I see you haven't lost your sense of humour," Brad smiled. "All I wanted to know was what happened to him in the end, that's all."

"I see," Walter replied. "Well, after an assortment of space chases, laser battles, close encounters, and magical kingdoms, Drax and Jed find themselves on the Glokorian home world."

"Which film is this?"

"*Rise of the Skellern Warrior*, the last film."

"Right, I'm with you."

"Anyway, Jed and Drax are having their final battle," Walter began enthusiastically. "We are talking heavy stuff. The set alone cost over a million pounds, designed by Jean-Marie Tréve, the French man. Very dark and gothic. The London Symphony Orchestra is giving it some serious whack with their string section."

"Can we stick to the story," Brad interrupted.

"Oh, yeah, sure," Walter apologised. "So Drax and Jed are having this fight. Things are pretty balanced, until suddenly Jed pushes Drax over this bridge. Now, Drax is just managing to hang on. Jed, however, doesn't want to finish him off. Of all things he wants to pull him up. Carina and Mahnja show up, and they are all for wasting him, but Jed talks them round and they pull Drax up."

"And Drax blows the fuck out of them, right?"

"Wrong. Drax actually turns a new leaf. He decides to start over. At first you aren't too sure about this. You don't know if you can trust him. Then, though, he saves Jed and the others from certain doom at the hands of Glokorian soldiers, and helps them escape. After that you know he's a good guy, like you always suspected all along."

"I never suspected," challenged Brad.

"Oh come on," retorted Walter. "You never really thought that Drax Mantis was really evil, did you? I mean, he was hardly Norman Bates or Freddy Kruger."

"So he was a wimp then?"

"No, he was just an anti-hero, a bit like Robin Hood. It's funny, when I was at college we had this big debate about Robin Hood and whether or not he was a good guy or a bad guy. Everybody else thought he was a good guy, when it was clearly obvious that he was a bad guy. Maybe I picked a bad example, I should have been speaking about Drax. It's the same but in reverse, Drax seems like a bad guy, when really he is a good guy."

"You are starting to get deep, Walter," said Brad, lifting himself off the broken mincer. "As far as I'm concerned, Drax Mantis was definitely a bad guy."

"Then you've proved the point," said Walter.

"What point?"

"That we never really know who the good guys and the bad guys really are."

"Huh?"

"Well take you and me," Walter suggested, "are we good guys or bad guys?"

"It doesn't matter," Brad replied, "it isn't the taking part, it's the winning that counts. Today we won, even if we didn't play by the rules. If you asked me, that makes us the good guys, but it doesn't matter at the end of the day."

Walter just smiled. Maybe Brad was right and maybe he was wrong. Maybe they were good guys and maybe they were bad guys. "I suppose we will just have to let history judge us," he concluded.

"More likely the tabloids," Brad smiled.

Jim Carley

The Smell of Bacon

Brad walked over to the van and climbed inside, pulling out a shock resistant metal box. From it he pulled out a small collection of explosive charges. He flicked a switch on each and arranged them around the van. The final item he took from the box was the remote control, which he slid in one of his pockets.

"Do you have to blow up the van?" Walter called across to him.

"Yeah," Brad called back. "This old van has got too many clues about Ralph and me inside. Too many fingerprints and computer files! We can't risk this falling into the wrong hands."

"But Danny Dellapicho has already told everybody who you are anyway," said Walter. Brad climbed out of the back of the van, kicking a leg of beef out of the way.

"Maybe he has," said Brad, "but no policeman in his right mind is going to use the evidence of a dead murderer on trust. Besides, Dellapicho isn't the last of our worries. If they went to the trouble to send him after Ralph and me because we screwed up, then the chances are they are going to send someone else to finish the job."

"What are you going to do?" asked Walter.

"Good question," Brad replied. "I hadn't really thought about that. It's certainly too hot to stay in

336

Britain at the moment, that's for sure. Personally, I've always fancied spending a bit of time in Spain. Barcelona, perhaps."

"You can't afford that," Walter pointed out. "Your van is wrecked, and all that gear will need replacing. This job has hardly been a money spinner for you, has it?"

"Walter," Brad said softly, "we won this job. That is all I ever hoped for. Sure, it was hardly our usual bread and butter work, but it was fun. Maybe we diverted from the original plan, but we got there in the end. That's what it is all about for me. Aren't you happy with Drax Mantis there?"

"Of course I am," said Walter, clutching the toy. "It's the coolest thing ever."

"That makes a good result then," Brad pointed out. "Don't worry about Ralph and me. Hard though it may seem to believe, we don't screw up every job we do. We've got a lot of money stashed away for rainy days. We also have a lot of good friends in Spain who can look after us. Tomorrow there will be another job lifting computer files in Berlin, or photographing military installations in Iraq, or stealing diamonds from Cape Town. The world goes on, and life with it."

"I wish I could come with you," said Walter.

"No, you don't," Brad replied. "You've got a shop to run, and films to see, and comics to read. I think you'd rather be doing that."

"I guess so," said Walter. "It was nice though. It was nice to be a part of the action for a change, rather than just a spectator." He reached inside his crumpled dinner jacket and pulled out a folded Polaroid photograph. "This is for you," he said, passing it to Brad.

Brad unfolded the picture and saw the image of himself sitting on an armchair in Walter's flat, his face a look of horror. Brad smiled, remembering that it was this photograph that had set the whole thing rolling in the first place.

"Keep it as a souvenir," said Walter. "It's only fair. After all, I've got Drax here. You should have something to remind you of all this as well."

"Did you have that in your pocket all along?" asked Brad.

"Yes," Walter replied. "All night."

"Thanks," said Brad, still smiling as he folded the picture again and placed it in one of the pockets of his boiler suit. Outside they could hear a car pulling up. The exhaust was too throaty to be that of a police car, so there was no cause for alarm. Ralph pulled the car up level with the hole in the wall left by the van, and wound down his window.

"What do you think?" he called.

"A Ford Capri!" exclaimed Brad. Ralph had indeed chosen a bright green Ford Capri, complete with go faster stripes, leopard skin seats, and fluffy dice hanging from the rear view mirror. The names Jason and Trina were splashed across the top of the windscreen.

"I guess Jason must be sorting out Trina in one of the other warehouses," said Ralph. "The stupid prick left it unlocked with they keys in the ignition. He must have been gagging for it. Have you set the charges?"

"The charges are set," reported Brad, pulling out the small remote control box from his pocket. "It looks like everybody in North London will be waking up to the smell of bacon today!"

Brad and Walter climbed into the Capri, and

Ralph turned the car away from the warehouse. Walter sat on the back seat, still clutching Drax Mantis as if he were some sort of life support machine. The meat merchants was left empty apart from a bust up van and a lizard suit with its mask missing. As the Capri reached the end of the road Brad pressed the button on the remote control, and W.G. Caruthers & Son exploded into a million pieces. A great fireball rose up into the sky, but none of the three men looked back. The car just kept on driving, heading north, towards the Celluloid Space Cowboy comic store, and then who knows where.

Epilogue

Helen Bridgenorth, now in her early fifties, watched the footage of the events at the Orbit Studio Experience on *Crimewatch UK*. She was convinced that the hostage who had been bundled into the van was her son, Walter. She had to ring him at his shop at least a dozen times before he could convince her otherwise.

The Gresham Corporation spent millions improving their security systems after Brad and Ralph's failed attempt to steal the AVREX files. The United States Government, however, hired another team of specialist operatives to steal them, which they did successfully. It is now believed that the first American mission to send a human being into the next galaxy will take place around the year 2015.

Todd Orchard, the director of *Galactic Encounter*, wrote new scripts for three sequels to the original films. Casting is already underway for the first of these, and filming is likely to start in the coming months.

Jimmy Lambourne successfully sued *Capital Night Out* for deformation of character. The trial created so much media interest that Jimmy ended up with his own TV chat show on Channel Five. It didn't work out though, and he has not been heard of since.

Jenny Lovelace lost her job as a result of the

Lambourne trial. She is now believed to be working as a lap dancer in a Soho bar in order to make ends meet.

Oswald Moriarty made a successful recovery from his injuries. Amnesia resulting from that night, however, made it impossible for him to remember who his original assailants were. He completely forgot that Walter Bridgenorth was even in the building. He has recently initiated legal proceedings against the Orbit Studio Group for his injuries.

Dana O'Brien and Marcus Clint were unscathed by the whole affair. Although *Capital Night Out* was subsequently axed, the two were given a new show in a prime daytime TV slot where their ratings soared.

Danny Dellapicho became the subject of a major police investigation. He was identified in both the murders of Helga the hotel receptionist and Buster Urman. In the end the police attributed him with eight murders over a period of as many days. The American Government denied any knowledge of Dellapicho, and his involvement with the CIA. His body disappeared shortly after his death, and has never been traced since.

The British Prime Minister was shown key evidence involved in the Dellapicho investigation. Within a week he had set up a crisis meeting with the President of the United States in Geneva. The contents of that meeting are bound by the Official Secrets Act.

Dilly Foxtrot sold her version of the events of that night to a major publishing house, and the film rights were sold to the Orbit Group. She became a millionaire over night. As part of the film deal she will be playing herself. Robert De Niro has been linked with the part of Warren Kingburger, Pierce Brosnan might play Nathan West / Brad Clusky, and Andy Garcia is in the frame as Danny Dellapicho.

Jim Carley

Warren Kingburger recovered from his injuries, and followed his dreams for the *Galactic Encounter* phenomenon. Despite his professional jealousy of Todd Orchard he agreed to finance the three new films. He also sold his entire restaurant chain after that night. The brand name survived, although the deal prevented an Orbit Studio Experience from ever being opened again in London. The new managers decided to open one in Birmingham instead, which was a resounding failure. Six months later Kingburger and Dilly Foxtrot married at a private ceremony in Las Vegas. The first baby is on its way.

Brad Clusky and Ralph Lee are known to have left the UK on the morning of the W.E. Caruthers' explosion. They were last spotted at Barcelona airport that afternoon. Interpol are investigating their whereabouts, and are questioning a number of big players in the European espionage circle. Word has it that they are lining up a big job in Madrid, stealing a secret paella recipe from one major food manufacturer on behalf of another.

Walter Bridgenorth returned to his shop, Celluloid Space Cowboy, and his flat upstairs. He added the Drax Mantis action figure to his collection. He looked at it and cleaned it every day, and recounted to it the chain of events that had brought it into his possession. As far as he was concerned, life was perfect. At that point, however, he was unaware that the shop was changing hands via an unsavoury deal being struck by its owner, Mr Chang. Faced with impending redundancy, Walter set about trying to trace Brad Clusky in an effort to gain his assistance in saving the shop. After some bizarre events, the two were eventually re-united. An elaborate scam to kidnap

Morton Bruce, the major Hollywood star who appeared as Jed Largo in the *Galactic Encounter* films, followed. Then again, that is another story.